THE LAST ARIES EXPRESS

"Come on, lad, come . . ." you hear a voice call, and, peering through the crowd for its source (so familiar, so familiar), you see him. There: past the sherbet sellers and the raucous pastry hawkers, past the crowds of hopeful Penitential Mendicants and Poor Sisters of Tharsis who press close to the dignitaries' rostrum, past the psalm-singing Cathars and the vendors of religious curios; there, he is coming for you, Naon Asiim, with hand outstretched. Through steam and smoke and constables wielding shockstaves who try to keep the crowd away from the man of the moment, here he comes, just for you, your grandfather, Taam Engineer.

The people part before Taam Engineer like grass before the scythe. Now you are on the rostrum beside him and every one of those thousands of thousands of people crushing into the station falls silent as the old man holds up the Summoner for all to see. There is a wonderful quiet for a moment, then a hiss of steam and the chunt-chunt of rumbling wheels, and like every last one of those thousands and thousands of people, you let your breath out in a great sigh because out from the pressure-shed doors comes the Greatest of the Great; the fabulous *Catherine of Tharsis* at the head of the last Aries Express.

THE STORIES

EMPIRE DREAMS

IAN McDONALD

BANTAM BOOKS
TORONTO • NEW YORK • LONDON • SYDNEY • AUCKLAND

Other Bantam Books by Ian McDonald:

DESOLATION ROAD

EMPIRE DREAMS
A Bantam Spectra Book / February 1988

PRINTING HISTORY

The following stories first appeared in Isaac Asimov's Science Fiction Magazine.

"The Catharine Wheel"—IASFM—January 1984
Copyright © 1983 by Davis Publications, Inc.

"Scenes from a Shadowplay"—IASFM—July 1985
Copyright © 1985 by Davis Publications, Inc.

"Empire Dreams"—IASFM—December 1985
Copyright © 1985 by Davis Publications, Inc.

"Christian"—IASFM—October 1984
Copyright © 1984 by Davis Publications, Inc.

ISBN 0-553-27180-6

Published simultaneously in the United States and Canada

PRINTED IN THE UNITED STATES OF AMERICA

KR   0 9 8 7 6 5 4 3 2 1

EMPIRE DREAMS

(GROUND CONTROL TO MAJOR TOM)

She can smell the sickness everywhere. Her nostrils are not duped by the desperate odor of antiseptic; there is a peculiar stench to sickness that nothing will conceal, a stench mixed in with the thick, glossy utility paint which, through years of overpainted overpainting, has built into layer upon layer of ingrained despair. From these hopeless strata sickness leaks into the air. There is no concealing the smell of a hospital, it squeezes out of the floor tiles every time a trolley rolls over them, and under the slightest pressure of a nurse's footstep.

As she sits in the chair by the bed she breathes in the sickness and is surprised to find how cold it is. It is not the cold of the snow falling outside the window, the snow that softens and conceals the outlines of the Royal Victoria Hospital like white antiseptic. It is the cold which encircles death, the cold of the boy on the bed, which draws the living heat out of her; cold and sickness.

She does not know what the machines are for. The doctors have explained, more than once, but there must be more to her son's life than the white lines on the oscilloscope. A person's life is not measured by lines, for if that is all a life is, which are the lines for love, and the lines for devotion? which is the pulsebeat of happiness, or the steady drone of pain? She does not want to see those lines. Catherine Semple is a God-fearing woman who has heard the steady drone of pain more than anyone should have to in any lifetime, but she will not hear it whisper any blasphemous rumors. Joy and pain she accepts from the fingers of the same God; she may question, but she never backbites. Her son lies in a coma, head shaved, wires trickling current into his brain, tubes down his nose, throat, arms, thighs. He has not moved for sixteen hours, no sign of life save the white measurements of the machines. But Catherine Semple will sit by that bed until she sees. At about midnight a nurse will bring coffee and some new used women's magazines; Nurse Hannon, the kindly, scared one from County Monaghan. By that time anything might have happened.

"Major Tom, Major Tom," booms out the huge voice of Captain Zarkon. "Major Tom to fighter bay, Major Tom to fighter bay. Zygon battlefleet on long-range sensors, repeat, Zygon battlefleet on long-range sensors. Go get 'em, Tom, you're the Empire's last hope." And down in the hangar bay under dome under dome under dome (the high curved roof of the bay, the plasmoglass blister of the ship, the decaled bubble of your helmet) you scrunch down in the rear astrogator's seat of the X15 Astrofighter and mouth the fabulous words, "You're the Empire's last hope." Of course, you are not the Major Tom whose name thunders round the immense fighter bay, you are Thomas junior, the kid, less than fifty percent of the Galaxy's most famed (and feared, all the way from Centralis to Alphazar Three) fighting duo, but it is nice to sit there and close your eyes and think they are talking about you.

Here he comes, Major Tom; the last Great Starfighter, Space Ace, Astroblaster, Valiant Defender, thrice decorated by the Emperor Geoffrey himself with the Galaxian Medal and Bar, striding across the hangar deck magnificent in tight-fitting iridescent combat-suit, and, cradled beneath his arm, the helmet with the famous Flash of Lightning logo and the name "Major Tom" stenciled in bold black letters. The canopy rises to admit him and the hero snakily wiggles into the forward command seat.

"Hi, Wee Tom."

"Hi, Big Tom."

Space-armored technicians are running ponderously to cover as the fighter deck is evacuated. The canopy seals, internal pressurization takes over and makes your ears pop, despite the gum you are looping around your back molars; the space door irises open and your fighter moves onto the launch catapult. What is beyond the space door? Vacuum, stars, Zygons. Not necessarily in that order. Tactical display lights blink green, little animated Imperial Astrofighters flash on half a dozen computer screens. You park your gum in the corner of the weapons-status display board.

"Primary ignition sequence?"

"Green."

"Energy banks at full charge?"

"Check."

"All thrust and maneuvering systems, astrogational and communications channels check?"

"All channels open, all systems go."

"Okay, Wee Tom. Let's go get 'em. We're the Empire's last hope."

A blast of acceleration stuffs your teeth down your throat, flattens your eyeballs to fifty-cent pieces, and grips the back of your neck with an irresistible iron hand as the catapult seizes Astrofighter Orange Leader and shies it at the space door. The wind whistles out of you; everything goes red as the space door hurtles up at you. Then you are through, and, before the redness has faded from your eyes and the air filled your lungs once more, Major Tom has looped your X15 up and over the semi-eclipsed bulk of the miles-and-miles-and-miles-long *Excalibur*, throneship of Geoffrey I, Emperor of Space, Lord of the Shogon Marches, Defender of Altair, Liege of the Orion Arm, Master of the Dark Nebula.

"Astrogation check."

"Enemy force targeted in Sector Green Fourteen Delta J. Accelerating to attack speed . . ."

"Good work, Wee Tom. Orange Leader to Force Orange, sign in."

One by one they climb away from *Excalibur*, the valiant pilots of Force Orange: Big Ian, The Prince, John-Paul (J.P. to his comrades *only*), Captain "Kit" Carson, Black Morrisey— nicknames known and respected (and, in some places, dreaded) right across the sparkling spiral of the Galaxy. Such is these men's fame that it brings a lump to your throat to see the starlight catch on their polished wing-fairings and transform their battlescarred fighters into chariots of fire.

"Force Orange reported in, Orange One through Orange Five, Orange Leader," you say.

"Okay," says Major Tom with that tight resoluteness in his voice you love to hear so much. He waggles his fighter's wings in the attack signal and Force Orange closes up behind him.

"Let's go get 'em. We've got a job to do."

PRESS CONFERENCE: 11:35 A.M. JANUARY 16, 1989.

Yes, the original diagnosis was leukemia, but, as the disease was not responding to conventional treatment, Dr. Blair classified it as a psychologically dependent case . . . No, sorry, not psychosomatic, psychologically dependent is Dr. Montgomery's expression, the one Dr. Blair would like used. Put simply, the conventional chemotherapy was ineffective as long as the psychological block to its effectiveness remained. Yes, the leukemia has gone into complete remission. How long ago? About twelve days.

Gentleman at the back . . . sir . . . This is the thirty-eighth day of the coma, counting from the time when the growth of the cancer was first arrested, as opposed to the complete remission. The patient had been in the orthohealing state for some twenty-six days prior to that while the chemotherapy was administered and found to be effective . . . Yes sir, the chemotherapy was effective only while the patient was in the orthohealing state. It was discontinued after thirty days.

Gentleman from the *Irish News* . . . The boy is perfectly healthy—now, don't quote me on this, this is strictly off the record, but there is no medical reason why Thomas Semple shouldn't take up his bed and walk . . . right out of this hospital. Our only conclusion is that there is some psychological imbalance that is keeping him, or, more correctly, making him keep himself, in Montgomery/Blair suspension.

Sir, by the door . . . No, the project will not now be discontinued; it has been found to be medically very effective and the psychological bases of the process have been demonstrated to be valid. International medical interest in the process is high. I might add that more than one university across the water, as well as those here in Ireland, have sent representatives to observe the development of the case and there is widescale commercial interest in the computer-assisted technology for the sensory-deprivation dream-simulation systems. In fact, Dr. Montgomery is attending an international conference in The Hague at which he is delivering his paper on the principles of orthohealing . . . Yes sir, I can confirm that Dr. Montgomery is returning early from the conference, and I wish I knew where you get your information from, because I only found out this morning; but this is not due to any deterioration in Thomas Semple's condition. He is stable, but comatose in the orthohealing state. Okay? Next question.

Sir, from the *Guardian*, isn't it? May I have your question . . . Yes, Mrs. Semple is in attendance by the bedside; we have a room set aside for her on the hospital premises; she is able to see her son at any time and spends most of her time in the ward with him. She will permit photographs, but under no circumstances will consent to be interviewed, so don't bother wasting your time trying . . . Yes, it was her idea, but we agree with her decision totally. I'm sure you must all appreciate, gentlemen, the strain she is under after the tragic death of her husband, her only child developing leukemia, and now the baffling nature of this coma. Next question. I.R.N?

We have no evidence to cause us to believe that he has drifted away from the programmed orthohealing dream. This would be most unlikely as the dream was designed specifically with his ideal fantasies in mind. We believe that he is still living out this *Star Wars* fantasy, what we call the "Space Raiders" simulation program. To explain a little, we have over a dozen dream archetypes specifically engineered for typical psychological profiles. Thomas

Semple junior's is a kind of wish-fulfillment arcade game, Space Invaders with an infinite number of credits, if you'll pardon me stretching the analogy. The cancerous cells are represented as alien invaders to be destroyed; he himself is cast in the role of Luke Skywalker, the hero. I believe it was the gentleman from the *Irish Times* who coined the expression, "Luke Skywalker Case," wasn't it?

Okay . . . any further questions? No? Good. There's a pile of press releases by the door; if you could pick one up as you leave it'd make it worth the trouble of having them duplicated. Afraid you won't find anything in them you haven't heard from me. Thank you, gentlemen, for being so patient and for coming on such a foul day. Thank you all, good morning.

(Shuttle flight BA 4503, London Heathrow to Belfast: after the coffee, before the drinks.)

MRS. MACNEILL:	I couldn't help noticing your briefcase, are you a doctor, Mr. Montgomery?
DR. MONTGOMERY:	Well, a doctor, yes, but not an M.D., I'm afraid. Doctor of psychology.
MRS. MACNEILL:	Oh, have to be careful what I say, then.
DR. MONTGOMERY:	Ah, they all say that. Don't worry, I'm not a psychiatrist, I'm a research psychologist, clinical psychology. I'm attached to the R.V.H. team working on orthohealing, you know, that Luke Skywalker thing?
MRS. MACNEILL:	I've heard about that, it was on *News at Ten*, wasn't it, and it was on *Tomorrow's World* a couple of weeks back. That's the thing about getting people to dream themselves into getting better, isn't it?
DR. MONTGOMERY:	That's it in a nutshell, Mrs. . . .
MRS. MACNEILL:	Oh, sorry, there's me rabbiting on and never thought to tell you my name. Mrs. MacNeill. Violet MacNeill, of Thirty-two Beechmount Park, Finaghy.
DR. MONTGOMERY:	Well, you've already guessed who I am, Mrs. MacNeill. Might I ask what takes you over the water?

MRS. MACNEILL:	Ach, I was seeing my son, that's Michael, he's teaching in Dortmund, in Germany, and he's always inviting me to come over and see him, so I thought, well, now I've got the money, I might as well, because it could be the last time I'll see him.
DR. MONTGOMERY:	Oh? How so? Is he moving even further afield?
MRS. MACNEILL:	Oh no. But you could say I am. (*Laughs, coughs.*) You see, Dr. Montgomery, I haven't got long. I'm a person who believes in calling a spade a spade. I'm dying. It's this cancer thing, you know? You can't even talk about it these days, people don't like you to mention the word when they're around, but I don't care, I believe in calling a spade a spade, that's what I say. I tell who I like because it won't go away if you don't talk about it, it's stupid to try to hide from it, don't you think? You're a medical man, you should know.
DR. MONTGOMERY:	Psychological, Mrs. MacNeill.
MRS. MACNEILL:	You see? The very man to talk to. The trained ear. They picked it up about eight months ago, stomach cancer, well on its way, and they said I only had about a year at the most. I reckon on longer than that, but I'm under no illusions it'll get better. My daughter, Christine, she wanted to put me in that hospice, you know, the place for the terminally ill, but I said away out of that, all you do there is sit around all day and think about dying and they call that a positive attitude. "Dying with dignity," they say, but if you ask me, I say you live a bit less and die a little bit more every day until finally no one can tell the difference. Me, I intend to keep on living until the moment I drop. Away out of your hospices, I says to Christine, rather than waste good money on that

abattoir, give it me in my hand and I'll spend it doing all the things I've always wanted to do and never had the time for. And do you know what, Dr. Montgomery, she gave it me and I took a bit out of my savings and I've been having the time of my life.

DR. MONTGOMERY: Now, that's what I call a positive attitude, Mrs. MacNeill.

MRS. MACNEILL: You see? That's the difference between a medical man; ach, I know you're a psychologist, but you boys with letters after your name are all the same to me, and an ordinary man. You can talk about these things, you can come out and say, "That's what I call a positive attitude, Violet MacNeill," while anyone else would only have thought that and been afraid to say it in case they offended me or something. But I wouldn't mind, wouldn't mind a bit, what offends me is people not saying what's on their minds. But I tell you this, there's just one thing bothers me and won't give my head peace.

DR. MONTGOMERY: What's that?

MRS. MACNEILL: It's not me, nothing to do with me, why, I'm having the best time, I've been to Majorca on one of those winter breaks, and to London to see the shows, you know, that Tim Rice and Andrew Lloyd-Webber thing, and I've a cousin in Toronto to see, and I have to get to Paris, I've always wanted to see Paris, in the spring, like that song, "I Love Paris in the Springtime," I'd love it any time of year, I've got to hang on till I've seen Paris. And then there was this joyride to Germany. Which brings me back to what I was talking to you about, don't I ramble on something dreadful? It's the kids I worry about, Michael and Christine and wee Richard, I say wee, but he's a full-time R.U.C. man; it's them worries me. Now, I don't care much for dying, but it has to happen and at least I'm not bothering to let it ruin my life, but I worry about what I'm leaving behind. Will the kids ever forgive me?

DR. MONTGOMERY: That's a very good question, Mrs. Mac-Neill. Do you feel guilty about dying?

MRS. MACNEILL: See? Asked like a true psychologist. It's all right, never worry, dear. In a way, it's stupid to feel guilty about dying; I mean to say, I'm not going to care, am I? But then again, I do feel bad in a sort of way because it's like I'm betraying them. I'm like the top layer between them and their own ends, and when I'm gone they move up and become the top layer. Do you understand that?

DR. MONTGOMERY: I do. Would you care for a drink? Trolley's coming up the aisle.

MRS. MACNEILL: Oh, please. Gin and bitter lemon for me. Should cut it out, but I reckon when you add up the harm it does and the good, it's six of one and half a dozen of the other. Now, what was I saying? Oh yes, do you think children ever forgive their parents for dying? When you're wee, your parents are like God; I remember mine, God love 'em, they could do nothing wrong, they were as solid as the Rock of Gibraltar and always would be, but they both died in the bombing in '41 and, do you know, Doctor, but I don't know if I ever forgave them? They'd built my life, they'd given me everything, and then it was as if they'd abandoned me, and I'm wondering if my Michael and Christine and wee Richard will think the same about me. Will they think I've betrayed them, or will I have given them that kick up the backside into being mature? What do you think, Dr. Montgomery? Do children ever forgive their parents for being human?

DR. MONTGOMERY: Mrs. MacNeill, I don't know. I just don't know.

(The drinks trolley arrives at seats 28C and D at the same instant as the Boeing 757 makes the subtle change of altitude that marks the commencement of its descent to snowbound Northern Ireland.)

She had wished upon a star, the star around which her son orbits, a shooting star, fast and low and bright, diving down behind Divis Mountain. When you wish upon a star, doesn't matter who you are, everything your heart desires will come to you: a cricket had sung that to her once upon a rainy Saturday afternoon in the sixties somewhen, but what if that star is a satellite or an Army helicopter, does that invalidate the wish, does that fold the heart's desire back on itself and leave it staring at its reflection in the night-mirrored window? The night outside fills the reflection's cheeks with shadows, and, in the desperate warmth of the hospital room heavy with the scent of sickness, she hugs herself and knows that she is the reflection and it the object. Every night the hollows fill up again with shadows from the shadowland outside where Army Saracens roar through the night and joyriders hot-wire Fords to cruise the wee small hours away round the neat gravel paths of the City Cemetery or stake their lives running the checkpoints manned by weary police reservists watching from the backs of steel-gray Landrovers with loaded rifles.

Stick them in neutral; he'd told her that once. We do that sometimes, stick the Landrovers in neutral and cruise for a couple of hundred yards, then shove them into second, and when they backfire it sounds like gunshots. Gets them ringing up the station: shots heard, Tennant Street, 1:15 A.M. Some of them make it sound like Custer's Last Stand, he'd said. It had made her laugh, once. Last Stand in Shadowland.

Somewhere in the room is the soul of a twelve-year-old boy, somewhere among the piles of junk Dr. Montgomery had suggested might trigger some response from him. Sometimes she thinks she sees it, like an imp, or like one of the brownies her mother had convinced her had lived behind the dresser in the farmhouse's kitchen: an imp, darting from under his American football helmet to hide behind his U2 poster, concealed like a lost chord in the strings of his guitar or looping endlessly through his computer like the ghost of an abandoned program. There are his favorite U2 albums, and the cassettes specially recorded for him by John Cleese to try and raise a smile on his face; there is the photograph of Horace, half-collie, half-greyhound, wall-eyed and wild-willed; there is the photograph of Tom senior.

Tom senior, who knew all about backfiring police Landrovers, and the room at the station with the ghettoblaster turned up loud outside it where they took the skinheads, and the twelve different routes to work each day: Tom, who had always been just Dad to him. No, the soul of a twelve-year-old boy, whatever its color, whatever its shape, is not something that can be captured by computer-assisted machinery or lured back to ground and trapped like a limed songbird by a junk-shop of emotional relics, not when it is out there in the night flying loops around Andromeda.

As many as the stars in the sky or snowflakes in a blizzard or grains of sand upon a beach, that is how many the Zygon fleet is; wave upon wave of fighters and destroyers and scouts and cruisers and battleships and dreadnoughts and mobile battlestations and there at the heart of it, like the black aniseed at the center of a gobstopper, the Zygon flagship. The enemy is so huge that it takes your breath away and there is a beat of fear in your heart, for the Imperial throneship *Excalibur* is but one ship and Major Tom is but one man. Major Tom points his fighter's nose dead into the densest part of the pack and leads Force Orange into the attack.

Is he totally without fear? you ask yourself, sweating under your helmet as the sudden acceleration pushes you deep into your padded seat, stamps all over your ribs, and stands forward on its head to become up.

"Where do they all come from?" you whisper to give your fear a name you can hold it by.

Major Tom hears you, for privacy is not a thing a fighting team with a Galaxy-wide reputation can be bothered with, and answers, "Survivors of the Empire's destruction of their

capital world, Carcinoma. Must have got the Zygon Prime
Intelligence off before we blasted Carcinoma, and now they're
here, grouping for another murderous attack on the peaceful
planets of the Empire. And we've got to stop them before they
destroy the entire universe. A battlefleet could fight for a
hundred years and still be no nearer the flagship of the Prime
Intelligence, but a small force of two-man fighters might, just
might, be able to slip past their defenses and attack the flagship
with pulsar torpedoes." And now he says into the relay
channels you have opened for him,

"Orange Leader to Orange One through Five, accelerate to
combat speed. Let's go get 'em, boys. The destiny of the
Empire is ours today."

How you wish you could make up lines like that, words to
inspire men and send them into battle, words that wave the
star-spangled banner of the Galactic Empire, words that make
the hair prickle under your helmet and proud tears leak from
the corners of rough-tough space-marine eyes. You think it
might not be such a terrible thing to die with words like that
ringing in your ears.

Your targeting computer has located the cluster of Zygon
dreadnoughts and fighters protecting the flagship of the Prime
Intelligence. The first photon blasts from the battleships' long-
range zappers rock your X15 as the enemy fighters peel out of
formation to intercept. Opaque spots appear on your visor to
screen out the searing light of the photon blasts.

"Orange Leader to Force Orange," says Major Tom, "I'm
going in."

"Tactical computer available," you say.

"Forget it, son, Major Tom does his own shooting." Your
thumbs twitch on imaginary triggers as Major Tom locks a
Zygon fighter in his sights and blasts it with his laser-zappers.
The black alien spacecraft unfolds into a beautiful blossom of
white flame. Already Major Tom has another in his sights.
Swooping up, up, and away from the nuclear fireball, he rolls
the X15 and downs another. And another, and another, and
another . . .

On your tactical display a green grid-square flashes red.

"Big Tom, one on your tail."

"I mark him. Orange Leader to Orange Two, Big Ian, I've
a bogie on my tail. I'm going in for the big one, the flagship."

He throws the astrofighter into a rapid series of bounce-about evasive maneuvers. A sudden flare of fusion-light throws your shadow before you onto the astrogational equipment as the Zygon pursuit ship explodes in a billion billion sparkling fragments. Orange Two thunders in to parallel your course. The daring star-pilots exchange greeting signals, and Orange Two rolls effortlessly away into a billion billion cubic light-years of space. Ahead, the Zygon flagship is sowing fighters like demon seed and now its heavy-duty laser turrets are swinging to bear on you. Photon blasts fill the air like thistledown on a summer's day.

"Hold on to your seat, kid, this calls for some tight flying," shouts the voice of Major Tom in your helmet-radio earphones, and he twists, turns, spins, loops, somersaults, and handstands the X15 past the crisscrossing Zygon fighters and the laserfire of the Flagship. The immense metal bulk of the enemy ship swells up before you, so close that you can see the space-armored crews at their batteries.

"Arm pulsar torpedoes' smart systems."

Click switch, press button; green lights reflect in your visor.

"Pulsar torpedoes armed." The infinitesimal white X15 Astrofighter hurtles over a crazy metal landscape bursting with laserfire. Before you loom the engine ports, ponderous as mountain ranges, vulnerable as free-range eggs. Your mouth is dry, your hands are wet, your eyeballs as desiccated as two round pebbles. Red lights . . .

"Squadron coming in behind us, fast." The metal landscape blurs beneath you; this alien vessel is so huge . . .

"Damn. Orange Leader to Force Orange, what happened to the cover? Mark three bogies on my tail, take care of 'em, I'm going for the engine ducts . . . five"—the iron mountains open like jaws—"four"—on your rear screen, three evil black Zygon pursuit ships slip into tight cover—"three"—you veer down a sudden valley in the huge geography of the flagship's drive section—"two"—ahead is the white dooms-day glow of the stardrives—"one . . . Fire." Orange Leader climbs away from the engine pods. The pursuit ships come after you, never seeing the tiny blob of light detach itself from your fighter at count zero and steer itself down the engine tubes into the miles-distant bowels of the enemy flagship. Major

Tom loops twelve thousand miles high above the doomed starship and declares, "Detonation!"

At first there is nothing, as if it has taken time for Major Tom's voice to travel across space and the torpedo to hear him, but then, as if by his express command, the Zygon flagship silently expands into a rainbow of glowing particles. The afterblast paints the cockpit pink, a beautiful bathroom pink. The glow takes a long time to fade, a man-made nova.

"Yahoo!" you shout. "Yahoo! We got him!"

"We sure did," says Major Tom. "Son, we sure did."

"What now?" you ask. "Take care of those pursuit ships and then back to *Excalibur*?"

"Not yet," says Major Tom and there is a strange note in his voice that reminds you of something you have purposefully forgotten. "We're pressing on, continuing the attack on our own, because there's a planet out there beyond the lines of Zygon ships, a planet hidden for a million years away from Galactic knowledge, and we, and we alone, must go there to destroy Zygon power forever."

PRESS RELEASE: DECEMBER 22, 1988 (EXTRACTS).

[This is] the concept of the "Mind Box," the baggage of beliefs and values which determine the individual's response to the events of his life. Research into depression has shown the relationship between psychosomatic symptoms and the state of the individual's "Mind Box." Dr. Montgomery hypothesized in his doctoral thesis that this Mind Box concept might account for many of the more severe medical cases which are never diagnosed as psychosomatic but which otherwise have no medical reason for their lack of response to conventional treatment.

[The concept of] "deep dreaming" [was developed] from Luzerski and Baum's work on lucid dreams, dreams in which the dreamer exerts conscious control over the content of his dream. It is a highly refined version of Luzerski and Baum's dream techniques whereby an individual enters a state of interactive dreaming through a hypnotically and chemically induced process and effects the necessary repairs to his damaged Mind Box, thus relieving the psychological pressures that have led to his deteriorating medical condition. It could be said that he literally dreams himself into a state of self-healing. Dr. Blair has related this effect to the Nobel Prize–winning Stoppard/Lowe theories of molecular iso-informational fields: zones of order generated by individual protein molecules which stabilize genetic material against interference and mutation from electromagnetic and gravitic fields. He argues the analogy of deep dreaming, returning the body's iso-informational fields to a state of biological and psychological metastasis, or harmony, which renders the patient—at the cellular level, at least—responsive to conventional treatment.

Thomas Semple, Jr., is the process's pilot case. The patient, a twelve-year-old boy, contracted leukemia shortly after the death of his father, a police sergeant. He was admitted to hospital but did not respond to conventional chemotherapy.

. . . Doctors Montgomery and Blair have created a deep-dream scenario for young Thomas analogous to the computer games of which he is very fond. In this dream simulation he plays the hero of a space-war arcade game shooting down invaders which are representations of the cancerous cells within him. He spends fifteen hours per day in this deep-dream suspension, during which normal chemotherapy is administered. His dream state is constantly monitored by state-of-the-art computer technology which also maintains his illusion of deep dreaming by direct stimulation (in sensory deprivation) of the neurons, both chemically and electrically . . .

. . . [D]uring his waking periods he talks constantly about how exciting he finds his space-war dream and Doctors Montgomery and Blair are confident that their first case using this orthohealing process will be a complete success.

* * *

(The front seat of a Vauxhall Cavalier, somewhere on the motorway between Belfast Airport and the Royal Victoria Hospital.)

DR. MONTGOMERY: How was the press conference, then?

MACKENZIE: Don't ask.

DR. MONTGOMERY: That bad? Oh come on, things haven't gotten any worse, the kid's stable, there's no cause for media panic, is there? Never was.

MACKENZIE: If you really want to know, they're trying a human-interest angle on the mother—you know, tragically widowed policeman's wife, her son struck down by you-know-what, can't mention cancer in the tabloids, hurts circulation; well, now, to compound her suffering, this ancy-fancy untested medical experiment goes sour on her. That's what they were trying to get me to say at the press conference. Never again. Do your own next time.

DR. MONTGOMERY: Bastards. I take it you didn't . . . say anything, that is . . .

MACKENZIE: Not a word.

DR. MONTGOMERY: Good girl yourself. Which papers?

MACKENZIE: As I said, tabloids: *Mirror, Sun, Star, Mail, Express.*

DR. MONTGOMERY: Bastards.

MACKENZIE: Mrs. Semple's keeping them all at bay at the moment, but it's only a question of how long it is before some hack cons his way past the ward sister and waves a checkbook under her nose.

DR. MONTGOMERY: Damn. Why all the sudden interest?

MACKENZIE: Don't know. Some local must have picked up on the story and now the crusaders are waiting to take you apart the moment you get back there, Saladin. Gave me a rough enough time of it.

DR. MONTGOMERY: And drag the hospital's name through the mire. You didn't, ah—

MACKENZIE:	Let them know that I was in charge of simulation software and the computer systems? Think I'm stupid? Not a breath.
DR. MONTGOMERY:	Thank God. *(Looks at the snow and is silent for a while.)* Roz, tell me, do you think children ever forgive their parents for dying?
MACKENZIE:	Wouldn't know. Mine are both disgustingly healthy. Better shape than I am.
DR. MONTGOMERY:	You tell me what you think of this, then. I'll review some facts about the case and you say what you think. One: Thomas Semple junior's leukemia is cured but he still remains in the orthohealing coma which cured him. We assume he's still deep dreaming because there's been no change in his vital signs between the two situations.
MACKENZIE:	Fair enough assumption. Two.
DR. MONTGOMERY:	Two: In such a state of lucid dreaming, he can be anything he wants to be, anytime, anywhere—subjectively speaking, he exists in his own private universe where everything is exactly as he wishes it to be.
MACKENZIE:	Within the program parameters.
DR. MONTGOMERY:	Well, that's your field of competence, not mine. Three: His father, a sergeant in the Royal Ulster Constabulary, was killed before his eyes by a bomb planted under his car.
MACKENZIE:	Deduced by yourself to be the neuropsychological basis of the leukemia.
DR. MONTGOMERY:	And his lack of response to conventional therapy, yes. Hell, twelve-year-olds shouldn't have death wishes, should they?
MACKENZIE:	You were the one thought it was displaced punishment behavior.
DR. MONTGOMERY:	Every other Tuesday I think the moon is made of green cheese and life is not a futile, worthless waste of time and energy after all. Listen to this: I think we have

given Thomas Semple junior the perfect environment to re-create his father. Now he doesn't have to die to join him, he has him all the time, all to himself, in that dream world of his. The kid can't face a world where his father was blown to bits by an I.N.L.A. bomb, he can't face the reality of his father's death—and now he doesn't have to, when he can be with his father, his perfect, idealized father, forever, in the deep-dream state.

MACKENZIE: That's spooky.

DR. MONTGOMERY: That's it. What do you think?

MACKENZIE: Did you think all this up on the plane over?

DR. MONTGOMERY: I got into conversation with the woman next to me—talk about strange bedfellows, airline booking computers have it down to a fine art—she had cancer, one of those six-months-to-live cases, and she was a talker, as they often are, it makes it easier for them if they can talk about it; well, anyway, in the middle of this conversation she mentioned that she feared her children would never forgive her for dying and leaving them alone in the world. Paranoid maybe, but it started me thinking.

MACKENZIE: It fits. It all fits beautifully.

DR. MONTGOMERY: Doesn't it? I reckon if we go through the printouts on the dream monitors we'll find Thomas Semple senior in there as large as life and twice as handsome, because his son cannot forgive him for being fallible, and mortal, and human, and so is driving him to prove his . . . godhead, I suppose, over and over and over again.

MACKENZIE: And what then? You going to exorcise his ghost?

DR. MONTGOMERY: Yes, I am.

(Overhead gantries bearing signs reading M1, City Center, M5, Carrickfergus, Newtownabbey, Bangor, Lisburn, appear above the car. MacKenzie slides the Vauxhall Cavalier into the lane marked City Center.)

She wishes they would go. She resents their noisy feet, their busy bustle, their muted conversation over rustling sheets of computer printout, their polite-polite "Mrs. Semple, excuse me buts" and "Mrs. Semple, do you know ifs" and "Mrs. Semple, could you tell us whethers." What are they doing that is so important that they must stamp around in their noisy shoes and remind her of the world beyond the swinging ward doors? She does not like them near her son, though the man is the doctor who invented the process and the woman is the one who developed the computers to which her son is wired from skull eyes ears throat. It worries her to see their hands near the machines; she fears that they might press buttons and throw switches and she would never know why they had done so. She hates not understanding, and there is so much she does not understand.

They are talking now, excited about something on a computer screen. She can see what it is that has excited them, though she cannot understand why. Who is this Major Tom? The empty coincidence of names does not fool her. Major Tom, Major Tom . . . she remembers a song she had once heard about Major Tom, the spaceman who never came down. Wasn't that it, Major Tom, the spaceman, still orbiting round and round and round the world in his tin can? She never knew Major Tom. But she knew Sergeant Tom, Sergeant Tom tall and lovely in his bottle-green uniform, Sergeant Tom photographed in his swimming trunks on a Spanish beach, brown and smiling with that little Tom Selleck mustache, Sergeant Tom sitting at the breakfast table in shirtsleeves, shoulder holster, and police boots waiting for the phone call which would tell him today's safe pickup point, Sergeant Tom putting on his jacket, kissing her on the lips and telling Wee Tom to have a good day at school and take care with his head-sums. Sergeant Tom walking out to the Ford Sierra, Sergeant Tom turning the key in the ignition—

"Mrs. Semple, Mrs. Semple."

Faces loom before her, changing size and distance as her eyes roll into focus.

"Yes, Dr. Montgomery?"

"We'd like your permission to try something we think will bring your son out of his coma."

"What is it you want to do?" The weariness in her voice surprises her.

"Adapt the program parameters slightly. Ms. MacKenzie wants to inject new material into the dream simulation."

"You've tried that before. You tried switching off the machines altogether."

"I know, Mrs. Semple. It didn't work." The young doctor (how can anyone so young have the experience to mold people's lives?) completes her thoughts for her. He is clever, but naive. She envies him that. "Thomas merely maintained the dream coma by exercise of his own imagination. No, what we want to do is inject something into the dream so unacceptable that his only escape is to come out of the deep-dream coma."

"And what is that something?"

"I'd rather not say at the moment, Mrs. Semple, in case it doesn't work."

"And if it doesn't work?"

"Then you and he are no worse off than you are now."

"And if it succeeds?"

"Do I really need to answer that question, Mrs. Semple?"

"Of course not. All right then. You have my permission, and my blessing."

"Thank you, Mrs. Semple. Okay, Roz."

What long fingers the girl has! She cannot get over those long, slender fingers as she types on the computer keypad. They are more like tentacles than fingers. Her attention is torn between those dancing fingers and the words that float up on the green screen.

PROGRAM "LUKE SKYWALKER": INTERRUPTIVE
MODE CHANGE: IRRAY 70432 GO TO 70863
READ: KILL MAJOR TOM
KILL MAJOR TOM

At the peak of the entry, when the X15 bucked and bounced like a bad dream from which you couldn't waken, and every bolt and rivet shuddered and your teeth shook loose in your head, the deflector shields glowed a violent blue and the fighter's ionization trail plumed out behind you like a shooting star on an autumn night. There had been a moment (just a moment) when the fear had won, when your trust in Major Tom's skill had not been its equal and you had seen your ship burst open like an egg and you hurled screaming and burning into three hundred miles of sky. The shriek had built in your chest and rattled the bars of your teeth and your brain had pounded pounded pounded against the dome of your helmet. Then you had come out and the air was smooth and the deflectors glowed a dull cherry red and your trusty fighter was dipping down through miles of airspace to the carpet of woolen piled clouds.

Now there is fear again, not the fear of disintegration in the ionosphere, for that is only death and to die is to leave the self and join the others, but the fear of what waits for you below the cloud cover, for that is more terrible than death, for it denies the others and leaves you alone with only yourself.

"Big Tom, we must go back! *Excalibur* has been calling and calling; Captain Zarkon, even the Emperor Geoffrey himself, have been ordering you to turn back. It's too dangerous, you are forbidden to go any further alone!"

Major Tom says nothing but thrusts your X15 Astrofighter lower, lower, lower. Clouds shred like tissue paper on your wingtips, the fog swirls and thins patchily, then you are out of the cloud-base and below you is the surface. The Montgomery/Blair engines thunder as Major Tom throttles back; he is coming in for a landing and your stomach, now gripped firmly by six billion billion billion tons' worth of gravity, is doing flipflops, a sicky-lurchy feeling that overcomes you as he throws the X15 into a left-hand bank.

The ground is tip-of-the-nose close beyond the canopy, a forbidden planet standing on edge in midbank: red-brick neo-Georgian bungalows in fifteen hundred square feet of white-chained garden, trailers in the drive, boats and hatchbacks parked outside, rosebeds flowering, children on BMXs stopping, pointing, gaping.

"Commence landing sequence."

You do not want to. You cannot go down there. To go down there is dying and worse. A billion billion billion miles away *Excalibur,* the Imperial throneship, hangs poised on the lip of jumpspace but its stupendous bulk is as insubstantial as a cloud compared to the painful truth of this place, so pin-sharp that you can even read the street name: Clifton Road. Suddenly you are no longer Wee Major Tom, half of the greatest fighting team the Galaxy has ever known. Suddenly you are a small boy who is twelve years old and more frightened than he has ever been before.

"Commence landing sequence," orders Major Tom.

"No!" you wail, wanting beyond want to hear the words which will make it all right, the words which will make men glad to die in the hollowness of space. "I want to go back! Take me back!"

"Commence landing sequence," says Major Tom, and there is nothing in his voice but determination and command.

"Landing sequence initiated," you sob, touching heavy fingers to cold control panels. Landing shocks slide from their fairings and lock with a thump. The engine noise rises to a scream. Major Tom brings the X15 Astrofighter in low above the rooftops like Santa Claus on his sled and stops it dead in the air over the turning circle at the end of the street. Housewives' morning coffees grow cold as their imbibers stand in their picture windows, babies in arms, to view the spectacle of the Astrofighter touching down. Whipped into tiny tornadoes, dust eddies chase down the street away from the downdraft. There is a gentle touch, as soft as a mother's finger upon a nightmare-snared cheek: touchdown.

"Power down," says Major Tom, but before the noise of the engines has whispered away to nothing his canopy is open, his harness unbuckled, and he is running down the street to a house with number thirty-two on the gatepost and a lovely tan-and-white hearth-rug dog lying on the front step. Behind that picture window, too, there is a woman, with a coffee cup in one hand and the head of a small boy of about twelve under the other.

Then the world folds up on itself like one of those origami fortune-tellers you used to make in school. Major Tom's tight shiny uniform rips and shreds as he runs and the wind whips the scraps away to reveal a new uniform beneath, dark green with silver buttons. An X15 Astrofighter lifts into the air above Clifton Road on a pillar of light, canopy open, and climbs away into forever. Your uniform is gone, and the gentle pressure on your head is not the pressure of a helmet but the pressure of a small, slender hand and you realize that you are the boy in the picture window as the X15 dwindles into a shining dot and winks out. You are held, you are trapped under the gentle hand, marooned on the Planet of Nightmares.

Now Major Tom is at the car and he waves at you and all you can do is wave back at him, for the words you want to shout, the warnings you want to scream, rattle round and round and round in your head like pebbles in a wave and will not be cast out.

Now he has the door open. Now he is in the car. Door shut, belt on, key in the ignition—

This time you know the blast for what it is. This time you are prepared and can appreciate its every vital moment in dreadful action-replay.

The ball of light fills the interior of the Ford Sierra. An instant after, still twilit by the killing light, the roof swells up like a balloon and the doors bulge on their hinges. Another instant later the windows shatter into white sugar and then the picture window before you flies into shards, a gale of whirling knives carried on a white wind that blasts you from your feet and blows you across the room in a whirling jumble of glass and smashes you into the sofa. The skin of the car disintegrates and the pieces take flight. The hood follows through the window to join you on the sofa. The roof has blown clean away and is flying up to heaven, up to join God. The car roars into flames and within, behind the flames, a black puppet thing gibbers and dances for a few endless moments before it falls into crisp black ashes.

A red rain has spattered the wallpaper. There is not a window intact on Clifton Road. Your mother is lying at a crazy angle against the door, her dressing gown hitched around her waist. Out in the drive the pyre roars and trickles of burning fuel melt the tarmac. Smoke plumes into the sky, black oily smoke, and there at the place where your eyes are drawn, the place where the smoke can no longer be seen, there is a bird-bright white dot: an Imperial X15 Astrofighter coming in from space, and now you know that it must happen all over again, the landing, the running Major Tom, the strange transformations, the man in the green uniform stepping into his car, the explosion, the burning, the Astrofighter coming in for a landing, the changes, the blast, the burning, the Astrofighter, the blast, the burning, the landing, the blast, the burning, landing blast burning, blast burning blast burning blast burning, over and over and over.

"Major Tom!" you cry, "Major Tom, don't leave me! Daddy! Daddy!"

When the alarms had sounded, when the flashing lights had thrown their thin red flickering shadows across the floor, she had said to herself, He's dead, they have lost him, and though the world had ended she could not bear any hatred in her heart for those who had killed her son. They had acted in good faith. She had consented. All responsibility was hers. She could forgive them, but never herself. God might forgive Catherine Semple, but she never would.

Gone, she thought, and had risen from her chair to leave. Empty coffee cups and women's magazines covered the table. She would slip away quietly while the alarms were still ringing and the lights still flashing. Nurses' running footsteps had come chasing down the corridors, but at the door the sudden, terrifying quiet had stopped her like ice in the heart. Then, after the storm had come, the still, small voice, pitifully frail and poignant.

"Major Tom! Major Tom! Don't leave me! Daddy! Daddy!"

"I won't," she had whispered. "I won't leave you," and everything had stopped then. It was as if the whole city had fallen silent to hear the cries of the new nativity, and then with a shudder the world had restarted. Lines had danced and chased across the oscilloscopes, rubber bladders had breathed their ersatz breaths, valves had hissed, and the electronic blip of the pulsebeat had counted out time. But even she had known the difference. The red lights which had been red so long she could not remember them being any other color were now defiantly green, and though she could not read the traces she had known that they were the normal signs of a twelve-year-old boy waking gently from a troubled, healthy sleep. She could feel the warmth from his bed upon her skin and smell the smell that was not the reek of sickness but the smell of sickness purged, disease healed.

She remembers all this, she remembers the nurses, she remembers the handshakes and the hugs and the hankies, she remembers Dr. Montgomery's lips moving, but the words escape her, for time has been jumbled up and nurses, reporters, doctors, photographers, are all stacked next to each other without meaningful order, like a box of antique photographs found in an attic. She remembers flashguns and journalists, video cameramen trailing leads and sound engineers, television news reporters; she remembers their questions but none of her answers.

Now she sits by the bedside. There is a cold cup of coffee on the arm which the friendly nurse from County Monaghan had brought her. Dr. Montgomery and the MacKenzie woman, the one with the look of computers behind her eyes, answer questions. She does not pretend to understand what they have done but she knows what it might have been. Ignored for a while she can sit and watch her son watch her back. Unseen by any cameras, eyes meet and smile. There has been pain, there will be pain again, but here, now, there is goodness.

Outside it seems to have stopped snowing, but by the cast of the darkening sky she knows that it will not be for long. The lights of an Army Lynx helicopter pass high over West Belfast, and if she squeezes her eyes half shut she can make herself believe that they are not the lights of a helicopter at all but the rocket trail of Major Tom, flying home from Andromeda.

SCENES
FROM A
SHADOWPLAY

O
h, but the Infanta Serenade is grace-
ful and the Infanta Serenade is fair
and when Dom Perellen sees her
descending the grand staircase on the
arm of the host, his ex-patron, the night of the pageant at the
House Merreveth, he knows someone will have to die. For but
two weeks previously his had been the arm she had taken
descending his grand staircase to greet his guests, his the halls
which had rung to her gay golden laughter, his the divan she
had graced with her long, languid huntress's limbs. Fury rising
in his gorge like bitter bile, Dom Perellen departs from the ball
as early as propriety permits and orders his gondola to return
him home without delay or detour. He sits like a dull cold
stone, wrapped in his mantle and street mask as the boat steals
down dark canals lined with yellow-windowed walls and low
bridges. Deafened by the imagined laughter of Dom Merreveth
and all the Gracious Castes of the city, he cannot hear the
desperate playing of the ensemble of mechanicals in the bow (a
selection of his own most celebrated quintets, no less), nor the
terrible distant cries of the Ragers as the night's madness
claims them again, nor the erosive slop of dark water against
the stones of the City of Man. Without his knowing, the chill
of autumn rises like fog from Elder Sea and steals through his
street gown into his soul. Upon arrival at the House Perellen he
locks himself in the music room and meets his servitors' well-
intentioned inquiries with a tantrum of temper that sends both
human and mechanical scurrying for their quarters.

From the walls of the music room portraits of the Doms
and Infantas of the House Perellen, separated forever by a

long, narrow strip of parquet floor, gaze upward into the tinkling chandelier, or wistfully toward the great oriel window with its commanding views of the Grand Canal and the Lagoon beyond. On a dais beneath this window stands the current Dom Perellen, thirty-fifth of his line, looking out toward the unseen sea. For a long time he stands thus and the retinue of the House hush each other in their duties and wait. Then as the uncounted campaniles and carillons of the City Imperishable ring out the Third Hour he turns to the device beside him. This is the Instrument, the wonderful contrivance of keys and stops, tabs and levers (capable of the faithful mimicry of any sound animate or inanimate) upon which he creates his compositions. Seating himself before the complex manuals, he touches a key here, a tab there, and swells the long room with music. He plays for many hours, filling the House with towering toccatas of dizzying virtuosity, intricate fugues, and moody sonatas until at dawn he emerges, his fury spent, and announces to his household that all is well, he will retire to his rooms for a short rest. As the doors close behind him the servitors all notice that the portraits of the Exalted Ancestors Beneath the Sea seem to be smiling the same smile.

Now we see a strange thing, for, since those of the Gracious Castes seldom visit those older parts of the city given over to the commonalty and the artisiers, there is a certain unseemliness in Dom Perellen's stealthy passage down branching waterways which grow out of each other, increasingly narrow and overshadowed by crumbling mansions. Slipping past sludge-boats and fishing-cogs, between the baroque barges of the transtellar merchants and the vigilant dark launches of the St. Charl Guards, he comes upon a quiet, deserted water alley enclosed by sheer walls of rusting iron balconies and peeling wooden shutters, overhung by the pale banners of fresh laundry. At the water-steps of St. Audeon's Place, he leaves his gondola and proceeds with two wardens (one fleshly, one mechanical) into the labyrinth of lanes and entries where he finds a place he knows well but has never seen.

Brothers Ho, says the sign above the door, *Importers and Purveyors of Exotic Creatures: Taxidermists.* Behind the latticed window a patchy stuffed padishant bows and curtsies to the passersby. Kittens in pinafores caper about a table in parody of a nursery tea-party, birds sing and display, gorgod-rills rise up upon their hind legs and open their ruffs, fritillaries flitter and fret, and the imported exotics lurk within their protective glass environments.

"Lo, Brothers Ho," whispers Dom Perellen, "a moment of your time for a dear sibling, a favor given, a favor taken?" The door pays no heed. There are no sounds of motion from within. "Lo, siblings, if you will not open the door to your dear brother, will you open it to good custom?" After a long time oiled bolts are drawn back and the door opens. Quick as thought, Dom Perellen is through it. He finds himself in a well-appointed parlor, low-ceilinged and lit by warm yellow gaslight. Every available inch of wall space is taken by some stuffed and mounted creature, every part of the room subjected to the scrutiny of their black glass eyeballs. Behind him the window displays perform their mechanical pantomimes for the amusement of the lanes and alleys. Before him stand two men, tall for the artisan castes, dissimilar in age but in every other way as alike as two peas in a pod.

"Which are you?" asks Dom Perellen. Both men answer together, "We are Adam Beth and Adam He," which is no answer at all. "So few?" asks Dom Perellen. One of the brothers shrugs, the other replies, "Brother Adam Zayin is in the workship, patron; the other four brothers are out among the Known Worlds procuring stock, thanks entirely to your continued patronage, Grace, in obtaining visas for us."

"It was the least I could do. We look after our own, even the discredited sons of our father. But I have some business for you; a matter of some delicacy which demands your particular skills and customary discretion. Now, if I may make myself comfortable?" Chagrined by their lapse of common etiquette, one of the brothers hurries to prepare tea while the other takes Dom Perellen's mantle and street mask. It is then that we see that the faces of Dom Perellen and Adam Ho are like one face reflected in a mirror. After tea has been served Dom Perellen leans forward confidentially across the low table. The swiveling glass eyes of the stuffed animals follow every motion from their high perches.

"I want someone killed."

The Brothers Ho smile politely.

"Go to the assassins, patron. Employ them. Our business is not in death of that manner."

"Where is the artistry in employing assassins? Where is the personal sense of triumph? It is like paying to hear another composer's sonatas; there is no satisfaction in the dry notification of a contract fulfilled. I must orchestrate it myself. It must be my own work, my own composition, my own personal vengeance."

"Ah, so it is the Dom Merreveth, then, patron."

"You pay close attention to the gossip of the Gracious."

"All the city has heard of your discomfiture, patron. Alas, but woman is as fickle and independent as—"

"It is nothing to do with you. Nothing."

"Apologies, apologies, patron. We presume too much on our kinship."

"This 'kinship' is too slender a thing by far to support your right to gossip about your superiors. Consider this: you have a business and a respected name among all castes of the city, although you have had to relinquish your gracious name and take a common appellation. How many other disinherited clones can claim such favorable treatment? Nobler families than the Perellens have sold their engineered sons and daughters to the licensed mendicants and seraglios."

"Nobler families than the Perellens would not perhaps have required seven attempts."

"Enough. I am not responsible for our father's whims. He wished his heir to be a composer, he cloned new sons until he had his composer, and that is it. Need I remind you that under the new law there may be only one legal claimant to any genotype? You live under sufferance and my good favor. Now, my dealings with the House Merreveth. I want to hear your suggestions for a fine present for the Gracious Dom as an apology for my behavior at his pageant."

From a high shelf the Brothers Ho (who we now see to be more than brothers, yet less) bring leather-bound volumes of sample books and a small imager which they employ to display their wares to Dom Perellen. They show him the wheeled gyropeds from the lava plains of Fafenny, helicoptera from the crystal forests of Chrios, fire-dwelling pyrogenes that seem mere lumps of dull stone until the moment they unfold in a blossom of flame; elegant, priceless agapanthas from Hannad, monstrous panjas from the mountains of Ninn; gooseberry-green vegemorphs that derive their motive power from sunlight and water; singing choirs of angels no larger than the palm of his hand; flocks of fritillaries on chains of silver filigree: he sees grampus, oliphaunt, kraken and werwulf; fur and feather, fang and fire. The imported exotica of a dozen worlds do not impress Dom Perellen.

"Something more homely," he says, "the gentle Dom is a home-loving fatherly man." So again the books open and the imager displays: hunting trophies of every conceivable species that can be followed with fowling-piece, crossbow, or light-lance; strange near-human creatures from the forgotten quarters of the city; diorama cases of prehistorical beasts from remote epochs; dumb-waiters and mechanical tray-boys in the shapes of gallimaufs and padishants; humorous novelty collages assembled from diverse pieces of reptiles, birds, fishes, and mammals; mounted grotesques, like the two-headed kitten and the pair of Siamese-twin calves; collections of insects, birds, and small mammals; amusing novelty automata . . . Here Dom Perellen stops them and exclaims, "The very thing!"

"What, patron, the House Mouse Family?"

"Precisely, citizen. The Dom Merreveth may be doubtful of a gift to himself from me, and rightly so, for I'll grant him a certain shrewdness, but a gift to his dear children could not possibly be suspect. And what could be more innocent, what better to delight a child's eye, than our little family of mice? How quickly can you have a set prepared?"

"Four days, patron?"

"Three?"

"It could be done, but not easily. The minutiae of detail, patron; we pride ourselves that our automata are indistinguishable from life."

"Your import licenses are due to expire shortly. I can arrange for another half-year's extension."

"Thank you, patron, but we live in difficult and trying times. Despite the quarantine and the best efforts of the St. Charl Guard, not a night passes without the shrieks of the Ragers, the carniphages, crying from our rooftops, nor morning break without some new poor victim having fallen to them."

"You are vulnerable, I understand. I shall have one of my personal wardens remain to guard your workshop by night."

"Thank you, Grace, but for the books . . ."

"Ah, the books; the books must balance, the gentlemen of

the exchequer never sleep. You will be paid fairly for your work, never fear. It is the least I can do for my unfortunate siblings. Now: the automata; there are a few minor changes I wish you to make."

Now it is noon, for the carillons of St. Maikannen's Chantry have rung out the Thirteenth Hour, and in the plaza beneath the bell-keep Dom Perellen takes wine with a few intimate friends from his circle of artists and aesthetes. They drink and laugh and stretch their elegant limbs in the weak autumn sunshine and exchange morsels of malicious gossip. But there is little pleasure in raillery for Dom Perellen for he knows that at other tables in other plazas beneath other bell-keeps other young bucks are lampooning and laughing at him.

Later they visit the Govannon Academy and fall in with a group of five young Gracious ladies, come like them to view the paintings. Dom Perellen drops a two-forent tip to the human chaperon, and his friends distract the mechanical conscience for the few moments necessary for him to slip aside with the Infanta Phaedra on pretext of showing her the exhibition. Later, at the House Perellen, he will entertain her with some short sonatas of his own composing. On their return from the Academy, with the campaniles sounding Nineteen o'Clock and the starlings flocking and swooping about the spire of St. Severyn's Cathedral, they are diverted from their course by the St. Charl Guards who have cordoned off an area surrounding a disused trading factor's warehouse.

"Ragers, Graces," says the fat perimeter sergeant. "Carniphages. Traced a chapter of 'em to this 'ere warehouse. Soon have 'em smoked out, rest assured. What you've got to do, Graces, burn out the Plague."

The Infanta Phaedra presses closer for reassurance and Dom Perellen commands his mechanical quintet to play and quench the sound of the screams. The little boat moves on. Behind, the sun-forged blades of the laser-lances cauterize the alien infection. Soon the cries are lost and all that can be heard is the gentle lilting of the music and the lap of dark water under the bow as the ebbing tide draws them down the confluence of conduits and channels toward Elder Sea.

* * *

Dawn finds Dom Perellen gazing into the ceiling. Confusing ripple-reflections move across plasterwork cherubs and peacocks. The Infanta Phaedra stirs contentedly in her sleep but Dom Perellen does not hear her, for he is far away in the passages of his mind. Dawn is the hour when the death-white corpse-boats slip from their moorings behind the Hall of Weeping and steal away into the sunrise to the funeral grounds. Only the gravely smiling boatmen who crew the water-hearses know the latitude and longitude of the funeral grounds, but in his imagination Dom Perellen can see them slipping the weighted coffins over the stern into fog-shrouded Elder Sea. For this is the vision that haunts him, a corpse-boat making its slow cold passage across the bar into Elder Sea. Between the somber upright figures of the boatmen is a white coffin bearing the crest of a Gracious Family unfamiliar to him. He sees the coffin sinking into the clean cold water without even a ripple, sinking with today's company of bakers and butchers and lawyers and priests, merchants and traders and lowly play-actors, poets and painters and wise men and fools. The citizens of the City of Man fall through the water to stand side by side in serried ranks of Grace and groveler, a submarine army waiting at attention on the silt and sediment of centuries for the fanfares of the Pantochrist on the Dawn of Resurrection when all will be summoned to the rising Land of Gold. The coffin rests in the blessed company of the Ancestors Beneath the Sea, those ancestors whose faces line the walls of the music room. It disturbs Dom Perellen that he cannot identify the armorial crest upon the sunken coffin.

For two further mornings this vision is to come to him. He lies alone under the startled scrutiny of cherubs on clouds and virgins pursued by stags, for his vengeful intensity has so disturbed the Infanta Phaedra that she will not consent to any further nights with him. "Like poison," she describes it. "Like a venom working behind the eyes." Dom Perellen shrugs and returns to the elaborate drawing out of his revenge. There is no doubt in his mind that the unidentified coffin is that of his enemy.

Just before noon on the second day the pneumatique delivers a message cylinder to his office. It states quite simply, *Work completed, awaiting your Grace's disposal. Respectfully, Adam Ho*. In reply Dom Perellen gathers together four important pieces of paper: a Mercantile Letter of Credit for the sum of five hundred forents, an importation permiso from the Port Wardens valid for the period of five months, precise instructions on the delivery of the automata collection, and an accompanying letter to the Dom Merreveth in which Dom Perellen extends his apologies to his onetime patron for having been out of sorts at the pageant and begs, for the sake of old affection, that the good Dom overlook his breach of etiquette by accepting this humble gift to his children. He places the documents in an empty cylinder, addresses it, drops it into the slot, and thinks nothing more about it. While the cylinder crosses beneath the city, he amuses himself by composing a set of complex improvisations about a simple, repetitive theme. It entertains him for the remainder of the afternoon.

Now the picture changes again, and we are in a Great House of grand halls and spacious galleries. Portraits of ancestors line its walls and the slow lap of water wears away at its stones, grain by grain, undermining the centuries. This is the House Merreveth, and we are in the nursery. Three children sleep by the glow of watch-candles, their faces folded to the pillows in simple dreams of childhood, nannies no more than a whisper away. It has been a good day; new toys to play with, a present from a friend of Papa's, a gift to make even the most blasé of aristocratic children gasp in delight. A family of mice, perfect in every detail: Grandpa in nightshirt with pipe, Grandma with her glasses and knitting, Mamma and Pappa Mouse, Mamma in apron and mop hat, Pappa in working bib-and-braces, and the three children in their neat little school uniforms. But more wonderful still, by repeating a magic word whispered to them by a tall, soft-spoken artisier in a street-mask, the tiny diorama comes to life. Mamma sews and Pappa saws, Grandpa puffs his pipe, Grandma knits and rocks her tiny rocking chair, and the children scamper about playing Chase and Blind-Man's Buff, tiny mouse voices squeaking.

The adventures of the mouse family entertained the children until bedtime, and now the minute, intricate automata lie where play has left them, transfixed by slats of moonlight beaming through the nursery shutters. Then two tiny ears prick upright in the moonlight. And two more, and two more, and two tiny red eyes blink open, and a tail twitches. From the frozen postures of abandoned games the mice stretch into animation. They seem almost alive, scurrying across the nursery floor and under the door, but they are no more than precise mechanisms dressed in flensed mouse-skins. It is the boast of the Brothers Ho that their creations cannot be distinguished from reality. By the secret run-ways and traverses known only to living mice they move through the sleeping House, to mice as vast and varied in its terrain as the City of Man to men. In time they come to the Dom's bedchamber. From behind a plasterwork rose on the coping they absorb the scene with pink sensor eyes.

The Dom Merreveth sleeps alone: this is well known among the Gracious Houses, for the Dom's attraction to women lies in his potency in the public world of the arts and commerce rather than in the private world of the quilts. The children dreaming in the moonlit nursery are his only insofar that he donated the culture cells to the genetic surgeons. All this is well; the plan hinges upon the Dom's solitary nature. No harm must be done to the Infanta Serenade. The Dom tosses and turns in the restless dreams of the powerful. The mice scamper unheard and unseen across the carpet, and up the carved legs of the divan. They stand for a moment on the pillow by the Dom's head; Grandma, Grandpa with his pipe, Mamma with her little apron, and Pappa in his dungarees, the children smart and neat in their miniature pinafores. They move to their programmed positions. Then on some silent order they flex their tiny soft paws and steel blades spring out. With surgical precision they slice open Dom Merreveth's throat and wrists.

By the time the servitors have rushed to answer the strange, croaking, flapping cry from the Grace's bedchamber, the toy mice have frozen into position once again, ready for another day's merry play.

The Chant Valedictory of the High Requiem dies away in the airy clerestories of the Hall of Weeping and the fog rolls in across the square like a breaking wave. In their white funeral gowns the small groups of mourners seem as insubstantial as ghosts. They are deathly silent as the fog muffles even their footfalls and respectful whispers. Above their heads, unseen in the fog, vast powers are moving: the seraphs of the Pantochrist, risen from Elder Sea in a cloud of mystery to descend upon the City of Man and summon the soul of a dead Dom to the company of the people beneath the sea.

The small group of young Graces part at the water-steps where their boats await them.

"Such a shock to lose your exemplar so suddenly, Perellen," says Dom Gerrever, the poet.

"Ex-exemplar, citizen; I have not had dealings with the Dom for almost a year. But he did embark me upon my musical career, and I owe him thanks for that. I am sorry he is gone."

"Oh, come now, Perellen," says Dom Harshadden, the playwright. "You couldn't stand the man; he cheated you, slighted you, and humiliated you every chance he could. I'll wager you're glad to see him gone. And at such an opportune time too."

"I would not wish an end like his upon even my worst enemy," says Dom Perellen, suddenly accused and guilty behind his mask. "He may have slighted me, and we have certainly had our differences in the past, but we are not men who murder on matters of shadowplay, are we?"

There are murmurs of consent, but Dom Hemmenveth the painter says, "Who said anything about Dom Merreveth having been murdered?"

"Well, he was."

"But not by someone of the Gracious Castes, as you seem to be implying." Dom Perellen's brain thumps against the front of his skull. His mouth is suddenly hot and dry.

"By me; is that what you are trying to say, Hemmenveth?" There is a deadly calm in his voice he does not feel. Dom Hemmenveth gives ground.

"Oh no, not at all, not at all, Perellen; as you said, we are not men who murder for shadows. Indeed, given your provocation, you did not even employ satirists; great restraint, citizen, great restraint."

"It was a Rager killed the gentle Dom," suggests Dom Perellen, and his friends mutter their agreement. There being nothing more to be said, they go down to their boats and Dom Gerrever calls out in parting, "Perellen, the masque at the House Kerrender, this Matinsday, remember." As the boats pull away from the mooring Dom Perellen remains awhile, head bent, breathing deeply, trying to regain his composure. He is trembling. It had been close. He forces the fear and the guilt down his gullet and draws himself up. It is then that he sees the solitary figure in white running across the empty, fog-shrouded plaza. For an instant the face is turned to him. Behind the funeral mask are eyes he knows.

"Serenade!" His lunge for shore sets the gondola rocking dangerously. "Serenade!" Far away at the edge of the cloisters the figure turns again for a moment, then hurries on. "Serenade." Doves explode into the air from the bell-keeps of the Hall of Weeping and the massive buttresses of pale stonework return his cry to him.

He is to see her again: spied from a high balcony, singular for a moment among the anonymous faces of the street entertainers and mendicants in the Bourse. Again, as a glimpsed figure hurrying up the steps of a water-gate in Harhadden. She turns for an instant at his call but there is no recognition and she does not wait. Again, on a water-taxi sweeping past his gondola on the Canal St. Nimien. Lastly, alone at a far table in a crowded cafe by the Damantine Fountain. By the time he presses his way between the chattering luncheoners she is gone, leaving only a five-pago tip and a musky wisp of perfume prepared from the powdered wings of night moths.

His discreet inquiries at the House Merreveth prove only that she is gone. Delving into past acquaintances from his rakish days discloses nothing. Her friends know less than he. She has vanished back into the city which raised and nurtured her. Looking out from the music-room window Dom Perellen knows that he can never find the one soul in the city's thronging millions who does not wish to be found, for what man could explore every laneway and waterway of a city that changes and grows every hour of every day so that it may never cease growing and thus stagnate and die? There is an infinity of canals and channels which reach back into derelict quarters abandoned so long ago by the slow migration to Elder Sea that their names are forgotten and their waterways choked and stagnant, where the funeral grounds of past millennia have, in their turn, become plazas and conventicles, chapteries and arcades, and are now, centuries later, returning to the ancestors who peopled them. The City of Man is upheld by the hands of the dead.

And she is there somewhere. She will come to him. She must. Otherwise Dom Merreveth's death is a hollow victory.

She will come in time, and time is as plentiful as water in the sea.

After that time at the Damantine Fountain he does not see her again, not even at the ball in the House Kerrender with every Dom and Infanta in the city in attendance. Though he dances a hundred waltzes and gazes into the eyes behind a hundred masks he does not find the eyes that glow in his memories or the body that quickens the beat of his soul. There are smiling invitations from Infanta and Dom alike but he does not accept them for he had hoped with a sure and certain hope that she would have been drawn here tonight like a moth to a candle. He has not yet found her, but there are still faces to be searched for well-known eyes.

So he dances too much and drinks too much and flirts too little and by the time his friends ask him to take them home he is obnoxiously drunk and bad-tempered. He is so unpleasant that his friends (considerably more drunk than he, but good-humored) drop him on the Florinthian Steps and sail off in his gondola in search of new diversions. The sounds of laughter and merry music recede into the fog. Dom Perellen breathes in the wet air, suddenly alone and vulnerable. It is so late it is early and there is no traffic abroad on the canals. He must walk. St. Devereux's Preview will take him to Rerren Square and thence over the Bridge-of-the-Virtues to Samtanavya Prospect. From there it is no distance through the Lido to the House Perellen. But this is a gloomy area of derelict warehousing, and Dom Perellen recalls with a shock the friendly face of a fat Guard saying, "Ragers, Grace, carniphages. Traced a chapter of 'em to this 'ere warehouse." That same warehouse which now looms before him. It puts an urgency in his step and a face in every shadow. Footfalls echo deceptively in the cold fog and the gas lanterns hiss like a slow exhalation. Scared sober, Dom Perellen stops, turns. The echo of his footfalls persists too long. They have a wrong sound, like the echo of high-heeled shoes, or claws, tapping on the cobblestones.

"Serenade?"

The scream shatters his soul like glass. He whirls to find himself face to face with snapping fangs and bulbous red eyes. The hot sweet stench of its breath drives him back, retching. The Rager twists its deformed body and hisses in its throat.

Dom Perellen's mouth is open but the words take an age to come. His heart surges against his rib cage.

"The Rage," whispers Dom Perellen. The Rage, the alien plague from beyond the edge of the world, brought, say some, by the vessels of the transtellar merchants which splash down in the Lagoon; sown by the agents of jealous foreign governments, say others; and yet others still maintain that it is caused by spores from an alien colonization vessel which crashed in Elder Sea thousands of years before. For the first time he is able to see the creature whole. By its shriveled breasts and wide pelvis it must once have been a woman of the City of Man. The Rage has deformed her skeleton until she stands no taller than a child, her muscles tied into powerful, tight knots beneath her fur. In the swollen bulbs of her eyes, adapted by the disease for better night vision, there dwells a certain unclean madness. Dom Perellen edges away from the creature, hands outspread in a human gesture of placation, but the Rager is beyond the reach of all things human for the plague has harrowed and violated her humanity and warped her body into an obscene travesty. She howls; the flames behind her eyes will not let her rest until she has tasted human flesh. She bares her teeth in the lantern-light and smashes Dom Perellen to the cobbles with a sweep of her arm. Then she is on him. Claws rip at his head, tearing away his flimsy party mask. Teeth the length of fingers snap in his face. The sweet stench of plague gusts hot in his nostrils. The jaws lock like cocked gin-traps for the killing bite through the throat. In his last moment Dom Perellen is aware of two things.

A searing blue flash.

A stench of burning meat.

The carniphage spasms and rolls from him to lie smoking gently on the cobblestones, teeth bared to the moon. The mask is clenched in her fingers. A charred hole has been stabbed cleanly between her breasts. Across the square the St. Charl Guard holsters his light-lance and runs to assist.

"Is His Grace all right? No wounds, bites, or scratches?" For this is the manner in which the Rage claims its victims, through spores transmitted in the saliva of the carniphage which infect the slightest wound. Dom Perellen shakes his head and mumbles, "All right, all right." Then the trembling starts, a spastic twitching so debilitating that the Guard must help him to the launch. He is taken to the House Perellen where his servitors fuss and fluster with warm quilts and healing broths and sleeping draughts. The Dom orders them out of his sight and shuts himself in the music room. Under the benign gaze of his ancestors he works the spasms from his fingers on the manuals of the Instrument. He commences with small whispering sounds, like the wind and the water and the scampering of mice. At the beginning of Fifth Hour he adds new tones, intricate repetitive sequences of pipes and bells. Then he brings in distant thunderous bass chords: storms and tempests in the mountains of the land beneath the sea from which his people came. Convoluted treble melodies occupy him for an hour or so, then he explores matching harmonies and subtle rhythms. He constructs his music hour on hour, layer upon layer like the strata of ancient sedimentary sandstones until the windows burst open under the pressure of music and the notes pour forth into the city in a waterfall of voices, singing down the empty canals and swirling around the eaves of the ancient houses in search of hidden things.

At last Dom Perellen lifts his hands from the manuals and the vast music dies away until only the tiny whispers and susurrations remain. In the silence after there is the sound of two hands clapping.

Dom Perellen turns and she is there, smiling and applauding.

She makes to leave and Dom Perellen is beside her.

"Why have you come? Why are you here?" She will not reply but leads him on a thread of perfume made from the crushed wings of night moths out of the music room and along the passage to the bedchamber. And there, under the plaster cherubs and peacocks and virgins, she gives herself to him and stops his questions with her mouth. By the light of cobwebbed candelabra their love builds like a symphony, like the stratified music by which Dom Perellen called her out from the hidden places of the city. Dom Perellen's hands grip great fistfuls of dark hair, he has never known such joy as she gives him her breasts and her mouth and the hidden places of her body on the divan that is wide as all the sea. Together they scale the pinnacles of pleasure in a love that threatens to consume them both and leave nothing but ashes. Yet there is something amiss in her lovemaking, something passionless and mechanical, as if they were two animals caught in the frenzy of rut. She does not utter a word, not a sigh or moan.

At the height of their passion she drives her teeth into his shoulder with such force that she draws blood. Dom Perellen scarcely feels it, swept away on the tide of his own pleasure. It is only afterwards, in the sadness that always follows, that he notices the smell, the smell of something sweet, something rotting, something ancient and foul. It is familiar but for the moment he cannot place it. Then it is forgotten as Serenade bends to his lips again. He looks into her gentle eyes and there sees a thing which freezes the very pith of his being.

Around each iris, in tiny stenciled letters, are the words *Brothers Ho, Taxidermists*.

Then he knows what his replicate brothers have done to him. He knows why Serenade has come here; and the nature of her business among the abandoned warehouses of Sessereth. He sees her opening her lips to the carniphage's poisoned kiss and recognizes the stench of the Rage. He feels the inhuman machinery beneath her skin, and the warm welling of blood from his shoulder. He makes a despairing lunge for the bell-pull but it was too late from the morning he saw her before the cloisters of the Hall of Weeping. Then the fire blossoms in his brain and red red pain sweeps away his reason as the Rage takes possession. He is given time for one final look at Serenade, the last memory he will take into insanity, then his humanity blows out like a candle and the animal is set free.

Last of all we see a boat waiting in the dawn light by the steps beneath the Bridge-of-the-Virtues. In it stand three men in white wearing identical funeral masks. In the bow sits a strikingly beautiful woman, but there is a touch of strange about her perfect stillness, something too precise, almost mechanical. The three men have their hands crossed on their breasts and the air of focused attention of those listening for a distant sound, perhaps the cry of some naked, twisted creature of the night turning away from the burning light of day. A corpse-boat glides by, silent and serene as a swan, journeying out to Elder Sea. Taking its passage for a sign of some kind, the three men turn their boat away from the Bridge-of-the-Virtues, away from the Sea, and journey inwards into the City of Man to claim their inheritance.

CHRISTIAN

When the day is so hot that it scorches the tips of the sea grass into tight brown spirals and sends the columns of ants stigger-staggering across the sand, the beach is a good place for a boy to play. He can splash through the waves as they wash on the shore. He can build castles and fortifications in the sand and watch the sea flood his moats and crumble his ramparts and capture his standard, a single gull's feather stuck into the topmost battlement. He can set a driftwood dreadnought afloat and bombard it into submission with stones from his shore batteries, or he can write his name with a stick in the damp sand and let the tide wipe his words away. There are a thousand different games a boy can play with the sea.

If the tide is low there are the hulks, tired gray men of the sea that have been slumping into the sand for centuries. Some have settled so deeply that only the points of their ribs protrude from the swallowing sand, and a boy can imagine that they are not the bones of ships at all, but the bones of prehistoric creatures.

But if the tide is high there is always the Cannery. It lies half an hour's walk down the beach, but is worth the effort, for it was made in heaven for a small boy. There are rusting steam cranes and disused canning machinery, there are chutes and slides and sluices, there are rails and dollies and hoists, but most of all there are the buildings, made from planks of that gray-brown wood that always feels warm to the touch, so old that they have begun to bulge at the sides. All the windows are broken and the doors off their hinges and light shines through the roof where the autumn gales have swept the shingles away. Parents do not trust it. They say the pier is unsafe and forbid children to play on it, but their restrictions take nothing from the magic of the place, a magic of a different kind from that of the hulks (for after all this pier has never sailed beyond the rim of the world), but no less magical for that. For above all other places, this is a boy's place.

Your place.

When the day is so hot that it drives the customers indoors and Ma wants you to run errands and Da wants you to collect glasses and Sister is too busy serving and Brother too busy practicing the mandocello, when not even Mr. Cat has time for you, the Cannery is a good place to be.

Ma's shout chases you along the beach but you easily outrun it and soon all there is to hear is the rush of surf and the mewling of the gulls slipping down the wind. The sun is bright and the sand is hot and you think that on a day like this anything could happen. So you search the sky for the telltale flickers of daylight shooting stars that you have been told are the trails of ships arriving at the edge of the world. You squint through your fingers, for the sun is very bright, but though you peer and peer you do not see even one.

But you do see three colorful shapes dancing high on the air. A moment's concentration reveals them: kites, one like a festival dragon with a long tail, one with a great smiling sun painted on it, and the third one, so high up that it is barely visible, no more than a dead black speck. Someone is flying kites from the end of Cannery Pier.

There is a gaily painted caravan with a skewbald pony munching the tough sea grass in the dunes by the foot of the pier. The caravan door is open and you decide to sneak a quick look. Why not? After all, isn't the kite flyer trespassing on the end of your pier?

The caravan is filled with kites. There are no pots, no pans, no sink and no stove, no bed or books or bootlocker, just kites of all shapes and sizes and colors. There is one with a painted moon, and another with a cross of stars that actually twinkle, and a blue kite with clouds on it, and one with a whirlwind and crisscrossing lightning bolts, and another blue one, but with a painted rainbow, and one so black that your eyes skid off it like glass, and many many more, too many to take in with one single glance, so that all you get is an impression of lightness and brightness and color.

You are so taken up with gazing that you do not hear the

creak of the step or the tired sigh or feel the cool of a shadow falling across your back.

"Oh," says a voice. You turn, seized up with dread. The tall gray man before you takes a step back in surprise. "Oh," he says again, at a loss for something better. It is hard to tell who is more surprised. You stand and stare openmouthed at each other for a long and silly time. Then the gray man frowns and says,

"But what are you doing in my caravan?"

At any other time you would have wilted with embarrassment, but the shock of discovery has made you defiant.

"What are you doing on my pier?"

The gray man gapes. A look of puzzlement crosses his face.

"I'm sorry, I was unaware that the pier belonged to anyone. It seemed to me just to be a good windy place well away from all the people where I could fly my kites in peace."

And because he has not laughed at you like any other adult would, you decide to trade this kiteman trespass for trespass.

"I don't actually own the Cannery, nobody does, but it's my special place. But because you think it's special too, you can fly your kites there anytime."

"Thank you," the kiteman says graciously.

"I came in here to look at your kites," you continue. "I saw them through the back door and came on in, because if you don't want people to go into your caravan, you shouldn't leave your back door open."

"True," the kiteman says. "Can't deny that. Well, having seen them, then, what do you think of my kites? Aren't they grand?"

What you think is that it is silly for a grown man to be playing with kites, but you keep your opinion to yourself.

"Aye, grand," you agree, but it is as if this gray kiteman can see right inside you, because he smiles and says,

"Ah, you're only saying that to keep a stranger happy. I can see that you know little of their true charms and mysteries. But you have the look of a boy with too much holiday time heavy on his hands; perhaps I might instruct you a little in the appreciation of kites? How would that sound? In return for the use of your Cannery?"

"Sounds fine, mister."

"Call me Christian," the kiteman says.

"Fraser MacHenry," you reply, remembering your manners.

"Glad to make your acquaintance, Fraser," the kiteman says, and he goes and picks up a great kite almost as gray as himself. On the kite is a painted cherub blowing a gale from apple-round cheeks and at its lowest point an ocean wave is breaking.

"What would you want with such a dull thing on a bright afternoon like this?" you ask.

"Because I think it's time we had a squall," Christian says, and, tucking the stormkite under his arm, off he sets; past the skewbald pony, who gives you a terrible look, up the dunes and across the tussocky grass to Cannery Pier where the three kites strain on the wind. A thought strikes you.

"Who's flying the kites if you're not there?" you ask, ready to feel betrayed.

"Oh, never worry, Fraser, I have this little black box I adapted from a ship's sheet monitor I picked up in the market in Corpus Christi. Clever little thing, but cost me a fair penny, as clever little things always do; it senses the shifting of the kites on the breeze and winds or releases line accordingly."

At the end of the pier lie the kiteman's few possessions: a crumpled coat of blue pilot cloth lying across a tall wooden staff with silver caps and the little black box clamped to an iron bollard. The kiteman sits himself down. He motions for you to join him and you come and sit down beside him and dangle your legs beside his over the glinting water. He nods at his kites.

"Well, which one would you like a go at?"

You squint into the painfully bright sky and pass your critical eye over the hovering kites. The sun one is pretty, the dragon exciting, but neither so exciting as the black one, which must be the twin of the one you saw in the caravan.

"The black one, please."

Christian shakes his head. "Sorry. Try again. You see, though I may be able, I hope, to teach you how to fly a kite forwards and backwards, and up and down, and side to side, that black one has to be flown *inwards* and *outwards* too, and to be honest, I don't think I can teach you that."

"*Inwards* and *outwards?* How do you fly a kite inwards and outwards?"

"Good question, Fraser. Wish I knew. But tell me, have you heard of people who can do something without being certain of how they do it? Well, I must be a bit like that with that kite. Now, which of the other two would you like, or would you prefer this one?" He holds out the gray stormkite, but you shake your head and say,

"The dragon kite, please."

"The dragon kite it is, then," says Christian, and unhooks the flying line from the little black machine and hauls down the big dragon kite. Close up, it is bigger than you had ever imagined. Then he shows you how cleverly it is constructed, how it generates lift from its geometry, how light and how delicate it is and yet how strong. He shows you how to fix the flying line to the bridle line, how to launch it and control it so that it holds steady in the windstream, not dipping and bellying like the rowdy gulls. Then he reels it in once more and hands kite and spool over to you.

You botch the first two attempts and your ears burn with horrible embarrassment. But again Christian does not laugh at you. "There's always time enough to do it well," he says, and on your third try the great sky-dragon skips and jumps and hiccups along the pier but then the wind catches it and whips it into the air so strongly that the line sings off the spindle in your hands. You cheer as your kite climbs high high past the startled delinquent gulls, high over dirty Cannery Pier, and the bright dragon's eye looks down to see the small dancing speck on the end of its line that is you and the larger gray spot that is Christian. He grins and unlashes the sunkite from the little black machine and together the sun and dragon tumble through the sky. Presently they are joined in their game by the gray stormkite, but within the hour you must hand the dragon kite back to Christian because the wind has grown too wild for you to master. A horizon-wide line of evil black cloud is advancing on the Cannery and gusts are tugging at your ears. Christian casts an eye on the sky and says,

"Go on, get out of here before it starts."

"Will you be here tomorrow?" you ask.

"Oh, I should think so. Look for me under . . . a blue kite, I think." And with that the first knuckles of rain rap on the shingles and chase you all the way up the beach to home. Da is bent over the wireless listening to the Coast Guard weather forecast and shaking his head.

Towards midnight the squall clears sufficiently for the storm shutters to be lifted and the refugee customers ushered gently home. For you, unable to sleep on account of all the wonders buzzing round in your head, this is a chance to unhook Da's binoculars from their peg and sneak up to the weather room. Despite the lateness of the hour it is still light, for this time of the year the sun never really sets, and by the gloaming you can clearly distinguish the caravan sheltered in the dunes, even the skewbald pony chewing contentedly at its thistles, and there at the end of the pier, is that Christian himself? You fumble the magnification up five and now you are certain, it *is* Christian, his coat of blue pilot cloth pulled on against the chill, and above him, his kites; one dead black, sprinkled with stars, the other a bold white half-moon riding up the sky. Far away around the edge of the world the real moon is rising to meet it, and on the face of the white moon is a sharp black spot: the black kite.

You return the binoculars to their case and are about to tiptoe back across the treacherous floorboards when something goes *click!* in your head, something you saw today, a wooden staff with silver heels. Close concentration reveals forgotten details: the notches on the staff, little nickmarks all the way down its length to within six inches of its foot. Memory clarifies: one of Da's hand-me-down sailing stories: that there's a mark on his staff for every passage of Cape Infinity a Pilot makes. Reason concludes: the man flying kites from Cannery Pier can be nothing other than a Pilot.

And now it is another hot, irritable day and you are getting underfoot even if you're just sitting playing with Mr. Cat on the window ledge. Ma throws a packed lunch at you and chases you out of the house, forbidden to return before tea. So away down the beach you go, secretly glad because there are a hundred questions you want to ask, each of which breeds a thousand more, and the answer to even one of them would be worth ten of Da's stupid old sailor stories. Your head rings with echoes of Pilots and SailShips, black suns and lightspeed horizons, sudden squalls and staffs and kites that fly inwards and outwards; half-understood fragments of overheard stories or lessons from school that have all solidified in the presence of a real Pilot flying his kites from the end of your pier. And as sure as eggs are eggs, there is the blue kite flying proudly in the clear morning air, so blue that it makes the sky seem pale in comparison.

As the tide is out you have planned to take Christian for a walk out to the hulks. Maybe they will prompt him to answer some of your nervous questions. Christian is only too pleased to fasten his kites, the blue, the black, and the bright yellow sun, to his little black box and follow you down the weedy-wet steps onto the sand.

"A fine morning for a walk," he declares and comes with you out over the sand ripples and through the shallow drift-locked lagoons to the damp place where the hulks lie. Behind you two lines of wet footprints meander over the glistening sand. Seagulls bicker above you and all around stand the tired old bones of the hulks. You squeeze puddingy sand between your toes and point to a barnacle-crusty cylinder of rusting plate about a mile off, slightly less decrepit than its two companions.

"My Da says when he was a wee boy he can remember that one coming down." Christian screws up his eyes against the glare and peers.

"He's not the only one," he says. Now what could that mean? Subtlety breeds subtlety, it seems. Time for a more direct approach.

"You were a Pilot once, weren't you, Christian?"

"Oh, you must have seen my staff yesterday, I left it on the pier, I remember. Well, yes, I am a Pilot, and let me see; yes, I am hundreds of worldbound years old, yes, I was conning ships around Cape Infinity when your grandfather's grandfather was your age, and no, I am not immortal, for not even a Pilot can cheat God, but perhaps I am a little less mortal than I once was, though my starfaring days are done. And that's your first question answered, Fraser."

Now it's your turn to gape.

"But how did you know that?"

"Foursight, Fraser, but it doesn't take foursight to tell me that you'd like to know every little thing I had to learn to be a Pilot. And I'd tell you that if I started now to tell you all that I learned I might be finished by St. Agnes's Eve, 1816, because it takes ten years for a man to learn the Pilot's art, and only then if he's the right man, for without the gift of foursight you might as well try teaching a handful of sand from this beach. Instead I think I'll tell you a story, and it's a story in three parts and this is the first part of it."

THE STORY OF THE BOY WHO WANTED TO BE HAPPY.

In the narrow lands that lie between the mountains and the sea there stood a city of warm red brick. In the winter the snow lay deep in its streets and in spring and autumn the sea-fog would hang for weeks over it like wet, gray wool, but in the summer the red brick buildings would sigh and stretch and release a gentle friendly warmth into the air.

Now, this city had but one Law, and it was the wisest Law ever made, for it held that nothing was higher than Happiness. To this end, every child who reached the age of twelve (for the years of that city are longer than yours, Fraser) was tested so that they might find the station in life which afforded them the greatest happiness. For everyone was happy in that city, from the street sweeper with his besom to the High Portreeve with his gold chain of office, for everyone was in the position to which he was best suited, and everyone who married, married someone who had been tested to be their perfect match in temperament and character, and there was no envy or greed or jealousy of another, for everyone was content. Tears were never seen in the streets of that city, nor the sounds of sorrow ever heard, for sadness and sorrow had been abolished.

Now, in this city lived a boy. In many ways he was like you, Fraser, for he loved to watch the steam-tugs laboring up the Musgrave Channel to Templemore Dock with laden transports wallowing in tow, or sometimes he might ditch school and cycle out along the pier to the Mole House with borrowed binoculars to wait for hours for the tremendous fountain of sunlit water that heralded the arrival of a ship in the bay. But though he loved the ships, as all boys can before life grinds the love out of them, there was something he loved better. For he was clever with his hands and had a quick and playful mind and what he wanted most in the world to be was a toymaker. He wanted to make little painted wooden farm animals, and clever, intricate puppets, and toy trains with real steam locomotives, and baby dolls so lifelike that you would hesitate to hug them for fear they might cry: this he knew would make him truly happy.

At the age of twelve he went to be tested, as everyone must if they wished to remain a citizen of that city. He filled the forms and completed the aptitude tests and submitted to the medical and psychological examinations, and in the middle of his gene-scan chart they saw a great peak in the graph and they knew then that he was that most singular of men, one possessed of the gift of foursight, who could see into a wider present than they did, one that went a little bit outward and a little bit inward into time.

So they summoned him to the Bureau of Happiness and told him that with such a gift he could never be truly happy as a toymaker, that he must go to Trinity House and learn the Pilot's Art, for such a great gift must be used for the good of the people of all the worlds and not be buried forever in some dingy toymaker's workshop. Finally convinced that he could not be happy any other way, the boy let them put him on an Admiralty ship called the *Edmund Foxx*, and the ship spread her sails to catch the winds between the worlds and sailed away from the city where Happiness was Law and the boy never returned there again.

And though many worldbound years passed, it only seemed a few days to the boy until he found himself treading the ancient halls of Trinity House. There they taught him to use his foursight to sense the possible futures that radiate away from the pivot-pin of *present* like the ribs of a fan, and the possible pasts that likewise converge upon it; they taught him to feel the tides on his skin, and the currents that flow under space and time; they taught him shipcraft in thrilling races round the sun in solos which were little more than a sail and a lifepod; they taught him the mysteries that lie at the unseen hearts of black suns and how they might be twisted to permit a ship to pass safely through to another place and time. And when they had taught him all they knew, they sent him out to sail the Nineteen Worlds under the staff of Navigator-Meister Koch to learn those things which cannot be taught. And at the end of all this, he was a boy no longer but a man, and a man but briefly, for when he took up the silver-shod staff and badge of Trinity House he became a Pilot. But do you know, Fraser, in all those years they never once thought to ask him if he was happy, for in the consideration of what is highest, Happiness always bows to the Law, and the Law to Expediency.

And that is the first part of Christian's story.

            "But how do you fly a kite inwards and out-wards?"

It is a gusty, roary sort of day. Overweight white clouds with dirty gray bottoms hurry across the sky. Too blustery for the sunkite, reckons Christian, so he has only the black kite, which no weather seems to worry, and a blue kite speckled with scuds of painted cloud, up flying this morning. Christian considers your question.

"Hard to explain, maybe easier to show. Try touching your fingers gently to the flying line, there . . . Now, what do you feel?"

You brush the line with your fingers. An odd sensation hums through them.

"It tingles," you whisper.

"But not unpleasantly?" You nod your head. "That's good. Now, close your fist on the line and pull it as hard as you like. Go ahead, pull, and don't forget to watch the kite." Puzzled, you keep one eye on the sky and tug the line firmly. Nothing happens. The line twangs from your fingers.

"Try again, harder, as hard as you can." You seize the line and heave for all your worth. It does not move one inch. It is like trying to pull an iron paling out of the school fence. Up there the black kite does not even waver.

"What's happening? Why won't it move?"

"Well, you see, most kites fly in the three dimensions that we're familiar with in our world, but some kites fly in four or even five dimensions and go a little bit outward and a little bit inward into time. So unless you can hold the flying line in those additional dimensions, the kite's not going to budge in these three. Then of course, the nature of the wind has a lot to do with it. Now, my weatherkites, they fly on the worldwind and respond to the world's weather, but the Black Kite (which is made from special, sensitive sail-fabric I buy from a man in Corpus Christi, and is as much a creature of the flyer's mood and whim as the wind's), it flies on the higher starwinds and responds not to the brightsun, but to the darksun out there at the edge of our system of worlds."

"But what would you want a kite like that for?"

"Many reasons, Fraser, but chiefly so that I know when anything arrives or departs from our universe at Cape Infinity. You remember that tingle you felt?" It had felt like a distant shout sounds when you cannot make out what the words are, like something you can never fully know. "Well, that's a foursight impression drawn down from the sky. In a way, it's sort of like . . ."

"The aerial on my Da's wireless!" you shout as things become clear.

"Well put. You see, over the years I've been waiting, my foursight has grown weak. Oh, I can still foursee big, obvious things, like the weather, or the first question that comes into your head, but I've lost the subtlety for the small things, like when a particular ship comes through Cape Infinity, or even when a small boy decides to have a look around my caravan. People muddy the timestream and cloud my foursight; they're always deciding, or not deciding, and from each decision, or lack of it, a whole new universe springs into being. You understand?"

"I think so. . . . So you need something to make the wee things louder," you say, thinking of Miss Latimer's ear trumpet from school. "And there're no people here to bother you. Except me."

Christian laughs, a wonderful sound like ripples chuckling on the shore.

"Oh, you're no bother, Fraser. You do me a power of good, because it's a man's duty to reflect upon his past in his retirement, and you remind me of that duty. Apart from that, I like having you here to talk to."

Something Christian had said prompts a question:

"Did you say you were waiting for your kite to tell you when a special ship came?"

"I suppose I did, in so many words. Mind you, she'd hardly qualify as a 'ship' anymore, though she'll be under sail and airtight: 'hulk' might be a truer description, but she's nothing like those poor old rusting things out there in the sand, she's a *true* ship, what you people call a 'Sail Module.' And she'll come down like a true ship, in a blaze of fire and glory, because like all Sail Modules she's too lightly built to survive entry into the atmosphere though she's laughed at Cape Infinity.

"Tell me, Fraser, have you ever seen meteors burn across the sky out of their proper season and wondered to yourself how they came to be there? You see, they might not be meteors at all, but the hulk of some SailShip burning away to nothing up there on the edge of the world. Despite our machines and our harnessing of foursight so that we can reach out over the lightspeed horizon and out of possible danger, travel between the worlds is still a perilous business. For although we created Cape Infinity, it is beyond our control and always will be, for in it we've finally made something which is our master."

And with that he will not say another word about ships or suns or black kites, but sits there gazing at the distant hulks with a look on his face that is a curious mixture of recognition and grief.

Your stomach reminds you that you have spent all morning talking and you are eager to unwrap your lunch. As usual Christian has forgotten to bring any, so you offer him a share of your cockelty pie and pickled onions.

"Oh, no, thank you, Fraser, I'm not all that hungry . . . I don't seem to have the appetite I used to."

The fact is, he doesn't seem to have an appetite at all because you have never seen him eat. And he mustn't need as much sleep as he used to either, because some mornings you have seen him sitting there at one or two or even three o'clock, just sitting there as still and solid as that iron bollard beside you.

"Christian, why do you tell me all these things?"

Christian smiles. "Who can really say why we do one thing rather than another? But, enough talking, for the wind's up and the sun's bright and the day's just perfect for flying a kite."

THE STORY OF THE PILOT AND HIS PUPIL.

This is a love story, and like all love stories there is more pain and cruelty in it than love.

Now, there are two types of men who sail between the worlds. There are those who love to adventure in uncharted skies and feel the long wind in their sails, and there are those who love to specialize in one part of space until they know the weave of its fabric like they know their own skin. The Pilot was one of the latter. For more worldbound years than you would guess, Fraser, he had conned SailShips through the singularity until it was said that he knew Cape Infinity better than he knew his own doorstep. And there was many a word of truth in that, for he was the kind of man who lived two months out of twenty years in his little house on Water Street, who was only truly happy with a ship's deck under his feet, and who had as many marks on his staff as a man of three times his subjective years. He remained changeless while the people he passed in the streets of the city grew older and they muttered to themselves that no one could cheat God and not reap the reward some day.

Now, about this time the Admiralty commissioned a ship for a seeding run to the then-uninhabitable New South Georgia Colony. Never a popular business, this planetary seeding; you'd think that in return for a whole new world the Admiralty would be a little more generous with their bonuses than they are. The name of this ship was *Esperanza* and there was never a ship quite as fine as she; bright and clean as a new-minted florin and still ringing from the hammers of the building docks at Coble. Everything about her was as new as ninepence, including her Master, and an apprentice sent from Trinity House to sail Cape Infinity under the staff of the Pilot. Two more different people than Master Roche and Apprentice Anelle you would be hard put to imagine, Fraser. Roche was a great heavy slug of a man; newly symbiosed and unable to do any wrong: his machineself was from an Admiralty warship crippled in a skirmish with Commonality privateers and his fleshself had been Chief Engineer on a decommissioned Company trader. A recipe, Fraser, for as boorish and insensitive a creature as ever aspired to the command of a star vessel.

Anelle was unlike him as black is white. Now, it's not unusual as you might think to have woman Pilots, for no one can say where the gift of foursight will rest, but it's said that for women and ships, where beauty leads sorrow always comes following, and Anelle was as beautiful as a Darkwinter's night is long. There was never one as lively, as quick to learn and laugh, as Anelle, and of course the Pilot soon came to love her for her dark beauty. But it is not wise for any teacher to love his pupil too much. And if the Pilot came to love his apprentice, he also came to hate his Master, and this is why.

The advice of a Pilot is never to be taken lightly, as every shipmaster knows. All save Master Roche, who believed only in his own infallibility. To impress the Admiralty Selectors who had symbiosed him to this command he programmed his machineself to take *Esperanza* on the fastest, most direct course through Cape Infinity to the New South Georgia Colony. Now, all Pilots make their approach to Cape Infinity through the north or south spinpoles, which, though slow, is safe, and only a fool would attempt to take a ship straight through the accretion disc where the event density is so high as to render even foursight unreliable. But though the Pilot argued day in, day out, Master Roche would not be swayed, and as the navigational computers were not just under his command, but an actual part of him, *Esperanza* held her course into the heart of the black hole.

One day, after another futile debate which only set Pilot and Master further at odds, the Pilot stormed from the flight deck in search of Anelle, for these days only her brightness and kindness made living bearable for him. He stamped into her room in a dreadful humor, and then stopped, and stared. He should have been horrified, he should have retched and covered his eyes, he should have turned his back and run away through the miles and miles of corridors to the furthest parts of the ship. But he did none of this. All he did was stare. For Anelle turned to greet him, and her breast was open and within delicate mechanisms moved and molecular circuits oozed.

Then she told him that she was the first of the new race, that after a thousand years of study the machines had identified and isolated the phenomenon of foursight and had learned how to duplicate it artificially. So that no human should needlessly cast wind and limb to the sky again, they had built a new race of machines ready to step forward to take man's place on word of Anelle's success. She was a machine, and still the Pilot loved her.

Then the Pilot felt the whole million-ton bulk of ship and transport shudder beneath his feet and he knew that they had arrived at the black hole and now he must call the Master's bluff. Reaching out with his foursight he beheld the rainbow ring of the accretion disc, and ordering short-sail, he took his ship down into the maelstrom. The buffets struck like the fist of God and *Esperanza* rolled and yawed like a pig, but he held her and the wind screamed into the singularity, seizing the ship like a glass float in a hurricane and driving her down that great gullet past shards of shattered planets, round gravitational whirlpools deep enough to drown whole worlds in. *Esperanza* plunged towards the shatter-point, and just as gravity reached out to smear her into a radio-stain on the thin edge of the accretion disc, the Pilot took her up and out and over and the ship howled across the face of that ring of solid ylem like every demon of Samhain Eve was after her soul, her way lit by insane neutron lightnings that crawled across the crust. Ahead lay the singularity and the sight of it awed every soul aboard into silence. Even Master Roche crawled from his cozy parlor to stare in wonder and horror, unaware that it was his foolishness and the Pilot's arrogance that had brought them to this terrible place. But at the sight of him the Pilot felt the rage boil over inside him, and his concentration broke and his foursight vanished like a burst bubble.

Then it happened that a gobbet of unimaginably dense matter broke away from the accretion disc and spun into *Esperanza*'s path. So close to the horizon it was invisible to normal senses, and though it brushed *Esperanza* as soft as a butterfly's kiss, that kiss swept away the portside arms and sails and crewmen in an instant. Worse, it threw *Esperanza* into a funeral orbit spiraling down to a final rendezvous with the Edge. Lacking enough sail to break free, the Pilot calculated that in less than an hour the ship would drop below the horizon and be lost. But if the crew could blast free from *Esperanza*'s hulk in the cargo modules, they could use the darksun's momentum to fling them into the polar approaches and safety. All agreed that this was the only means of survival.

All save Master Roche. His mission would not be abandoned, his ship would be repaired using the automated systems of his machineself, passage would be effected and no dissent brooked. Twice he called for all hands to damage-control. Twice he was refused. A third time he ordered them, and, being refused a third time, turned to face the Pilot and ordered the men to arrest him. And the Pilot's fury broke. With a cry he swung his silver-shod staff high and brought it down on Master Roche's head. There was no doubt that he died then for everyone heard bone snap. For an instant they stood stunned at the thing the Pilot had done, and then hurried to save themselves before Roche's machineself recovered from the death of his flesh.

But Anelle would not come. You see, Fraser, she was a machine and machines are not as free as you or I. The Pilot pleaded and begged and told her she would surely perish, but she thought not. Working at machine speeds, she could indeed repair *Esperanza* as Roche had maintained and return her to port.

Then the Pilot said that if she loved him she would come and at that she was sad and said, "But I am not yours, Mr. Christian Pilot, that I am free to come. I must remain here where time runs out and centuries pass like seconds, but I will not forget you if you will not forget me. Look for me in the steely-bright flash of summer shooting stars or the winter-shadow of my sails across the moon, for one of these years I will return to you, I promise." And with that she turned a joyful cartwheel across the flight deck and the Pilot went down to the waiting cargo module and never saw her face again.

Now, Fraser, they say there's no sin in a man loving a machine, for all men agree that in love the outward form is of no consequence and many men have loved machines that are not even remotely human. But what if the machine loves him back?

And this is the second part of Christian's story.

* * *

Above the dirty skylight, wisps of blue are at last showing through the wet-cotton clouds where the gray rainkite keeps watch. You sit together in the airy space of a disused packing shed, each of you absorbed with your own thoughts. Christian's fingers play over the bottom end of his staff, like a blind piper, over the place where there are no notchmarks. Who can tell what he is thinking? Your head is full of heroes and villains. Which was the Pilot? Hero, for playing the brave navigator saving his crew? or villain, for letting his stupidity get them into trouble in the first place? He killed his captain with one blow from his silver-shod staff; does that make him a hero or a villain? Villain in the eyes of the Law, but a hero to you, you decide.

Kicking your way home through the damp sand you find that the circle of your thoughts has brought you round to Christian's caravan in the dunes. It looks old and shabby on this gray afternoon. Paint blisters are popping on the door panels and the steps are worn white with traffic, but there is really no better place for you to be with Christian's story rattling round in your head. How nice it would be, you think, to have a Black Kite of your own to float on the edge of the world like one of your little driftwood dreadnoughts. And with that thought comes a terrible certainty of what you want to do, and you creep up the stairs into the caravan.

Its perfect blackness outshines any of the other gaudier kites. "Black as the Black Sun," you whisper and reach out to take it, to feel an echo of that neutron lightning. Your fingers sink into the blackness, there is nothing there to touch. Startled, you jerk your hand away and the fabric comes with it. Stuck to your fingers, the black material tears silently.

Horror drives all the air out of you. It is like heaven has fallen. For a numb second you cannot breathe. You imagine Christian's iron tread coming up the stairs, finding you as he found you that first time. You search for a place to hide the pieces of shredded kite but there is nowhere where Christian will not see the desecration.

In your ears is a tight singing like you are going to cry, but you dare not afford that luxury. You scoop up the Black Kite, its delicate ribs snapping like sparrow's bones, and hide it under your raincoat. Ribbons of black nightmare trail from below the hem. You run from the caravan, run from the skewbald pony who is watching and knows, run all the way home as if Hell itself has opened up behind you.

Now that you have had time to think about it, everything seems so very much worse. Of course it is only a matter of time until Christian finds his replacement Black Kite missing, and that makes you a thief, which is much much worse than a vandal. How you wish you had not taken the Black Kite, how you wish you had never touched it, how you wish you had never met Christian and his wretched kites! It is no use wishing now.

Consumed with dread, you sit by your bedroom window. Downstairs you can hear the faraway, safe sounds of the patrons making merry. You can clearly pick out Da's voice and the cheeky step-a-jig of brother's mandocello. The binoculars are by your hand on the windowsill. You could pick them up and see if Christian is still flying the first Black Kite, but you are afraid that if you do you will see only empty sky. The wind is rising, quarreling round the rooftiles, but you daren't look out to watch it. And you daren't look under the bed either, for there you have hidden the splinters of kite.

The later it gets the more the fear grows. What if Christian already knows what you've done through foursight? Will he then forgive, or is he preparing some punishment too dreadful even to think about? Hero, or villain? There is no doubt about which role you play. You wrap your quilt around you and wish wish wish that this night was over.

Tomorrow you will explain. You will take the kite and tell him it was an accident, and you won't mind what he does because anything, *anything,* is better than this waiting in fear. Firm with resolution, at last you slide into a shallow, dream-ridden sleep.

The tapping wakes you. The wind is really wild now, snatching at the guttering and beating the pear trees in the garden together. Lashing branches and storm-driven clouds racing through the twilight throw crazy, scary shadows over the carpet. For a moment terror holds you, because you think that he has stepped out of your dream into the world of shapes and substances. Then you listen. The inn is quiet. It is well past even the unofficial closing time, but there is this tap, tap, tap; clearly audible over the shrieking of the storm, like a little winter-blighted bird seeking entrance at the window. You turn to look, and there it is.

A great black kite as wide as the sky is flying outside your window and tapping gently on the glass as it dances on the edge of the storm. The stormkite.

At that same instant of horrified recognition there is a hammering on the door downstairs. That door is six-inch ship-timber, but under those blows it sounds as fragile as dried drift.

"Open up, Mr. MacHenry, open up, I say!" That bellowing voice drains all motion from you.

Christian.

Locks are being drawn back, latches lifted. The door scrapes open.

No, Da, don't let him in, don't let him near me! you want to shout but the words have died in your throat. The stormkite scratches malevolently at the glass. It is almost as if it has *summoned* this evil wind to come hunting you.

"Where is he, where is the boy, the thief, the little thief who stole my Black Kite?" Christian's voice sweeps Ma and Da away like leaves in a tempest.

"No, Christian, I didn't steal, I didn't," you whimper and dive to lock the door. Da is shouting loudly now, demanding names and reasons, ordering your brother to run up to the Coast Guard Station for help, but Christian roars "Silence!" and even the storm falls quiet for an instant.

In that instant you know he has fourseen and found you.

Now he is coming up the stairs, one step, two step, three step, four, now he is on the landing, now he is at the door.

The door handle rattles, the door jars against the lock. There is a pause for a second, then an ugly shout with nothing of the pebble-worn old voice of the kiteman left in it:

"Boy, open the door! Open this door; give me back my kite and I will go in peace, just return my property to me, I have dire need of it."

There is no way you will ever open that door.

Then the blows come, each one twice as heavy as the one before. The doorframe shudders under the impacts. Surely no human fist could strike that hard, and every second the blows double in strength.

There is an explosion and the door blows into splinters.

Christian stands there like a tree riven by lightning, holding his staff in both hands. Blue fire shimmers around its silver heels.

"Fraser, where is my kite?" There is a grief too heavy for whole worlds to bear in those words.

Time freezes over like a winter estuary; Christian, your Ma, your Da, your sister trembling by the bannister, all stand frozen like bulrushes in January as you present the dead, ruined thing to Christian.

"It was a mistake," you plead, holding it up before him. "I touched it."

Christian looks down at you from light-year's distance.

"Oh, Fraser," he says, with aching gentleness, "Fraser!" and that final syllable howls out in a roar that goes on and on and on and on and you tear at your ears and squeal, "Stop it, Christian, stop it, stop it, stop it!" And at last it does stop and the room is empty.

Christian and his kites are gone.

Replaced by—a hall full of grim people with lanterns and weapons—someone asking, "Where, Fraser, where where?"—light catching on shotguns and polished Coast Guard cap-badges—all these come to you like an album of summer snapshots. What is real is that dreadful, dreadful scream ringing round and round in your head. You know it will echo there for always.

"Where, Fraser, tell us where!" the voice insists.

"Caravan by the Cannery, in the dunes," you sob and in seven words betray him.

"Right!" Heavy men in heavy boots stamp in the hall. Hastily wrapped in a heavy sea-coat, your own brother carries a ponderous whaling lance and a look on his face that he will not have to use it. The men crunch off down the path in puddles of lantern-light. Ma takes you upstairs, but you struggle free and skip away from the snatching hand. Then you are after them into the twilight.

How fast they are! You had hoped to dash ahead of them and warn Christian, but the heat in their blood must drive them on like ship's boilers. They are easy to follow: the sway of their lanterns and the mumble-grumble of their angry voices carry over the windswept dunes and when those are lost there are their heavy, nailed bootprints pressed hard into the sand. Boots are good in the sand, that is why they are so far ahead of you, slithering and sliding in your slippers. The sky hangs huge above yet the stars feel as close and familiar as thistledown. Meteors kindle away to nothing on the edge of the horizon.

There are no kites flying in the gloaming above Cannery Pier.

In the hollow in the dunes is a yellow knot of lantern-light. Men's voices are raised, ugly and angry, and Da's ugliest and angriest of all. You scrabble up the dune face and part the grass to peer down unnoticed into the valley.

In a circle of yellow light, Christian sits on the steps of the caravan turning the smashed frame of the Black Kite over and over in his hands. The stormkite sits propped against the rear of the caravan by his side. Da is shouting questions and the faces of the men come to arrest him are grim, but Christian does not look up. They might as well not be there.

Tiring of Christian's obstinacy, Da gives an order. The men close in. Two of them grasp Christian and drag him to his feet. He does not resist. The kite falls from his hands and is unheedingly trampled under the heavy boots.

You cannot bear to see this. You cannot let them take him without a word. You climb to the crest of the dune and shout, "Christian!" You wave to him, he must see you. "Christian!"

Heads turn. Every eye fixes on you standing there in your dressing gown and slippers.

"Fraser," your Da cries, "Fraser, you shouldn't be here. Away home with you; Dougal, take him home." Obediently, your brother drops his whaling lance and comes for you, feet sinking deep in the sand. Christian stirs, sees you.

"Ah, Fraser," he rumbles like sad stones rolling on a beach. With a slow flex of his muscles he throws his captors away from him and comes to you. There are shouts. Men surge around Christian. There is scuffling. Christian is incredibly strong, strong as iron. Men tumble and wrestle in the sand. There are oaths and cries. The sudden crack of a shotgun splits the night in two.

The old skewbald pony goes mad with fright, plunging and kicking. The hollow is full of frantic motion.

"Hold the horse, the damn horse, somebody hold him," a man shouts. One man dives for the frenzied pony's halter, the others try to hold Christian down. The pony shies away from the looming man and kicks out.

From your forgotten vantage point you are perfectly placed to see the awful thing that happens next.

In its skittering dance the pony kicks a lantern against the caravan wheel. Glass shatters and burning oil splashes all over the woodwork. Paint blisters, blackens, burns. Within seconds the caravan is a bonfire.

The wind fans the greedy flames; with an ugly, gleeful roaring and sucking they snap and shrivel the lovely thing. The beautiful kites are seared away like so much scrap paper: the sunkite and the moonkite, the dragon and the butterfly and the hawk, the windkite and the kite with clouds on it, all turned to ash in a second. Even the stormkite by the door shrivels and bursts into flame. The blazing timbers crumble and the burning caravan folds up and collapses inwards in a gout of fire.

There is nothing left of the stormkite but a white metal skeleton. With its death the wind dies down.

The fire knocks the fight out of everyone. The men watch with horror. This was not their intent, to burn the beautiful caravan, they only came to bring justice to this man who stands looking with eyes nailed open by the flames. The blaze settles lower. Soon it will be out.

Christian turns away. His eyes search for you, but you know that it is his foursight, though so blinded by the actions of other people that he was unable to avert any of this night's tragedy, which finds and fixes you. He holds you with his gaze and you cannot look away. He raises his hands to his face. The men close in, hasty to act. He holds them back with a gesture. This is for you only. Then he will go.

"Fraser, I can't blame you though heaven knows I ought to. But does any snowflake in an avalanche feel responsible? No less you for your simple, good-hearted ignorance. Perhaps I'm still paying the price of the Pilot's pride; if so, it was bought dearly."

He touches his hands to his cheeks in a curious motion. And his face falls into his hands.

The men gasp and step back, reaching for weapons.

Up on the dune you feel like your soul is being torn out by its roots.

Delicate mechanisms ooze and pulse where Christian's face once was. The gray eyes sunk in gray metal look into you.

"You had to rush ahead and find the end of the story before

I led you to it, didn't you, Fraser? So now you know, and I hope you're the wiser for it.

"You see, if you'd listened I'd have told you how I had the surgeon on the transport make me into this unchanging thing, for otherwise how could I have borne all those years of waiting past and those yet to come? Mere flesh will be dust when she returns across the sky, so I must clothe the perishable in imperishability to be there for her. And, how else could I truly love a machine, unless I became one too?

"But look at this face, Fraser, look at it and know that it is agony to be a machine, to be only the memory of flesh. Ask yourself, what could ever be worth that price? Only the certainty of her love. I have her promise that she will return, and unlike men, machines are bound by their word. I had that certainty, the only valid coin I possessed, and you took it from me, Fraser. Oh, the kite was pain enough, but even then I could still have hoped, but what if they now take me and try me and put me in a cell? I cannot fool myself. For that shadow across the face of the moon could be hers, or those footsteps passing beneath the bailey wall. And then my mortal soul in this immortal frame will die a little. You see, I'll never be certain, and only the certainty made life bearable. Now I will never know. But you know, Fraser."

And he nods to the men with his machine head, and they reluctantly come and take him away.

And that is the last part of Christian's story.

But his face still looks up from the sand into the dawning sky and you know you will never be able to meet the gaze of those empty eyes.

Though the days no longer hold the frenzied heat of summer, there is still a lingering warmth as they dwindle towards the perpetual midnight of Darkwinter.

The beach is still a good place for a boy to play on the short afternoons, when school is done and friends gone home, when Da is serving and Ma busy with mussel soup and soused gurnards, when Sister is reading in the weather room and Brother in town for a new set of strings and even Mr. Cat prefers the company of the bugs under the veranda. The Cannery is still there, though folk don't go there so often now that they've chained it off and hung warning signs giving notice of its demolition, and the hulks remind you rather too much of things you would sooner forget. But there are always the games a boy can play with the sea.

Thousands of games, some as old as the sea itself, others that swim up like new-hatched elvers out of your imagination. There are imaginary countries to be mapped, peopled, and invaded on the uncharted wastes of the shore. There are springs to be forded, bridged, dammed, and then blasted back into their original state. There are messages, some cryptic and coded, some just a hopeful call for a reply, to be sealed into bottles and re-addressed to the waves. There is never any want of things to do on the beach.

And when he tires of games, a boy can always beachcomb along the tideline for whatever treasures the ocean chooses to release. Glass fishing floats, rusty chunks of metal that might once have been ship's fittings, bottles (always empty) worn opaque by tumbling sand, lengths of rope, oddly shaped pieces of driftwood, sea-purses holding a fortune in grit, pieces of crumbled cork, feathers and bones . . .

The sea casts up some funny things: you never know what a boy might find if he searches long enough.

KING OF
MORNING,
QUEEN OF DAY

DR. EDWARD GARRET DESMOND'S PERSONAL DIARY: APRIL 12, 1909.

Last night, upon the occasion of my daughter Emily's sixteenth birthday, I took the liberty of drawing Lord Fitzgerald, a keen amateur astronomer and fellow of the Society, aside from the celebrations (such girlish things doubtless holding little appeal for the Marquis of Claremorris) and showed him through my telescope the object referred to by my philistine colleagues in the Royal Irish Astronomical Society as "Bell's Comet." Lord Fitzgerald I know to be a highly educated and intelligent man (a rare commodity in these days of inbred gentry and fossilised aristocracy) and a close friend who would receive openly and without prejudice my speculations upon the nature of "Bell's Comet."

Whilst at the telescope the Marquis observed one of the object's periodic flarings (which I have calculated to occur once every twenty-eight minutes) when, for a second or so, "Bell's Comet" becomes as bright as a major planet. Lord Fitzgerald expressed a great and open curiosity in the phenomenon, and as he had previously intimated to me that he would be unable to attend the meeting of the Society which I am to address four days hence (due to a commitment in that great cauldron of muddy thought and confusion, the House of Lords in London), I explained my hypothesis briefly to Lord Fitzgerald, partly as a preparation for my lecture to my peers, partly, I must confess, to win a favorable ear. Here I must add that it is more than the Marquis of Claremorris's ear I mean to win; I have need of his considerable fortune if "Project Pharos" is to be brought to fruition.

On a personal note, how good it was to have Emily about the house again! She is like a beam of spring sunshine, flitting through the house like a faery brightening whatever she touches. Why, I had not realised what a dark and gloomy place Craigdarragh is without her until she arrived from Dublin and the Cross and Passion School this morning. I rather fear that I have grown engrossed in my work to the exclusion of all else, even my dearest daughter!

Domestic memo: I must remind Mrs. O'Carolan to have a man up from the town to look at the electricals: last night's current failure caused great distress to the young ladies at the party. Voltage fluctuations apart, the birthday tea was most successful; Emily was clearly delighted. Young girls are so easily pleased!

EMILY'S DIARY: APRIL 13, 1909.

How wonderful it is to be home again! All the dreary hours I spent in Sister Immaculata's Latin 5th dreaming of home have not dulled Craigdarragh's wonderfulness: for three days I have gone round hugging every wall, window, and door in the place! I almost hugged Mrs. O'Carolan when she met me off the train in Sligo town; oh, the look there would have been on her face! How good it is to see people who are round and plump and happy after the pinched black and white nuns. They are like magpies, the nuns, always miserable, always cackling and rubbing their black wings together. I hate them and I hate Cross and Passion, it is like a prison, old and grey, and it is always raining.

I had forgotten the colors of Craigdarragh in the spring, the new greens of the hills and the woods, the blue of the sea and beyond it, purple Knocknarea, the red of the early rhododendrons, my father's red cheeks and beard: it is funny how easily you forget the colors when there is only grey around you. But oh, nothing has changed, and that is so good; everything is as it was when I left after Christmas, Mrs. O'Carolan is fat and fusty and kind. Mama is Mama, pretending she is an artist and a poet and a tragic queen from a legend all rolled into one; Papa is Papa, worried and hurried and so busy with his telescopes and sums I'm sure he has already forgotten I'm here. And Craigdarragh is Craigdarragh: the woods, the mountain, the waterfall. Today I revisited the Bridestone up above the woods on the slopes of Ben Bulben. How peaceful it is there with only the wind and the song of the blackbird for company. Peaceful, and, dare I say, magical? It is like nothing has changed for a thousand years, one can imagine Finn MacCumhall and his grim Fianna warriors hunting the leaping stag with his red-eared hounds through some woodland glade, or the sunlight glinting from the spearpoints of the Red Branch Heroes as they march to avenge some slaughtered comrade.

Perhaps my imagination is too vigorous after months of confinement in that grey prison of Cross and Passion: I could have sworn that I was not alone as I came down through the woods from the Bridestone, that there were shadowy shapes flitting from tree to tree, unseen when I looked for them, giggling at my foolishness. Ah well, I did say it was an enchanted, faery place.

EXCERPTS FROM DR. EDWARD GARRET DESMOND'S LECTURE TO THE ROYAL IRISH ASTRONOMICAL SOCIETY, TRINITY COLLEGE, DUBLIN, APRIL 16, 1909.

Therefore, gentlemen, it is clearly impossible for these fluctuations in luminosity from Bell's Comet to be due to the differing albedos of its spinning surfaces, as my mathematical proofs have demonstrated. The only explanation for this unprecedented phenomenon is that these emissions of light are artificial in origin.

(*General consternation among the learned fellows.*)

If artificial, then we must address ourselves to the disturbing truth that they must, *must,* gentlemen, be works of intellects: minds, learned fellows, as great as, if not greater than, our own. It has long been held that we are not the unique handiwork of our Creator; the possibility of great civilizations upon the planets Mars and Venus and even beneath the forbidding surface of our own moon has been many times mooted by respected men of science and learning.

(*Heckler: "Intoxicated men of absinthe and bourbon!" Laughter.*)

What I am now proposing, if I may, gentlemen, is a concept of a whole order of magnitude greater than these speculations. I am proposing that this artifact, for artificial it must be, is evidence of a mighty civilization *beyond our solar system*, upon a world of the star Wolfe 359, for it is from the direction of this star that the object called Bell's Comet originates. Having ascertained that the object was indeed no mere lifeless comet, I attempted to ascertain its velocity. As the learned fellows are doubtless too aware, it is difficult in the extreme to calculate the velocity of astronomical phenomena; nevertheless, I estimated the object's velocity to be three hundred and fifty miles per second.

(*Murmurs of amazement from the learned fellows.*)

However, over the four-week period during which I kept the object under daily observation, weather permitting, the velocity decreased from three hundred and fifty miles per second to one hundred and twenty miles per second. Clearly, the object is decelerating, and from this information only one conclusion is possible—that the object is a spatial vehicle of some form, despatched by the inhabitants of Wolfe 359 to establish contact with the inhabitants of our earth.

(*Heckler: "Oh come now."*)

While the exact design of such a spatial vehicle is beyond my conception, I have some tentative suggestions as to its motive power. Our French colleague, M. Verne has written most imaginatively (*Heckler: "Not as imaginatively as you, sir."*) of how a great space-gun might propel a capsule around the moon. Intriguing though this notion is, it is quite impractical for a journey from Wolfe 359 to our earth. The velocity imparted by such a space-gun would not be sufficient for the journey to be completed within the lifetimes of its voyagers. (*Heckler: "Will this lecture be completed within the lifetimes of its audience?" Laughter.*) Therefore I suggest, if I may do so without interruption, learned fellows, that the vehicle accelerates and decelerates through a series of self-generated explosions, of titanic force, which propel the vehicle through transtellar space at colossal velocities. Of course, such star-crossing velocities must be shed to rendezvous with our earth at the completion of the journey, and I would submit that the immense flarings of light we are witnessing are the explosions by which the vehicle slows its headlong flight.

(*Heckler: "Are we in any seriousness meant to accept these fanciful vaporings over the Astronomer Royal's reasoned arguments?"*)

Gentlemen, I cannot say with any measure of scientific certainty (*Catcalls, booing. Heckler: "What scientific certainty?"*) what such a propulsive explosive might be, certainly no earthly explosive would possess sufficient power for its weight to be a practical fuel for such a transtellar flight. (*Heckler: "Oh certainly!" Laughter.*) However, I have conducted a spectral analysis of the light from Bell's Comet and found it to be identical to the light of our own familiar sun. (*Heckler: "Of course, it's reflected sunlight!" Laughter.*) Could it be that the extrasolar stellanauts of Wolfe 359 have learned to duplicate artificially the force that kindles the sun itself and tamed it to power their space vehicles? (*Heckler: "Could it be that the Member from Drumcliffe has learned to duplicate artificially the spirit of the mountain dew and used it to fuel his somewhat active imagination?" Uproarious laughter.*)

Learned fellows . . . gentlemen, please, if I might have your attention; since it is now clear that we are not unique in God's Universe, it is therefore of paramount importance, even urgency, that we communicate with these representatives of intelligences immeasurably superior to our own. Therefore, in the August of this year, when Bell's Comet makes its closest approach to earth (*Heckler: "I don't believe it! Gentlemen, a fact! A cold, hard fact!"*) I will attempt to signal the presence of intelligent life on this world (*Laughter grows louder.*) to the extrasolar intelligences. . . . (*General laughter: cries of "Poppycock," "Shame," "Withdraw." A rain of pamphlets falls upon the platform. The President calls for order; there being none, he declares the meeting adjourned.*)

EMILY'S DIARY: APRIL 22, 1909.

I do believe there are strange and magical things in Bridestone Wood! Real magic, magic of sky and stone and sea, the magic of the Old People, the Good People who live in the halls beneath the hills. Oh, this sounds foolish, this sounds like whimsy, but last night I looked out of my bedroom window and saw lights up there on Ben Bulben, like the lights of many lanterns there on the slopes of the hill, like there were folk dancing by lantern light in a ring around the Bridestone. Mrs. O'Carolan used to tell me stories of the faery lords who would take their mortal brides by the joining of hands through the hole in the middle of the Bridestone. Could this have been such a faery wedding? For as the hour of midnight struck the dancing lights lifted from under the shadow of Ben Bulben and flew through the air into the west; over Craigdarragh, over this very roof! As I leaned out to watch I imagined I could hear the whinnying of the faery horses and the laughter of the host of the air and the playing of the faery harpers.

Oh diary, it was such a wonder! My heart would still be full to the brim with it but for the shadow that has fallen across both it and Craigdarragh. Ever since Papa's return from Dublin there has been the most horrid atmosphere in the house. I wanted to tell him all about the wonderful things I have seen, but Mama warned me not to disturb him, for he has locked himself up in his observatory and works like a man possessed by demons, growling like an angry dog at the least annoyance. Whatever has happened in Dublin has so soured the atmosphere that my Easter has been quite spoiled, and now there is another shadow hanging over me; in two days I must return to Cross and Passion. That horrible place . . . oh, come quickly, summer! Even now I am counting the hours until I am home again, in Craigdarragh, beneath the shadow of Ben Bulben, where the faery folk are waiting for me . . .

> Craigdarragh
> Drumcliffe
> County Sligo
> April 26th

My dear Lord Fitzgerald,
    I am deeply, deeply grateful for your letter dated April 24th in which Your Lordship expressed an interest in, and indeed pledged support for, my project to communicate

with the transtellar vehicle from the star Wolfe 359. I am glad that Your Lordship was spared the humiliation of my embarrassment before the Society; would that I had been spared it myself. Christians to the lions, my dear Claremorris, were none such as I in that lecture hall. Yet like those early martyrs, my faith is undiminished, my zeal for the successful pursuance of Project Pharos is greater than ever: we shall teach these arrogant pedagogues a thing or two when the star-folk come! And I am delighted, no less honored, to hear that Your Lordship has submitted a letter of support for my propositions to the Chairman of the Society, though I regret that, for all Your Lordship's cogent arguments, it will achieve little: the gentlemen of Dublin are not as open-minded to revolutionary concepts as we men of the West.

Now ensured of support, we may proceed apace with "Project Pharos," and I enclose blue-prints for the signalling device. Nevertheless, I will here summarise in my own hand the principles of the signalling device, lest my enthusiasm in draughting the designs has rendered my diagrams a trifle incomprehensible.

The device takes the form of a cross of floating pontoons supporting electrically powered lanterns. The cross must necessarily be of immense size: I have estimated that to be visible from astronomical distances the arms will have to be five miles in diameter. This of course necessitates the use of the pontoons; an artifact of such size could not be accommodated on land, but on sea it is a relatively simple task to construct, and possesses the additional benefit of being clearly distinguishable from the humbler lamps of civilization, namely, those of Sligo town. The electrical supply for the pontoons can be cheaply supplied by my brother-in-law, Mr. Michael Barry, of the Sligo, Leitrim, Fermanagh and South Donegal Electrical Supply Company. How useful it is to have relations in places of influence! Indeed, he has successfully influenced the recent disruptions of Craigdarragh's electrical supply, which Your Lordship will recall from the night of my daughter's birthday. The man he personally despatched, a Mr. MacAteer of Enniskillen, a dour Presbyterian but quite the man with the electricals, has eradicated the power failures which plagued us that night and indeed for most of the Easter time.

Here, Your Lordship, I must beg leave to conclude. I once again thank the Marquis for his kind patronage of this experiment which will surely be regarded by history as one of the epochal events of the millennium. I will keep Your Lordship closely informed of further developments, particularly my compiling of a code with which to signal the presence of guiding intelligence to the "Wolfii," as I have termed them, and finally wish God's richest blessing upon Your Lordship's self and all at Claremorris House, especially the Lady Alexandra, who is never far from our affections here at Craigdarragh.

I remain Your Lordship's devoted servant,
Edward Garret Desmond Ph D

(*Submitted to the Cross and Passion School magazine* Veritas: *not accepted.*)

to my Faery Lover

Oh, would that we were many things,
My golden-shining love and I;
Bright-flashing scales, a pair of wings
That draw the moonlight down the sky,
Two hazel trees beside the stream,
Wherein our fruit in autumn drop,
A trout, a stag, a wild swan's dream,
An eagle's cry on mountain top.
For we have both been many things:
A thousand lifetimes we have known
Each other, and our love yet sings.
But there is more that I would own.
Oh, that we could but naked run
Through forests deep and forests fair,
Our breasts laid open to the sun,
Our flesh caressed by summer's air,
And in some hidden, leafy glen
My striving body you would take;
Impale me on your lust and then
Me Queen of Daybreak you would make.
And we would dance and we would sing
And we in passion's fist would cry;

Loud with our love the woods would ring
If we were lovers, you and I.
If we were lovers, I and you,
I would cast off all mortal ills
And you would take me, Shining Lugh,
To feast within the Hollow Hills.
For the world of men is filled with tears
And swift the night of science falls
And I would leave those tears and fears,
To dance with you in Danu's Halls.
So let us cast our cares away
And live like bright stars in the sky.
Dance dream-clad till the break of day,
For we are lovers, you and I.
Emily Desmond, Class 5a Cross and Passion School.

DR. EDWARD GARRET DESMOND'S PERSONAL DIARY: MAY 28, 1909.

Work is proceeding apace on the signalling device. The laborers are addressing themselves to their tasks with an enthusiasm I would like to attribute to their desire to communicate with higher intelligences but I fear is due rather to Lord Fitzgerald's generous purse. Already the first pontoon sections have been floated into Sligo harbor and the lanterns have been tested and found to work satisfactorily. Such successes are heartening after the delays and confusions of the early weeks. The plan is to assemble the cross from one hundred and seventy-six pontoon sections each one hundred yards long. This sounds a daunting proposition, given the brevity of time before the space vehicle attains perigee, but the sections have been largely preassembled in the town boatyards and only remain to be floated and bolted into their final form. Observing the great legion of laborers (of which there are no shortage in this poverty-stricken county) I have no fear that "Project Pharos" will not be completed by the allotted date.

My outstanding concern, that of devising a universally comprehensible mode of communication with which to converse with the Wolfii, has been recently resolved to my complete satisfaction. It is a universal truth that the laws of mathematics are the same upon the worlds of Wolfe 359 as they are upon this one; to wit, the ratio of a circle's circumference to its radius, which we call *pi,* must be as familiar to the Wolfii as to us. Therefore I have designed an electrical relay whereby one arm of the cross will flash its lights twenty-two times for the other's seven, this being the approximate fractional ratio of *pi.* Such a signal cannot fail to attract the attention of our stellanauts and pave the way to more intimate conversation, a code for which I am currently devising using primes and exponents.

>   Craigdarragh
>   Drumcliffe
>   County Sligo

My dearest Constance,

Just a brief note to express my heartfelt thanks for your generous invitation to visit you at Lissadell House to attend a reading by Mr. W. B. Yeats of his most recent poetic works. I shall certainly accept your kind invitation and, if it is not presuming too much upon your generosity, I wonder if perhaps I might bring my daughter Emily? She will shortly be returning from Cross and Passion School (where, I fear, she is far from happy, the dear child, constantly fretful and distressed in her work, and, so I am informed by Mother Superior, given to strange delusions and fantasies) and I know nothing would thrill her more than to hear Mr. Yeats reading his own incomparable poetry: she, like myself, is a great admirer of Mr. Yeats, especially his earlier works: his mythological world of gods and fighting men has quite stimulated her! I was recently sent a copy of a poem she wrote in English class; not bad, quite racy even, and showing definite promise, though it was not this promise that prompted Mother Superior to send it to me, I think, but the overtly sensual content of some of the imagery. Honestly, Constance, these church schools! I cannot understand Edward's insistence that she be educated by the sisters, this is the twentieth century, this is the age of the new Renaissance, the Celtic dawn! Forgive me, the affair has made me quite flush with outrage. What I am trying to convey is that if it is acceptable, I will bring Emily on the date you suggest, and I thank you once again for your kindness, generosity, and hospitality,

yours sincerely,
Caroline Desmond.

EMILY'S DIARY: JUNE 29, 1909.

Oh, to be in Craigdarragh now that summer's here! I do declare that the moment the train steamed out of Kingsbridge station I could smell the wild honeysuckle and the purple heather on the slopes of Ben Bulben! Despite the warnings of the guard I must have travelled almost the whole way home with my head out of the window, just breathing in the smell of wild summer.

After I said hello to Mama and Papa (what a strange mood he is in still, the silly man!) the first thing I did was to revisit Bridestone Wood and taste again the ancient magic that I have felt calling me, calling me, every hour of every day I was imprisoned in Cross and Passion. And now, as I try to write about what I experienced, my hand trembles and I feel guilty, though I should not, for then I did not care, not one bit.

Today Bridestone Wood was alive as I have never known it before. Every leaf, every twig, every blade of grass, every drop of dew breathed magic, the Old Magic of stone, sea, and sky, and it was so quiet I could hear the trees breathing. The air was full of the perfume of green growing things and the soft green grass was calling out for the touch of my bare feet. I imagined I was a fair princess, a woman of the de Danaan, the Ever-Living Ones, and I slipped, quickly, willingly, under the spell of the green-woods. In an instant I had cast off my horrible, tight, constricting clothes and I ran naked and free as a sunbeam through the summer glens. How wonderful I felt! It was like the poem I had written for the school magazine, but this time there was no Sister Assumpta, black and white like a folded-up newspaper, to tell me I was proud, sensual, and sinful. I was beautiful, I was proud, I would not be driven onto my knees to pray and pray for deliverance from the sins of the flesh; I loved the flesh, I loved the grass beneath my feet and the thin willow wands which whipped my body did not scourge me for my sins but blessed me with their golden pollen. I did not care if I ever saw my clothes again, I wanted to be like this forever, free from the petty, jealous restrictions of the human world, free from the sterile bleakness of Cross and Passion and my poor father. At length I collapsed onto a bank of moss beneath an ancient druid oak.

When the voice called my name I was afraid and ashamed of my nakedness, but it called again, my name, Emily, in a voice so sweet I thought it was the singing of a bird. Three times the voice called before I could reply with a "Who's there?" Then I saw a golden glow moving through the trees towards me. I should have been frightened but I was not, I could not be, I knew that no harm was intended me. As the light drew nearer I saw that it was a golden wheel, rolling by its own power, with five spokes, like a cartwheel, only smaller and finer, much as I have always imagined a chariot wheel to be. It rolled towards me and spoke to me, telling me not to be afraid (and indeed, I was not afraid, not one bit), that the time was not yet come for me to meet the wheel's faery master, but that it would come soon and now I was to follow it so that I might return to the realm of men again.

I cannot remember, dear diary, where I followed that magical wheel, nor the least part of what transpired until I found myself upon the south edge of Bridestone Wood, but it must have been something strange and exceeding wonderful, for clasped upon my left arm was a golden horse-shoe torc of the kind that faery kings give to their faery queens as token of love and faithfulness. The torc I have hidden in my secret hidey-hole, for no one would understand it, but I am setting everything down in your pages, dear diary, so that I will never forget the wonderfulness of it. But diary, my secret, most trusted friend, if it was so magical, so wonderful, why do I feel I have sinned?

EDWARD GARRET DESMOND'S PERSONAL DIARY: JULY 8, 1909.

I here pause in my records of "Project Pharos" (which is proceeding to my complete satisfaction) to comment upon a matter of a personal nature which is causing me not inconsiderable distress. I refer of course, to the increasingly irrational behaviour of my daughter Emily. Since her return from Dublin she has floated around Craigdarragh as if in a daydream, paying only the scantest attention to her father and his epochal work, head filled rather with fantastic nonsense about faeries and mythological creatures haunting Bridestone Wood. And as if this was not enough, she has borrowed (taken without permission, rather!) one of my portable cameras which I was using to photograph the Wolfii vehicle to take a series of photographs of these "faery folk" at play in the woods around the demesne. I have seen these photographs, they are doubtless forgeries of greater or lesser skill; what I cannot understand is my daughter's absolute insistence upon the objective truth of these fantastical notions. She believes utterly that she has taken factual photographs of supernatural creatures! Is she doing this out of spite for me and my rational, scientific philosophy of life in a pique of adolescent rebellion? We had the most fearful row, Emily demanding that she was not a little girl any longer, that she was a woman and that I treat her accordingly, and I, arguing with gentle persuasiveness and calm rationality, maintaining that to be treated like a woman she cannot revel in the childish hysterias of little girls. Alas, nothing was resolved, and worse still, Emily has won Caroline over to her side.

Caroline intends to take Emily to Lissadell House and show these photographs to Mrs. Gore-Booth and Mr. William Butler Yeats, the famous poet, who will be delivering a reading there. Mr. Yeats is a man for whose poetry I have the highest regard but for whose superstitious fancies of gods and warriors and mythological hosts of the air I have no time, and I know with sure and certain knowledge that no good will come of his involvement on these ludicrous proceedings.

But that I had more time to spend with Emily! Maybe then she would not have wandered heedless into the realms of fantasy and whimsy! I fear I have not been a proper father to her, but the advent of the star-folk will turn all our human relationships upon their heads.

Finally, the electrical fluctuations that bedevilled the house at Easter have resumed and are more frequent and of longer duration. I shall have to have words with Mr. Michael Barry of the Sligo, Leitrim, Fermanagh and South Donegal Electrical Supply Company, and his dour employee Mr. MacAteer. What is more disturbing, and mystifying, is that objects have been moved around my observatory at night after I have locked up and left. Papers, books, chairs, tables, all have gone stray, and, most perplexing of all, my antique brass orrery, weighing nigh on a ton, was moved right out of the observatory into the gardens! The lesser items I could attribute to Emily in a pique of spite, but the orrery takes ten strong laborers to even budge! Alas that I have not the time for such mysteries at present; the demands of the Wolfii are paramount.

> Craigdarragh
> Drumcliffe
> Co Sligo
> 16th July 1909

My dearest Constance,

Just a short note to let you know how thrilled I was to read in your letter that Mr. William Butler Yeats in person will be coming to talk with Emily about the faery photographs, and what is more, bringing with him Mr. Hannibal Rooke, the celebrated hypnotist and investigator of supernatural phenomena. Of course I would be delighted to accommodate Mr. Yeats and his colleague for a few days towards the end of this month, if they, for their parts, will excuse my husband's small insanities and the somewhat chaotic state of the house; my husband's experiments, you understand, he has everything quite topsy-turvy. Quite frankly, Constance, I cannot see any benefit from what he is doing; are not our photographic proofs of another world co-existent with our own more significant than his fanciful communications with the inhabitants of another star? Poor Lord Fitzgerald, I sometimes think he agreed to this quixotic escapade merely to humour Edward. Be that as it may, I must once again thank you, Constance, for all your support and hard work and I look forward enormously to seeing you on the 27th when Mr. Yeats comes.

Yours sincerely,
Caroline Desmond

Excerpts from the Craigdarragh interviews: July 27, 28, and 29, 1909, as transcribed by Mr. Peter Driscoll, B.A., of Sligo. (The first interview: 9:30 P.M., July 27. Present: Mr. W. B. Yeats, Mr. H. Rooke, Mrs. C. Desmond, Miss E. Desmond, Mrs. C. Gore-Booth, Mr. P. Driscoll. Weather: windy with some rain.)

W. B. YEATS:	You are quite certain she is in the hypnotic trance and receptive to my questioning, Mr. Rooke?
H. ROOKE:	Quite sure, Mr. Yeats.
W. B. YEATS:	Very well then. Emily, can you hear me?
EMILY:	Yes sir.
W. B. YEATS:	Tell me, Emily, have these photographs you have shown me been falsified in any way?
EMILY:	No sir.
W. B. YEATS:	So these are genuine pictures of faery folk, then.
	(*No reply.*)

H. ROOKE:	You must question the subject directly, Mr. Yeats.
W. B. YEATS:	Forgive me, I forgot. Tell me, Emily, are these photographs actual representations of supernatural beings? Faeries?
EMILY:	Faeries? Of course they are faeries, the Old Folk, the Ever-Living Ones.
W. B. YEATS:	Thank you, Emily, that is what I wanted to know. Now that we have established that these are real photographs of real faeries, could you tell me, Emily, on how many occasions were these photographs taken?
EMILY:	Three occasions; once in the morning, twice in the early afternoon. Three days. Then . . .
W. B. YEATS:	Go on, Emily . . .
EMILY:	It was as if they didn't want me to take any more photographs of them, they grew cold and distant, like there was a cloud over the sun. They don't like mechanical things, the Old Folk, they don't like cold, hard, iron human-made things.
W. B. YEATS:	Thank you, Emily.

(The second interview: 9:50 P.M., July 28. Present: as above. Weather: wind gusting from the west, with showers.)

W. B. YEATS:	As we have no photographic evidence of either the earliest or the most recent encounters with the faery folk, could you describe for us please these Lords of the Ever-Living Ones?
EMILY:	(*Her face becomes ecstatic.*) They are the fairest of the fair, the sons of Danu; there are none to compare with the comeliness of the dwellers in the Hollow Hills: no son of Milesius, no daughter of proud Maeve aslumber on cold Knocknarea. Their cloaks are of scarlet wool, their tunics of fine Greek silk. Upon their breasts they wear the badge of the Red Branch Heroes, upon their brows circlets of yellow gold; their skin is

white as milk, their hair black as the raven's wing, the glint of iron spear-points is in their eyes and their lips are red as blood. Fair they are, the sons of Danu, but none so fair nor so noble as my love, Lugh of the Long Hand. Strong-thewed he is, golden-maned, golden-skinned; clad in the green and the gold of the royal Dun at Brugh-na-Boinne; he is Lugh, my love, my King of the Morning, and I am his Queen of the Day, and this token of his everlasting love he has given to me . . .

(*Several murmurs of astonishment are heard among the witnesses as Miss Desmond produces a golden bracelet from beneath her dress.*)

H. ROOKE:	Good grief! A Celtic arm torc!
W. B. YEATS:	Emily? Can you hear me, Emily?
EMILY:	I can hear you, Mr. Yeats.
W. B. YEATS:	Emily, where did you get this from? This is most important— Damnation, what was that?
MRS. C. DESMOND:	I'm so sorry, it's another of those mysterious electrical failures I mentioned to you yesterday. Mrs. O'Carolan . . . Mrs. O'Carolan . . . lamps please. Gentlemen, if you wish we may continue by lamplight.
H. ROOKE:	Thank you, Mrs. Desmond, but with this new evidence being produced in such a dramatic way I think it would be best if we were to retire to draw up a new line of questioning.
W. B. YEATS:	Yes, we have put poor Emily through quite enough for one evening. Mr. Rooke . . . the trance . . .

(The third interview: 3:30 P.M., July 29, 1909. Present: as above, with the addition of Dr. E. G. Desmond. Weather: cloudy, threatening rain from the west.)

W. B. YEATS:	This faery lover who gave the torc to you, Emily; tell us about him, will you?

EMILY: (*Grows animated.*) Ah, Lugh, Lugh, King
                  of the Morning, Master of the Thousand
                  Skills; there is none to compare with him in
                  music or archery, poetry or the feats of war,
                  hunting nor the tender accomplishments of
                  love. (*Here Dr. Desmond blushes.*) We are
                  riders on the wings of the morning, he and
                  I, we are dancers in the starlit halls of Tir-
                  Nan-Og, and with the sun setting we rise in
                  the shapes of swans, joined at the necks by
                  chains and collars of red, red gold and
                  journey to the Land of the Sunrise where we
                  begin our wondrous journey of love again.
                  We have tasted the hazelnuts of the Tree of
                  Wisdom; we have been many things, many
                  shapes; wild swans upon the lake of Coole,
                  two arbutuses twined together upon a moun-
                  tainside, white birds upon the foam of the
                  sea, we have been trees, we have been
                  leaping silver salmon, wild horses, red
                  foxes, noble deer; brave warriors, proud
                  kings, sage wizards . . .

W. B. YEATS: Thank you, Emily. Now, if you could please
                  tell us, what is the precise significance of
                  the torc which was given to you in this
                  otherworldly drama?

EMILY: (*Shows consternation.*) Why, I am the
                  Queen of the Morning, I am the mortal
                  woman taken to be the immortal bride
                  through the hole in the Bridestone . . . I
                  am . . . I have . . . They have told me I
                  have the power of the deep magic.

W. B. YEATS: Deep magic? What is that, Emily?

EMILY: The power of wishing, the power of trans-
                  formation, the power to change nature at the
                  most fundamental level of its being.

H. ROOKE: Excuse me, Mr. Yeats, but this is incred-
                  ible.

W. B. YEATS: Yes? Oh, thank you, Emily, that will be all
                  for the moment. Go on, Mr. Rooke.

H. ROOKE:	This is incredible: the girl seems to be referring to herself as the embodiment of the Morrigan, the Celtic myth of the shape-changer. The mythological sources seem to hint that the Morrigan does not transform herself so much as transform the perceptions, even the reality itself, of those about her. This is quite fascinating, Mr. Yeats. We must continue immediately.
E. G. DESMOND:	I am afraid not. I must protest. My daughter is not some sideshow or circus freak for your amusement. I will not tolerate her further humiliation before her own father and mother, no, I will not tolerate it, nor will I tolerate any more of this . . . idle superstitious tommyrot masquerading in the guise of science and reason! Gentlemen, I must demand that you terminate these . . . these . . . parlour tricks forthwith! My daughter's childhood years will not be muddied by your unscientific vapourings! Caroline, I wish to speak with you . . .

Extracts from Dr. Edward Garret Desmond's and Lord Fitzgerald of Claremorris's paper submitted to the Irish Astronomical Bulletin: *not accepted for publication.*

On the 8th August at 12:15 P.M. it was observed that the transtellar vehicle had ceased generating explosions, having shed sufficient velocity to match the pedestrian pace of our solar system. Its final proper motion was approximated to be fifteen miles per second.

The vehicle maintained course and velocity over the days preceding perigee. It was not until the night of the 27th August that conditions were suitable for the experiment. That night the sky was clear, Sligo Bay uncommonly calm, and the extrasolar vehicle two days from perigee of 156,000 miles. At 9:25 P.M. the signal was activated and for a period of two hours the primary communication code was transmitted; that is, *pi* expressed as the approximate ratio of twenty-two over seven. This sequence was repeated every two hours for two hours until local dawn at 6:25 A.M. Simultaneous with the operation of the stellagraph, the vessel was closely observed through the Craigdarragh 18-inch reflector telescope. No change in luminosity was observed.

After nightfall on the following day, August 28th, it again being clear and calm, the floating stellagraph was again activated, transmitting the *pi* ratio for an hour, then flashing the natural exponent *e* expressed as the approximate fraction of nineteen over seven. As before, this cycle was repeated every two hours for two hours. As before the spatial object was closely observed through telescopes.

At 3:19 A.M. the luminosity of the object suddenly increased drastically for an extremely short period of time: a flash. After a short pause came another flash, a short pause, then a third. The flashes were observed to be regular in interval, and timing of the intervals proved them to be 3.141 seconds in duration: *pi* to three decimal places. Sensitive and accurate timing equipment would doubtless reveal the period to be accurate to a far greater number of places. It was also discovered, quite by chance, that the interval between flashes themselves corresponded with similar accuracy to the natural base *e*.

(Several sections omitted here.)

EMILY'S DIARY: AUGUST 28, 1909.

I know they are there, I can feel them, I can hear them, calling for me, calling me by harp and flute, calling me away away away, away from the mortal world, into the dream-time, into the never-ending dance. They are afraid, they hide themselves under the eaves of Bridestone Wood, but I know they are there, waiting for me. It is the great light in the sea they are afraid of, it is evil, they say, it is steel and iron and hard hard coldness, but they have braved its man-light to fetch me to the Bridestone: the bride to the Bridestone.

All the day long my heart has yearned for my Lugh, and now as the silver spearpoints gather in Bridestone Wood and the faery steeds stamp their hooves in impatience, I long to cry to the mountains, "Not long, not long, the mortal bride comes, she comes." All is ready. I have braided my hair, I have cast off my confining human clothes, and on my wrist I wear the token of Lugh's love, the golden torc; I only delay to set down these words in you, dear diary, for after tonight I do not know if I shall ever return to you again. Maybe then someone will read your pages and sigh and pine for the love they contain, and maybe understand. I am a woman! I am a woman! I am not a child! I am Queen of Morning, my heart has passed through the hole at the centre of the Bridestone into the land of the Ever-Living Ones.

DR. EDWARD GARRET DESMOND'S PERSONAL DIARY: AUGUST 29, 1909.

I awaited last night with the thrilled expectancy of a child awaiting Christmas. I could hardly wait for darkness to descend and communications be reestablished with the otherworlders. At the pre-arranged hour Lord Fitzgerald down in Sligo town operated the floating stellagraph and transmitted our recognition signal. From my observatory I could see the floating cross of pontoons, filling all of Sligo Bay, flashing our proud message of will and intellect to the stars. Almost immediately the space vehicle replied in kind with a series of pulsed emissions from its mighty star-engine: again, *pi* and *e*.

It was then that the first of the night's bizarre occurrences happened. All of a sudden the observatory was plunged into Stygian gloom. By now accustomed to these failures of the electrical supply, I lit the oil lamps I have had installed with just such a contingency in mind. Then Mrs. O'Carolan rushed in from the main house in a terrible to-do, flustered and flapping and gabbling something about the current having failed over the whole county. I abandoned my telescope and reached the window just in time to see the lights of my fine floating stellagraph plunged into darkness. Just as abruptly the glow from Silgo town vanished as if some vast hand had snuffed it out. As I was later to learn from the pages of the *Irish Times,* the electrical supply for the entire North West of Ireland was blacked-out (a good descriptive phrase for a semi-literate journalist) at its source in the generator chambers of the Sligo, Leitrim, Fermanagh and South Donegal Electrical Supply Company for a period of four hours. As yet ignorant of this, I was greatly fearful at the time and imagined for an instant that my signal attempt had brought some dreadful star-doom down upon our earth. Then the second bizarrity occurred.

The star-vehicle, which I had kept under observation in my telescope, suddenly emitted a stream of pulsed lights. It took me a moment to clear my befuddled wits and recognise the underlying pattern, and I must confess that when I did, I was astounded to the point of stupefaction. It was Morse code! What is more, a Morse code transmission in English! How the Wolfii achieved this feat I cannot imagine; all I could do was hastily jot down the signals which I noted, even in my incredulous state, were in the form of repeated cycles of messages. I have since transcribed them and note them down herewith.

> Greetings . . . greetings . . . greetings
> He of dawn to:
> Transformer
> Translator
> Shaper of Reality
> We return thy power to thee:
> Shaped we
> Translated we
> Transformed we
> By she of the sunlight.
> Greeting . . . greetings . . . greetings.

The message was repeated over three hundred times. And now I must record the greatest mystery of that mysterious night. At 12:16 A.M. the object flared again, taking me quite by surprise and momentarily blinding me. When I regained my customary clarity of vision I observed that the space-vehicle was accelerating by the same means I had hypothesised: titanic explosions of stellar force, one every four and one half minutes. The object was leaving the proximity of our earth and travelling in the direction of the constellation Lyra. The star-crosser accelerated thus for fifty-three minutes and then, at three minutes past one, it abruptly vanished from my telescopes. There was no evidence of any explosion, no burst of light; the object had vanished as utterly as if it had never been: no conjuror vanishing a lady into thin air upon the Dublin stage could have matched that feat and the vacuum of space is thinner by far than the most rarefied of airs.

I searched the heavens frantically for some trace of the great star-vehicle but it was quite gone. As I was musing what might have befallen that brave vessel the electrical supply was restored, all at once and, as I subsequently learned, to the whole of the Western sea-board of Ireland.

My head was spinning with imponderables as I tried to ascribe some sense and order to the events of the night. Could there possibly be any connection between the strange happenings? What of the extrasolars' enigmatic message and their mysterious fate? It was upon such musings that I was intent when Caroline burst in upon me to inform me of the dreadful news that Emily had been found wandering in high distress on the Sligo Road by a police constable. . . .

FROM THE REPORT OF CONSTABLE MICHAEL O'HARE, DRUMCLIFFE R.I.C. STATION.

Upon the night in question I was proceeding on my bicycle along the Sligo Road towards the Rosses Point Police Station where there had been numerous complaints of the sudden failure of the electrical supply to certain well-to-do households. At approximately half past midnight, as I was passing the place on the road where Bridestone Wood comes down to the sea, I heard a noise like crying and sobbing coming from the edge of the road. I advanced with caution and by the light of my bicycle lamp I saw a young lady huddled by the forest wall in a state of great and obvious distress. She was quite naked, I am ashamed to say, and covered in cuts and bruises. I was unable to console the young lady, so great was her distress, but for the sake of decency and the coolness of the air I lent her my police cape to cover her modesty. I decided to take the young lady to the O'Bannon residence, Mullaghboy, not a quarter-mile distant, where a doctor might be fetched. However, she would not consent to be moved from the side of the road. I attempted to glean some inkling of what might have befallen her but what information I did glean was fragmentary and incoherent.

Between sobbing fits the young lady mentioned the Bridestone, brides, the King and Queen and some person, possibly of foreign origin, whose name I took to be Lew. More significantly, she spoke of violation, stolen maidenhood, ravishment, and unfaithful lovers. From these statements, her unclad state, and her general air of distress, it was apparent to me that some form of improper assault had been made on the young lady. It was therefore imperative that I get her to a safe place where I could summon the necessary medical, police, and priestly assistance. Knowing that any attempt to force her to accompany me would only increase her distress, I finally persuaded her to mount my bicycle, and wheeled her to Mullaghboy House. As we turned into the drive, the local electrical supply was suddenly restored. . . .

EXTRACTS FROM THE REPORT OF DR. HUBERT ORR, ROYAL COLLEGE OF SURGEONS, DUBLIN.

Physical examination of the patient revealed her to have indeed suffered some form of sexual ravagement, resulting in pregnancy, undoubtedly upon the night in question. However, it is not the physical aspects of this case which are so intriguing as the psychological ones . . .

The recent works of the Viennese Dr. Sigmund Freud have aroused great interest in the subliminal processes of the mind, particularly in the field of repressed sexual feelings. In the patient's case I feel this to be a significant contributing factor. The repressive regime of the teaching sisters at Cross and Passion School has been well testified to in the girl's diaries, and, coupled with her hints as to juvenile dalliance in illicit love with its consequent fear of censure and punishment, would certainly drive her sexual longings deep into what Dr. Freud terms the "subconscious" and seal them there under layer upon layer of guilt. On her return to the romantically idealised home environment, these restraints would be loosened, the patient's sexual imagination permitted full play, generating hosts of hysterical delusions: faeries, goblins, warriors, kings, druids, lovers. It is significant that many of the patient's fantasies are unconscious recapitulations of her own earlier imaginings: her poems, the works of W. B. Yeats, the stories of the locality told to her by the cook, Mrs. O'Carolan: the seeds of hysteria had been sown and only needed the proper soil to germinate.

. . . The role of the father is most interesting. It is clear from her early diary entries that the patient idolised her father and his work, yet at the time of the "Craigdarragh incident" she was quite hostile both to him and to his work. Why should this be? Perhaps a clue lies in the patient's response to her sixteenth birthday. She clearly considered herself to be a woman in the fullest sense of the word, but her father refused to see her as anything but a little girl, immature and dependent, and it is quite likely that such a hysterical retreat into superstition and mythology was a subconscious backlash against her father and his scientific work. Through her fantasies, the patient was attacking her father.

. . . However, I am utterly at a loss to explain the photographs of the faery folk: it is not within my sphere of professional competence to proffer any authoritative statement concerning them, though I think it likely that they may have been cleverly falsified and that it was vital for the patient's desire for them to be true that she lie even under hypnosis . . .

> Glendun
> Blackrock Road
> Blackrock
> County Dublin
> September 20, 1909

My dear Mr. Yeats,

I have studied all the material pertaining to the Craigdarragh case with the greatest scrutiny, and though I find Dr. Orr's conclusions interesting and far-sighted, I do not feel they quite adequately explain the remarkable events to which we were partly privy.

Recent research has uncovered a close relationship between emotionally (read sexually) disturbed adolescents and bizarre psychic activity, such as poltergeists, phantom noises, and strange lights in the sky. The admirable Dr. Orr has applied Freudian theories in one fashion; I would now apply them in another to suggest that in the Craigdarragh case, the patient's repressed sexuality was lashing out from the subconscious in paroxysms of supernormal activity, including the electrical failures, the moving furniture, and, ultimately, the faery manifestations.

With regard to this last point I must warn you that I am engaging in the purest speculation when I wonder if it is possible that at a deeply subconscious level, far beyond any yet tapped by hypnosis or theorised by Dr. Freud, the human mind is in direct contact with the underlying structure of the universal all? What I am thinking is that in certain individuals, or under certain circumstances, the barriers between this deep preconsciousness and normal consciousness may be lowered, even abolished, allowing the nature of reality itself to be changed. The power of mind over base matter, the power of generating material objects by force of will, has indeed been long maintained by certain Eastern mystics. What I am proposing here is a scientific rationale for this phenomenon.

By now my reasoning should be obvious to you, my dear Willie: in the Craigdarragh case it could indeed be that the faeries were real, generated out of the patient's frustrated sexual longings touching upon the ancient reality-shaping consciousness at the core of her psyche, and that power in turn taking the form of her fancies and fantasies. That she mentioned the Morrigan, the Celtic Shifter of Shapes, is highly significant in this respect: it was the very shape of reality itself that was being shifted!

At first I was convinced that these manifestations were purely subjective; it being a simpler matter to shape a person's perceptions than obstinate matter. Then I paused to reconsider. The evidence of the photographs is compelling, also the golden torc which Dr. Hanrahan of the National Museum has authenticated, and the tragic conclusion of the Craigdarragh episode is proof that the apparitions were sufficiently real to turn on Emily and ravage her. Her guilt never left her and in the end it was the guilt that took hold of her reality-shaping ability to punish her for her sins. Such, I fear, may ever be the penalty for dabbling in powers too mighty for men. We are vessels too weak by far to hold the power of God.

One final observation, and this, my dear Willie, is the most outrageous of all. If Emily could generate a host of the Sidhe (possibly out of the electricity stolen during the power failures?) she could have as easily generated the astronomical object Dr. Desmond maintained was an unearthly space-vehicle. It is only a matter of scale and projection. . . . Forgive me, Willie, if these words sound like the ravings of a lunatic; I rather fear that some of the implications of this case frankly scare me. But there are too many co-incidences between the faery and the astronomical for any other conclusion to be tenable. The alien craft's signal, in Morse code, in English, is meaningless unless interpreted in terms of Emily's reality-moulding imagination; indeed, any other explanation is impossible. Emily created both faery host and Wolfii, and at the moment of her sexual completion, her guilt, her fear, her ultimate destruction, shut the door between merely subconscious and preconscious and burst her power like a bubble. The faery host returned to Other-world, and the alien star-crossers and their incredible vessel dissolved into the nothingness out of which Emily's mind had called them and imbued them with their brief phantom lives.

In so doing, Emily has made Dr. Desmond the laughing-stock of the astronomical fraternity: I hear that both he and the Marquis of Claremorris have been severely financially embarrassed by this episode; never-theless, it is a fitting punishment for a daughter to visit upon an inadequate and inattentive father. As the saying goes, my dear Willie, "Hell hath no fury like a woman scorned," and I feel that that small word, "woman," lies at the heart of the whole Craigdarragh case. Emily wished to be a woman; now she is a woman, more woman, perhaps, than she desired. I am reminded of another proverb, one of our Chinese brethren's sayings: "Beware what thou wishest, to thee it may be granted." The power of the preconscious mind is too mighty, too lofty, too terrible a thing to indulge in irony, yet perhaps the saddest thing of all this sad chapter of events must be the child Emily Desmond carries in her womb. For be it mortal or be it god, it will forever stand before her as a haunting reminder of the Otherworld she glimpsed, just for a single, searing moment, and which she has lost forever.

Yours sincerely,
Hannibal Rooke, Esq.

Craigdarragh
Drumcliffe
County Sligo
September 5th 1909

Dear Mother Superior,

Just a brief note to inform you that Emily will not be returning to Cross and Passion School in future. Alas, the poor child has recently suffered a major breakdown of health, and, after a spell in Dr. Hubert Orr's renowned Harcourt Street clinic, will be convalescing at some length here at home in Craigdarragh. It will be many months, I fear, before Emily regains her health fully. However, her education will not suffer; a governess is being hired to school her in a style I feel is more suited to her particular disposition. Therefore I take this opportunity to thank you, Mother Superior, for what you have done in the past for Emily: education truly is a gem beyond price in this modern world, and I know that Emily's private tutor will build soundly upon the solid foundation you have laid at Cross and Passion. In parting then, I would ask for your prayers for Emily's safe and full recovery; as ever, my own thoughts and prayers are all for my misfortunate daughter,

sincerely,
Caroline Desmond.

THE CATHARINE WHEEL

(OUR LADY OF THARSIS)

"Come on, lad, come . . ." you hear a voice call, and, peering through the crowd for its source (so familiar, so familiar), you see him. There: past the sherbet sellers and the raucous pastry hawkers, past the crowds of hopeful Penitential Mendicants and Poor Sisters of Tharsis who press close to the dignitaries' rostrum, past the psalm-singing Cathars and the vendors of religious curios; there, he is coming for you, Naon Asiim, with hand outstretched. Through steam and smoke and constables wielding shockstaves who try to keep the crowd away from the man of the moment, here he comes, just for you, your grandfather, Taam Engineer. You look at your mother and father, who swell with pride and say "Yes, Naon, go on, go with him." So he takes your hand and leads you up through the pressing crowd and the people cheer and wave at you but you have not time to wave back or even make out their faces because your head is whirling with the shouts and the music and the cries of the vendors.

The people part before Taam Engineer like grass before the scythe. Now you are on the rostrum beside him and every one of those thousands of thousands of people crushing into the station falls silent as the old man holds up the Summoner for all to see. There is a wonderful quiet for a moment, then a hiss of steam and the chunt-chunt of rumbling wheels, and like every last one of those thousands of thousands of people, you let your breath out in a great sigh because out from the pressure-shed doors comes the Greatest of the Great; the fabulous *Catharine of Tharsis* at the head of the last Ares Express.

Do you see pride in Taam Engineer's eye, or is that merely the light catching it as he winks to you and quick as a flash throws you into the control cab? He whispers something to you which is lost beneath the cheering and the music, but you hear the note of pride in it, and you think that is just right, for the Class 88 *Catharine of Tharsis* has never looked as well as she does on this her final run. The black-and-gold livery of Bethlehem-Ares glows with love and sacred cherry branches are crossed on the nose above the sun-bright polished relief of the Blessed Lady herself. Well-wishers have stuck holy medals and icons all over the inside of the cab too. Looking at them all leads you on to realize that the cab is much smaller than you had ever imagined. Then you see the scars where the computer modules have been torn out to make room for a human driver, and you remember that all those nights when you lay awake in bed pretending that the thunder of wheels was the Night Mail, the Lady was far away hauling hundred-car ore trains on the automated run from Iron Hills to Bessemer. Since before you were born *Catharine of Tharsis* has been making that slow pull up the kilometer-high Illawarra Bank. You have never seen her as she is today, the pride of Bethlehem-Ares, but your imagination has.

Now the people are boarding: the dignitaries and the faithful and the train enthusiasts and the folk who just want to be there at the end of a little piece of history; there they are, filing into the twenty cars and taking their seats for the eight-hour journey.

"Hurry up, hurry up," Taam Engineer says, anxious to be off. He pours you a sherbet from the small coldchest and you sip it, feeling the cool grittiness of it on your tongue, counting the passengers, eighty, ninety, a hundred, still a bit dazed that you are one of them yourself. Then the doors seal, *hsssss*. Steam billows, the crowd stands back excited and expectant, but not as excited or expectant as you. Down the line a red light turns green. The old man grins and taps instructions into the computer.

Behind you the drowsy djinn wakes and roars in fury, but it

is tightly held in its magnetic bottle. Just as well, you think, because your grandfather has told you that it is as hot as the center of the sun back there.

The crowds are really cheering now and the bands are playing for all they are worth and every loco in the yard, even the dirty old locals, are sounding their horns in salute as *Catharine of Tharsis* gathers speed. The constables are trying to keep back the crazy wheel-symboled Cathars who are throwing flower petals onto the track in front of you. Grandfather Taam is grinning from ear to ear and sounding the triple steam-horns like the trumpets of Judgment Day, as if to say, "Make way, make way, this is a *real* train!"

The train picks up speed slowly, accelerating up the long upgrade called Jahar Incline under full throttle, up through the shantytowns and their thrown-together ramshackle stations whose names you have memorized like a mantra: Jashna, Purwani, Wagga-Wagga, Ben's Town, Park-and-Bank, Llandyff, Acheson, Salt Beds, Mananga Loop.

Now you are away from the stink and the press of the shanties out into the open fields and you cheer as Grandfather Taam opens up the engines and lets the Lady run. *Catharine of Tharsis* throws herself at the magical 300 km/hr speed barrier and in the walled fields by the side of the track men with oxen and autoplanters stop and look up from the soil to wave at the black-gold streak.

"Faster, Grandfather, faster!" you shriek and Grandfather Taam smiles and orders "More speed, more speed!" The fusion engines reply with a howl of power, *Catharine of Tharsis* finds that time barrier effortlessly and shatters it, and at 355 km/hr the last ever Ares Express heads out into the Grand Valley.

For a long time I moved without style or feeling, wearing simple homespun frocks and open sandals in cold weather. My hair I let grow into thick staring mats, my nails began to curl at the ends. When I washed (only when people complained of the smell), I did so in cold water, even though some mornings I would shiver uncontrollably and catch sight in the mirror of my hollow blue face. I permitted myself that one vanity, the mirror, as a record of my progress towards spirituality. When I saw those dull eyes following me I would hold their gaze and whisper, The mortification of the flesh, the denial of the body, until they looked away with an expression other than disgust.

I allowed myself only the simplest foods: uncooked, unprocessed, and as close to natural as I could take it—for the most part vegetable. Two meals a day: a breakfast, and in the evening a dinner, with a glass of water at midday. Cold, of course, but with the taste of Commissary chemicals to it.

Patrick fears that I am wasting to a ghost before his eyes. I reassure him that I am merely abolishing the excess and taking on a newer, purer form. Purity, I whisper, Spirituality.

Purity! he says, Spirituality! I'll show you purity, I'll show you spirituality! It's us, Kathy; we are purity, we are spirituality, because of the life we share together. It's the love that's pure, the love that's spiritual.

Poor Patrick. He cannot understand.

I've seen the needle and it said, This is purity. Some showed me the secret spaces of their bodies and said, Here is spirituality. Others held up the bottles for me to see: Look, purity: escape. And I've seen the books, the red books, the blue books, the great brown ones dusty with age which say, Come inside, many have gone this way to wisdom before you. What a pity the blue books contradict the red books and the brown books cannot be read because they are so old. And you, Patrick, you are the slave of the book. You call it freedom: I have another name for what you give the name of Political Expression.

I've seen a thousand altars and breathed a thousand incenses, sung a thousand hymns, chanted a thousand canticles to gods a thousand years dead, and been told, This is the way, the *only* way to spirituality. Dancing-dervish under the love-lasers till dawn with men so beautiful they can only be artificial, I've been to the heart of the music where they say purity lies. Lies lies lies lies. The paintings, the altered states, the loves, the hates, the relationships: lies of the degenerates we have become.

Someday I will have to make Patrick leave. For his own sake as much as for the sake of my path to purity.

But he is my conscience. He makes me constantly ask, Am I right, am I wrong? and he must be a strong man indeed to be able to sleep night after night with the stinking animal into which I am changing. But I will cast him off, on that day when

I achieve purity, because then I won't have any further need of my conscience.

In an age of decadence, I alone strive for purity. I saw it once, I saw spirituality in the face, and since that day I have sought in my own human way to embody it. But give Patrick his due: I am learning that perhaps my daily denials and asceticisms are not the best way to attain my goal. Perhaps the human way is not the way at all.

For the greatest spiritual experience (I would almost call it "Holy," but I don't believe in God) comes when I taphead into the ROTECH computers, in that instant when they cleave my personality away from my brain and spin it off through space.

To Mars.

I can't explain to Patrick how it feels, like I couldn't explain it to my colleagues on the terraform team how it felt that first time when I tapheaded into the orbital mirrors we were maneuvering into position to thaw the polar ice-caps.

I've tried to tell him (as I tried to tell them, hands dancing, eyes wide and bright) of the beauty of the freedom I felt—from the strangling stench of our decaying culture, from the vice of material things, from my body and the arbitrary dictates of its biology: eating, drinking, pissing, crapping, sleeping, screwing. He doesn't understand.

Kathy, don't deny your body, he says, touching it. Yours is a beautiful body.

No, Patrick, only spirit is beautiful, and the machine is beautiful, and only what is beautiful is real.

"But was she real?" you ask, and your grandfather replies, "Oh, certainly. I tell you, she was as real as you or me, as real as any of us. What use is a saint who isn't real?" So you look out through the screen at the blurred steel rail that stretches straight ahead as far as you can see, right over the rusty horizon, and you think, Real, real, real as steel, real as a rail, rail made from steel. It is easy to make up rhymes to the beat of the wheels: diddley-dum, diddley-dum, real, real, real as steel.

An hour and a half out. Back down the train the passengers are having lunch; the dignitaries in the first-class restaurant, everyone else from packages and parcels on their laps. Taam Engineer is sharing his lunch with you, savory pancakes and tea, because you did not bring any lunch with you as you never expected to be riding high at the head of the Ares Express deep in the magic Forest of Chryse.

You have heard a lot about the Forest of Chryse, that it is under the special protection of the Lady herself, that travelers come back from it with tales of wonders and marvels, with unusual gifts and miraculous powers, that some come back with only half a mind and some do not come back at all. Look at the trees: giant redwoods older than man reaching up three hundred, four hundred, five hundred meters tall; it is easy to believe that the machines that built the world are still working under the shadow of the branches and that Catharine of Tharsis walks with them in the forest she planted a thousand years ago. Aboard her namesake, you hurtle past at 300 km/hr and wonder how Saint Catharine could possibly have built an entire world.

"Look, son." Grandfather Taam nudges you and points to a place far up the valley where a great patch of brightness is sweeping across the Forest of Chryse towards you. You hold your breath as the huge disc of light passes slowly over you on its way to the distant rim walls. If you squint up through your fingers you can just about see the intensely bright dot of the sky-mirror way up there in orbit behind all the glare. Then you feel a blow to the back of your head . . . you see hundreds of intensely bright dots.

"How many times have you been told, boy, don't stare at the sky-mirrors!" your grandfather bellows. "You can look at the light, but not at the mirror!"

But you treat yourself to one small extra peep anyway and you think of the men from ROTECH who are focusing all that light down on you, Naon Asiim.

"Remote Orbital Terraform and Environmental Control Headquarters." You whisper the name like a charm to keep the wind and the storm at bay and you remember what your friends told you: that the men who move the sky-mirrors have grown so different from ordinary people up there that they can never ever come down. That makes you shiver. Then you pass out from under the light, but out of the rear screens you can see its progress over the valley to the plateau-lands beyond. In its wake you see a tiny silver bauble bowling across the sky.

"Look, Grandfather! A dronelighter!"

He gives it the barest glance, spits, and touches one of the tiny icons of Our Lady fastened above the driving desk. Then you realize what a mistake you have made, that it is the dronelighters and the 'rigibles of the world that have made your grandfather the last to bear the proud name of Engineer, they are the reason why the museum sidings are waiting for the Lady just beyond the crowds at Pulaski Station.

"I'm sorry, Grandfather." A hand ruffles your hair.

"Never mind, son, never worry. Look: see how that thing runs . . . It's getting out from under the skirts of the storm, running as fast as it can . . . They can't take the weather, they're flimsy, plasticky things, like glorified Festival kites."

"But we can take the weather."

"Go through it like a fist through wet rice-paper, my boy! I tell you, Bethlehem-Ares never lost a day, not even one single hour, to the weather: rain, hail, blizzard, monsoon, none of it stops the Lady!" He reaches out to touch the metal window-frame and you feel like shouting "hooray!" Taam Engineer (what, you wonder, will he call himself when the Lady is gone?) stabs a finger at the sky-screen.

"See that? Because of those things cluttering up the sky they have to move the weather about to suit them. That's what the mirror's for; those ROTECH boys are moving the storm up onto the plateau where it can blow itself to glory and not harm one single, delicate dirigible. Puh!" He spits again. "I tell you, those things have no soul. Not like the Lady here, she's got a soul you can hear and feel when you open those throttles up, she's got a soul you can touch and smell like hot oil and steam. You don't drive her, she lets you become a little part of her and then she drives you. Like all ladies. Soul, I tell you." He hunts around for words but they evade him like butterflies. He waves his hands, trying to shape the ideas that mean so much to him, but the words will not come to him. "I tell you, how can you feel part of anything when you're flying way up there above everything? You're not part of anything up there like you're a bit of the landscape down here. I tell you, they've no soul. You know, soon it will be just them and the robots on the freight runs and then one day even they'll be gone, it'll be just the lighter-than-airs. The only engines you'll see'll be in the museums and God forbid that I should ever come to see that day." He looks at you like he wants you to back him up in what he has said, but you didn't really understand what he said because the rumble of the engines and the sway of the cab as it leans into the curves and the drumming of the wheels saying *real, real, real as steel* is sending you off to sleep.

When I wake the sight disgusts me. Gap-toothed crack-skinned filth-haired hag holding splintered nails up to the mirror whining, The mortification of the flesh, the denial of the body. Hideous. Futile.

Sleep came hard to me last night. Lying beside Patrick, staring at the ceiling, I had time and plenty to think. Letting the pieces tumble through my head, I saw how I was wrong, so wrong, so magnificently wrong. The mortification of the flesh is empty. It only serves to focus the mind more closely on the body it seeks to deny. Disciplining the body does not discipline the mind, for the greater the denial the greater the attention the body must be given. This is not the way to spirituality.

So before Patrick wakes I shower. I wash my hair, I trim my nails, I depilate, I deodorize, I even repaint the tekmark on my forehead and dress in the most nearly fashionable outfit I own. On the train downtown I just sit and watch the people. They do not know that I was the girl with the sunken eyes and the stinking hair they were so careful not to be seen staring at. Now I am just another face on a train. By denying the body I only drew more attention to it. The only way to achieve purity is to escape totally from the body. But that is impossible while we are on this earth. Not so on Mars.

Tapheading, for me, is like waking from a dream into a new morning. Eyes click open to the vast redscapes of Mars. You can hear it shouting, Real, real! with the voice of the polar wind. Let me tell you about the polar wind. For a hundred thousand years it blew cold and dry from the ice itself, but we have moved our orbital mirrors in over the pole and are thawing the cap. So now the winds have reversed direction and great thunderheads of cloud are piling up, layer upon layer, in the north. Someday it will rain, the first rain on Mars for fifty thousand years. I will rejoice at the feel of it on my plastic skin, I will laugh as it fills the ditches and dikes of our irrigation systems and I shall doubtless cry on the day when it touches the seeds of the Black Tulips I have planted and quickens them to life. But that is in the future. Maybe this year, maybe next year, maybe five years from now.

For the present I take joy in lifting my head from the planting and seeing the rows of Johnny Appleseeds digging and dropping and filling and moving on. They are mine. No. They are *me*. I can be any one of them I choose to be, from Number Eleven busily spraying organic mulch over the seedbeds to Number Thirty-five trundling back to base with a damaged tread.

But I can be much more than that. If I blink back through the ROTECH computer network I can be a dronelighter blowing tailored bacteria into the air, or a flock of orbital mirrors bending light from round the far side of the sky, or an automated hatchery growing millions of heat-producing oxygen-generating Black Tulip seeds for the Johnny Appleseeds, or a channel cutter building the fabulous Martian canals after all these millennia, or a Seeker searching deep beneath the volcanic shield of Tharsis for a magma core to tap for geothermal energy, or an aviopter flying condor patrol high over the Mare Boreum, which will one day indeed be a Sea of Trees . . .

I can be whatever I want to be. I am free. I am pure spirit, unbound to any body. And this is my vision of purity, of spirituality: to be forever free from this body, from earth and its decadence, to fly on into a pure future and build a new world as it ought to be built; as a thing of spirit, pure and untainted by human lusts and ambitions. This is a future that stretches far beyond my human lifespan. They say it will be eight hundred years before a man can walk naked in the forests we are growing in Chryse. Two hundred years will pass after that before the first settlers arrive on the plains of Deuteronomy. A thousand years, then, to build a whole world in. That will give me enough time to make it a proper world.

This is my vision, this is my dream. I am only now beginning to realize how I may achieve it . . .

But first I must dream again. . . .

It is not the rattle of the rain that has woken you, nor the slam of a passing ore train on the slow up-line; it is something far less tangible than that, it is something you feel like the crick in your neck and the dryness in your mouth and the gumminess around your eyes that you get from having fallen asleep against the side window. So knuckle your eyes open, sniff the air. You can smell the rain, but you can smell something else too, like electricity, like excitement, like something waiting to happen.

Look at the screen, what do you see? Wind blowing billows across endless kilometers of wet yellow grass that roll away to the horizon. Low rings of hills like the ancient burial mounds of Deuteronomy lie across the plain: eroded impact craters, Taam Engineer tells you. This is Xanthe, a land as different as different can be to the forests of Chryse or the paddies of the Great Oxus. A high, dry plainland where the Grand Valley begins to slope up to the high country of Tharsis. But today the rains have come out of season to the stony plain, carried on an unnatural wind, for the ROTECH engineers and their sky-mirrors are driving the storm away from the peopled lowlands to the Sinn Highlands where it can blow and rain and rage and trouble no one. The sky is hidden by a layer of low, black, curdled cloud and the wind from the Sea of Trees blows curtains of rain across the grassland. Miserable.

You ask your grandfather how much longer and he says not long, the storm will blow out within the hour and Xanthe's a poor land anyway, fit only for grazers and goatherds and getting through as quickly as possible. Grandfather Taam smiles his special secret smile and then you realize that, according to the story, this is where it all happened, where Taam Engineer—your own grandfather!—met the saint and so averted a dreadful accident. Now you know where the feeling of excitement has come from. Now you know why Grandfather Taam has brought you on the great Lady's last haul.

So you ask the old man, this is where it all happened? And he smiles that secret smile again and says yes, that this is where it all happened all those years ago, long before you were even thought of; it was here the Lady worked a miracle and saved five hundred lives, yes, we'll be there soon, and look, even the weather is deciding to improve, look.

Out across the hills the sky is clearing from the northwest. Light is pouring through the dirty clouds and the rain has blown away leaving the air jewel-bright and clear. *Catharine of Tharsis* explodes out into the sunlight, a shout of black and gold, and the plains about her steam gently in the afternoon sun.

Lights flash on the control desk. Even though you do not understand what they mean, they look important. You direct Taam Engineer's attention to them, but he just nods and then ignores them. He even sits back and lights a cheroot. You thought he had given up those dirty things years ago, but when you ask him if there is anything wrong, he says, "Nothing, boy, nothing," and tells you she's only doing what her high station expects of her, but you haven't time to think about that because the train is slowing down. Definitely, unmistakably. Her speed is now well under 100. You look to Taam Engineer, but he grins roguishly and does not even touch the keypad to demand more speed. He just sits there, arms folded, puffing on his cheroot as the speed drops and drops and it becomes obvious that the train is not just slowing, but stopping.

The nonstop Rejoice-to-Llangonnedd Ares Express grinds past a stationary chemical train down-bound from the sulfur beds of Pavo. The engines whine as they deliver power to the squealing brakes, and the seven-hundred-ton train comes to a stand right out there in the middle of the pampas with not a station or even a signal pylon to mark it as special and worthy of the attention of *Catharine of Tharsis*.

A hiss of steam startles you, it is that quiet. Cooling metal clicks. Even the hum of the engines is gone, the fusion generators are shut right down. The rust-red chemical train looks almost sinister in its stillness.

"What now?" you whisper, painfully aware of how loud your voice sounds. Grandfather Taam nods at the door.

"We get out."

The door hisses open and he jumps out, then lifts you down to the ground. You can see the staring faces pressed to the windows all the way down the train.

"Come on," says Grandfather Taam and he takes you by the hand and leads over the slow down-line (you glance nervously at the waiting chemical train, half-expecting the automated locomotive to suddenly blare into life), down the low embankment, and into the tall grass. He grinds his filthy cheroot out on the ground, says "It should be around here somewhere," and starts thrashing about, *whish whish swush*, in the wet grass. You can hear him muttering.

"Aha! Got it! A bit overgrown, but that just goes to show how long it is since a human engineer ran this line. I tell you, in my day we kept the weeds down and polished the silverwork so bright you could see it shining from ten kilometers down the track. Come and look at this, son . . ."

He has cleared the grass away from a small stone pedestal. Inlaid in tarnished metal is the nine-spiked wheel symbol of Saint Catharine. You can feel the devotion as your grandfather bends to rub the dirt of the years from the small memorial. When it is clean and silver-bright again he bids you sit with him on the damp crushed grass and listen as he tells you his tale.

I have told Patrick what I am going to do. I used the simplest words, the most restrained gestures, the shortest sentences, for I know how incoherent I become when I am excited. I did my best to explain, but all I did was scare him. Seeing me transformed, my body clean, my face pretty, again the Kathy Haan he had once loved, and then to hear me tell him of how I am going to cast this world away and live forever on Mars is too great a shock for him. He does not have to tell me. I know he thinks I am mad. More than just "mad." Insane. My explanations will do no good, he can't understand and I'm not going to force him to.

One favor, Patrick. You know people who can get these things, could you get me two lengths of twistlock monofiber?

What for?

I need it.

For your mad "escape"—don't tell me. Forget it. No, Kathy.

But listen, Patrick—

No no no, I've listened enough to you already, you're a persistent bitch, if I listen to your voice long enough I'll find myself agreeing with whatever insane notion you suggest.

But it's not insanity. It's survival, it's the only way for me to go.

Yes yes yes, the only way you can be pure, the only way you can achieve spirituality . . . What is it that's driven you to this, Kathy? It's suicide, that's exactly what it is!

The Crazy Angel, Patrick. At some time or another the Crazy Angel touches us all and we just have to go with the flow.

But he doesn't see the joke: if there is no God, how can there be any angel at all, crazy or otherwise, unless it is me?

Are we not enough? There was a time when it was enough for us to have each other. What more do you want, what more is there?

Do you really want me to answer that, Patrick? I give him one of my fascinating half-smiles that used to excite him so much. Now it only angers him.

Then, what does Mars offer that I don't?

Same question. This time I choose to answer it.

Sanity.

Sanity! Hah! You talk to me about sanity? That's rich, Kathy Haan, that is rich.

I remain patient. I will not allow Patrick to disturb me. I will not lose my head or shout at him. To do so would only be to play the game according to his rules, and his sick society's rules.

Sanity, I say, in a world where words like hunger and fear and disease and war and decadence and degeneration don't have any meaning, in a world that one day will be so much more than your earth could ever be. Freedom from a world that registers its terrorists, Patrick Byrne, and lets them kill who they will for their high and lofty registered ideals!

That stings him, but I am relentless, I am the voice of final authority: the angel is speaking through me and won't be silent.

And you will let me go, Patrick, you will get me those lengths of monofiber from your Corps friends, because either I go or your sick, sick society will have me off the top of a building in a week, and that is a promise, Patrick Byrne, a Kathy Haan promise: either way I go, either way you lose.

Bitch! he roars and spins round, hand raised to strike, but no one may lay hands on the Crazy Angel and live and the look in my eyes stops him cold. Serenity.

Bitch. God; maybe you are an angel after all, maybe you are a saint.

Not a saint, Patrick, never a saint. Sure, don't I not believe in God? Not Saint Kathy, just a woman out of time who wanted something more than her world had to offer. Now, will you get me those bits of twistlock fiber?

All right. I can't fight the Crazy Angel. How long? I hold my hands about half a meter apart.

Two of them, with grips at both ends and a trigger-release twistlock set to fifth-second decay so they won't ever find out how I did it.

I'll get them. It'll take some time.

I can wait.

Words flow as expressions across his face. Then he turns away from me.

Kathy, this is suicide!

So what? It's legal, like everything else from political murder to public buggery.

It's suicide.

No. Not this. To stay behind, to try and live one more year on this rotting world, that's suicide. More than that, it's the end of everything, because then I'll have even thrown all my hope away.

It is a story old and stale with telling and retelling, but here, sitting on the damp grass under the enormous sky, it feels as if it is happening to you for the first time. Taam Engineer's eyes are vacant, gazing into years ago; he does not even notice how his stained fingers trace the starburst shape of the Catharine Wheel on the pedestal.

"I tell you, I thought we were done then. I'd given up all hope when that pump blew, with us so far out into the wilderness (and it was wilderness then, this was years back before ROTECH had completed terraforming the Grand Valley). We were so far out that no help could ever reach us in time, not even if they sent the fastest flyer down from their skystations, and there were five hundred souls aboard, man, woman, and child . . .

"So I ordered them to evacuate the train, even though I knew right well that they could never get far enough away to outrun the blast when the fusion engines exploded . . . But I had them run all the same, run to those hills over there—you know, to this day I don't know if they have a name, those hills—but I thought that if they could reach the far side then they might be safe, knowing full well that they never would . . .

"All the time I was counting off the seconds until the pressure vessel would crack and all that superheated steam would blow my beauty to glory and us with her. I can remember that I had one thought in my head that kept running round and round and round: 'God, save the train, please, save the train, God . . .' That was when the miracle happened."

An afterbreath of wind stirs the grass around you. It feels deliciously creepy.

"I don't know if it was my calling or the train's agony that brought her, and I don't think it matters much; but on the horizon I saw a black dot, way out there . . ." He points out across the waving grass and if you squint along the line of his finger into the sun you too can see that black dot rushing towards you. "An aviopter, black as sin and big as a barn, bigger even, circling over the line, and I tell you, it was looking for me, for the one who called it . . ." Taam Engineer's hands fly like aviopters, but he is too busy watching the great black metal hawk coming lower and lower and lower to notice them. "And I swear she took the loco in her claws, boy, in her metal claws, and every bit of brightwork on her ran with blue fire. Then I heard it. The most terrible sound in the world, the scream of the steam-release valve overloading, and I knew that was it and I scrambled down this bank as fast as I could and threw myself onto the ground because death was only a second behind me, and do you know what I saw?"

Though you have heard the story a hundred tellings before, this time it takes your breath away. So you shake your head, because for once you do not know.

"I tell you, every one of those five hundred souls, just standing there in the long grass and staring for all they were worth. Not one of them trying to run, I say, so I turned myself belly-up and stared too, and I tell you, it was a thing so worth the staring that I couldn't have run, though my life depended on it.

"They'd stripped her down and laid her bare and unplugged the fusion generators and, by the Mother-of-Us-All, they were fusing up the cracks in the containment vessel and running the pumps from zero up to red and down again, and those pumps, those God-blind-'em pumps, they were singing so sweetly that day it was like the Larks of the Argyres themselves."

"Who, Grandfather?" you say, swept away by the story, "who were they?"

"The Angels of Saint Catharine herself, I tell you. They had the look of great metal insects, like the crickets you keep in a cage at home, but as big as lurchers and silver all over. They came out of the belly of the aviopter and a-swarmed all over my locomotive."

He slaps his thighs.

"Well, I knew she was saved then and I was whooping and cheering for all I was worth and so was every man-jack of those five hundred souls by the time those silver crickets had finished their work and put her back together again. Then they all just packed back into the belly of that big black aviopter and she flew off over the horizon and we never saw her again, none of us.

"So, I got up into the cab and everything was all quiet and everything smelt right and every readout was normal and every light green, and I put the power on as gentle as gentle and those engines just roared up and sang, and those pumps, those pumps that so near killed us all, they were humming and trilling like they were fresh from the shop. Then I knew I'd seen a miracle happen, that the Blessed Lady, Saint Catharine herself, had intervened and saved us all. And I tell you this, I would still never have believed it had it not been for those five hundred souls who witnessed every little thing she did and some of them even had it recorded and you can see those pictures to this day."

Up on the track the chemical train fires up. The shocking explosion of sound makes you both jump. Then you laugh and up on the embankment the robot train moves off: *cunk cunk, cunk cunk.* Taam Engineer rises to watch it. When it is gone he pats the small stone pedestal.

"So of course we named the engine after her and put this here to commemorate the miracle. I tell you, all the engineers (in the days when we used to have human engineers) on the Grand Valley run would sound their horns when they went by as a mark of respect, and also in the hope that if they gave the Lady her due, one day she might pull them out of trouble. You see, we know that the Lady's on our side."

He offers you a hand and drags you up damp-assed from the ground. As you climb the embankment you see all the faces at the windows and the hands waving icons and charms and medallions and holy things. It makes you look at *Catharine of Tharsis* again, as something not quite believable, half locomotive and half miracle.

Grandfather Taam lifts you up the cab steps. Suddenly a question demands to be asked.

"Grandfather, then why do the trains stop now if they only used to whistle?"

He reaches for the flask of tea and pours you a scalding cup. Behind you the djinn rumbles into life again.

"I'll tell you for why. Because she is not a saint of people but a saint of machines. Remember that, because the day came when the last engineer was paid off this line and they turned it over to the machines and then they felt that they could honor their Lady as best they knew."

Lights blink red white green yellow blue all over the cab. The light glints off the holy medals and icons but somehow it is not as pretty as it once was.

As if it was aware of my imminent escape into spirituality, the ugliness is drawing closer to me. Yesterday in the train I saw a licensed beggar kicked to death by three masked men. No one raised voice or hand in protest. For one of the masks held out a Political Activist Registry card for us all to see while the other two beat the old man to death in accordance with their political ideals. Everyone looked out of the windows or at the floor or at the advertisements for sunny holidays and personal-credit extensions. Anywhere but at the beggar or at each other.

I am ashamed. I too looked away and did nothing.

We left him on the floor of the car for others to take care of when we stepped off at our stop. A smart man I vaguely know with a highcaste tekmark glanced at me and whispered, We certainly must remember to respect people's right to political expression, goodness knows what terrible things might happen if we don't.

Oh, Patrick, how many beggars have you killed in the name of political expression? Damn you, Patrick Byrne, for all the love I've wasted on a man who a hundred years ago would have been hunted down and torn apart for the common murderer he was. Dear God, though I know you aren't there, what sort of a people are we when we call terrorists heroes and murder "political expression"? What sort of a person is it who would dare to say she loved one? A Kathy Haan, that's what. But I will be rid of him.

Escape is two lengths of twistlock monofiber wrapped up in my pouch, but have I the courage to use it? Cowardice is a virtue now, everyone has their Political Activist card to wave as justification for their fear. Be brave, Kathy.

I like to think of myself as the first Martian at these times.

It's not the loneliness that scares me. I have been alone for twenty-four years now and there is no lonelier place than the inside of your skull. What terrifies me is the fear of gods.

Deiophobia.

Maybe you are an angel after all, maybe you are a saint, Patrick said. What I fear most is that I may become more than just a saint, that the ultimate blasphemy to all that the sacrifice of Kathy Haan stood for will be for me to become the Creator God of the world I am building: the Earth Mother, the Blessed Virgin Kathy, the Cherished and Adored Womb of the humanity I despise.

I do not want to be God, I don't even particularly want to be human. I only want to be free from the wheel.

Smiles and leers greet me from friend and satyr alike.

Morning, Kathy (thighs, Kathy); 'day, Kathy (breasts, Kathy) . . .

I take my chair, still warm from the flesh of its previous occupant whom I have never known and probably never will now. Warm-up drill: codes, ciphers, and calibrations. The sensor helmet meshes with my neural implants and nobody sees me slip the coils of monofiber from my pouch and throw a couple of loops around the armrests.

Lightspeed will be the death of me. The monofiber is merely the charm I choose to invoke it.

Okay, Kathy, taphead monitoring on . . .

Needles slip into my brain and I slip my wrists through the loops, concealing the twistlock control studs in my palms. I had not thought death would be so easy.

Brainscans worm across the ceiling.

Listen: I have not much time to tell you this, so listen well. It takes two minutes for the oxygen level in the brain to fall to the critical point after which damage is irreversible. It is easy to do this. Damage to two major arteries will do very nicely, provided there is no rapid medical attention.

But, it takes four minutes for the coded tadon pulse containing the soul of Kathy Haan to reach Mars. You can add: you know that if you add another four minutes' return time from ROTECH to Earth, that leaves you with a brain so like shredded cabbage that there's no way they'll ever be able to pour poor Kathy back into it again. I shall be free and I shall live forever as a creature of pure spirit.

I have invented a totally new sin. Is it fitting then that I should become a saint?

All I need do is press the buttons. The molecular kink in the monofiber will contract, neatly severing my wrists. A fifth of a second later they will dissolve completely. Lightspeed will

do the rest. All I need do is press the buttons. They are hidden
in my palms, slick with sweat.

Okay, Kathy, counting down to persona transfer. Prelimi-
nary tadon scan on, transfer pulse in five seconds . . .
four . . .

The mortification of the flesh, I whisper. Behind me
someone shouts. Too late.

. . . one.

I press the buttons.

Green lights all the way down the line on the final
run into Llangonnedd. Clear road: dirty freighters pulled into
sidings blare their horns and ugly, ugly robot locals squawk
their nasty klaxons as the Lady races by. Suburban passengers
blink as she streaks by; by the time the shout reaches their lips
she is around the next bend and leaning into the one after that
like a pacehound.

And all the lights are green. More magic. Grandfather
Taam tells you that you never get a full run of greens coming
into Llangonnedd, no, not even for the Ares Express. Never
ever. It must be more magic, of the same kind that let the Lady
reach the incredible 450 km/hr out there on the flats beyond
Hundred Lakes. Grandfather Taam tells you that she never
touched 450 before, never ever, not even 400. Why, the people
who built her had told him themselves that she would blow
apart if she went over 390.

You reckon the engineers know nothing about engines and
their special magic. After all, they are just engineers, but
Grandfather Taam is an Engineer. Looking out of the side
windows, even a leisurely 250 seems frighteningly fast in these
crowded suburbs. Canal flash houses flash fields flash park
flash factories flash: you can feel your eyes widening in appre-
hension as the stations and the signals hurl themselves out of
the distance at you. And all the lights are green.

That can mean only one thing.

"She's doing this, isn't she, Grandfather?"

A station packed with round-mouthed commuters zips by.
Taam Engineer lights a cheroot.

"Must be. I've hardly had to lay a finger on those buttons
for the past hour or so."

Beneath you the brakes start to take hold, slowing you
down from your mad rampage through outer Llangonnedd to a

more civilized pace. You say, "She must really love this train very much."

Grandfather Taam looks straight ahead of him down the silver track.

"After all, she did save it."

"But it wasn't the people, was it, Grandfather? It was nothing to do with those five hundred souls; she saved the train because it was the train she wanted to save. All those people were extra, weren't they?"

"They didn't matter to her one bit, boy."

"And you said she's a saint of machines, didn't you? Not a saint of people? That's why she loves the train, why she loved it enough not to let it die, isn't it? If there hadn't been a single person there, she would still have saved the train, wouldn't she? But, if that's true, why do people love her?"

"Love her? Who said anything about loving her? I tell you, boy, I have little love for Catharine of Tharsis. Respect, yes, love, no. And I'll tell you why. Because if she hadn't thought the train was worth saving, if she hadn't loved the train, she would just have let it blow those five hundred people to hell without a single thought. That's the kind of God those crazy Cathars are worshiping, but as to why they love her, I don't know. Do you have any idea why people would love someone like that?"

He looks straight at you. You have been expecting this question. You know that he has never been able to answer it himself, and that it is the reason why he brought you along on this ride.

"I don't know what I think . . . If she's really like that, then I think that most people must be very foolish most of the time, especially when they have to look for someone to help them when things go wrong and then put the blame on when things don't happen like they want. People are like that. I think if I were a saint like Saint Catharine I would be a saint of machines, too. Then I wouldn't care what people said about me or thought of me because I wouldn't be doing anything for them and they could cry away and pray away all day like those silly Cathars and Penitential Mendicants and Poor Sisters of Tharsis and I wouldn't care one bit, because machines are never foolish."

Catharine of Tharsis has slowed right down. The end of

the journey is near now. Tomorrow Taam Engineer and you will be flying home on one of those dreadful dirigibles, and *Catharine of Tharsis* will be taken away to the museum for the foolish people to stare at and marvel over her record-breaking final run. And now you understand.

"Grandfather, of course I'd be a saint of machines! Because I could fly with the aviopters and the sky-mirrors and even the great SkyWheel herself and I could burrow with the Seekers and swim with the 'Mersibles, but most of all I could run with the Lady of Tharsis faster than she ever ran before and show off to everyone what a wonderful engine she is before they put her away for good in a museum. People are always moaning and complaining about their troubles and their problems; they won't let you run and be free from them, people won't let you do things like that!"

"Ah, the ways of saints and children," Taam Engineer says as the Lady rumbles over the Raj Canal into the glassite dome of Pulaski Station. Already you can hear the roars and the cheers of the crowds and every loco in the yards is sounding its horn in salute.

"Here, button three," Grandfather Taam says and you reply to the people with the wonderful blare of the steam horns.

You press and press and press that button and the trumpets sound and sound and sound until the notes shatter against the glass roof of the station. And how the crowds cheer! Taam Engineer is hanging out of the window waving to the mobs of petal-throwing Cathars as *Catharine of Tharsis* glides in to Platform Three as smooth as smooth. You are sliding the other side window open, ready to cheer, when something stops you. An odd feeling, like a persistent itch in the nose that suddenly stops, or a noise in your ears that you never hear until it goes away. A kind of click. You shake your head but it is gone and you shout and wave for all you are worth to the excited people. They wave and call back to you, but you do not see them because you are really thinking about that click. For a second or so it puzzles you. Then you realize that it is nothing very important, it is only the empty space filling in where once there might have been a saint.

UNFINISHED
PORTRAIT OF
THE KING
OF PAIN
BY VAN GOGH

Vincent: that is how he signs all his paintings; just his name, "Vincent," in the bottom left corner. Sometimes, if the day has been good and the yellow sun of Provence has been warm and kind to him, splashing a paint-pot of color across the fields swept bare and clean by the cold wind from the north, then he will date it: *Spring 1888,* so that he will remember for always the good day when the sun was kind to him. *The sun, the sun,* he writes in his letters to his brother, *I am a servant of the sun,* and on the walls of his bedroom he hangs six paintings of sunflowers to remind him always of the sun. Yellow is the color of the sun, yellow is the color of friendship: "The House of Friends," he christens his little yellow house on the corner of place Lamartine and dreams through the hot Provençal nights of the friends with whom he might fill its walls: a brotherhood of visionaries, a painters' colony dedicated to the service of the sun.

Every other day he writes to his brother Theo in Paris. He asks for more yellow; *Send me more yellow,* and begs Theo to once again try and persuade Paul, implore Paul, go down on his knees and beg Paul, to come south to Arles to lead the artists' colony. Letter after letter after letter he writes, letter after letter after letter arrives, brought to him by his friend the postman Roulin (who he will paint someday soon, he thinks), letters saying *Not yet* and *In a little while* and *Patience,*

patience, my dear Vincent. Vincent sits late, very late, too late, in the Cafe L'Alcazar, writing letter after letter after letter to his brother.

"Monsieur, we are closing, monsieur, you must go now, we are taking the tables in; monsieur, have you no home to go to?" say the waiters in their white aprons and Vincent, who drinks too much and eats too little and sleeps hardly at all, crosses the square and climbs the stairs to his Yellow House. In his blue-walled bedroom, under six paintings of sunflowers, he dreams. He dreams of a brotherhood of artists, he dreams of the arch-backed bridges of Japan under needles of rain, but most of all he dreams of the boiling solar disk of the sun.

In these dreams the sun speaks to him. It calls him its child touched with divine madness, and shows him its paintings: a hat caught in a tall treetop; a rose pierced by a silver thorn; a king upon a burning throne; a raven with a cherry in its beak; a crown in a cornfield, the sky dark with birds of ill-omen.

See, Vincent, says the sun, these are my paintings of you. Are they not fine, works of note and merit?

When Vincent awakes, the canvases of the night are still with him and he packs them up with his own canvases and brushes, his oils and easel, and takes them out with him onto the roads of Provence, into the heat and the dust and the scent of wild thyme and the yellow sun. When he has walked quite far enough he sets up his easel and his canvas and paints until the shadows grow long. He paints until the images of the night are emptied out of him, for he fears that to nurture them in his imagination will surely bring the black birds of madness flocking round his soul. When he is drained, as empty as a summer well, he looks at what he has done and sees his bold colors, his solid brushstrokes of red and green, his beloved blues and yellows. He sees the sun captured on canvas and remembers his teacher at the Academy in Paris. "Who are you," the man had asked, incredulous before potato-faced peasants and Bible-black skies of Borinage. "I am Vincent the Dutchman!" Vincent had replied, and remembering that in the evening-shadowed byways of Provence, Vincent the Dutchman smiles and signs his name in the bottom left-hand corner.

One night, having surrendered to exhaustion, an image comes out of the heart of the sun like none he has ever seen before. He stands upon an endless shingle beach by the side of a silver sea. The air is filled with the knocking of the rolling pebbles and the cry of unseen seabirds. Beyond the silver sea a haze of sick yellow smoke clouds the air, as if the billion belching chimneys of some world-encompassing city, some universal Borinage, were pouring a blanket of filth to hide the sun. In the far distance, along the beach, is a tree springing from the sterile shore and as Vincent begins to walk towards it he sees that it bears both blossom and ripe fruit, and its leaves are both summer-green and withered brown. Beneath this tree a man is seated. His face cannot be distinguished, so great is the glare reflected from the glass sea, but from his posture he seems absorbed in musings. But as Vincent draws closer the man looks up and Vincent is shocked to see that it is not who he thought it would be. It is not himself.

And then there are the days when the mistral blows from the north. It bows the trees to the ground before it and ruffles the cornfields like cat's fur and dries up Vincent's soul, sending him a little crazy so that he puts big rocks on the corners of his canvases to hold them to the ground. When the mistral blows, the brown-leather people of Provence clap their hats to their heads and wonder at this crazy foreigner who paints when the wind is in the north and who is always, always, peering into the sun as if looking for something hidden in its glare that no one else can see. He is looking for the windswept hat and the pierced rose, the king, the crown, and the raven. He is looking for the beach by the shining silver sea. He is looking to see if the dark freckles on the sun's face are only the birds of madness diving down for him.

Oh, Vincent is crazy, yes, Vincent is mad, and Vincent fears the madness around which the round earth rolls more than he fears the black realisms of death. He fears his sanity blowing away on the mistral wind like an unweighted canvas, like a hat snatched up into the branches of a high tree—his hat! his hat! his favorite straw hat, snatched from his head by the cold, dry wind from the north and whisked teasingly along just above the grasp of his reaching fingers. It hurdles hedges, leaps stone walls and whitewashed pickets. All the brown-leather people crease up into wrinkles of laughter at the crazy Dutchman chasing after his jumbling, tumbling hat. Then a final wintery breath from out of the Low Countries whips it straight up, high beyond his snatching fingers, and sweeps it along above a line of flowering walnut trees until it capriciously fails and deposits his hat in the topmost branches of the tallest tree.

"Damn," says Vincent, and with a Dutchman's stubborn single-mindedness he sets about the recovery of his hat. He can see it there, held tantalizingly in the branches of the last tree in the row. How long since Vincent last climbed a tree? He cannot remember, but climb this one he must. The yellow sun beats down upon his head, and standing in the middle of the lane Vincent thinks he hears the mewling of white gulls—yes, and the crashing of surf upon a shore, how can this be? and instead of the hard-packed provincial earth beneath his feet he is sure he feels rolling, sliding pebbles. He is running down the lane, he is running down the beach; he breathes harder now and with each breath he inhales the fragrance of wild thyme, yes, but also the great salt of the ocean. Before him he sees not a row of tall walnuts, but a single tree, impossibly both blossoming and bearing fruit, its leaves both green and brown. In the branches of the tree is his hat. Beneath it sits a man who rises to greet him.

"Madness!" says Vincent, dreading that he has walked off the round world into the swirling chaos without hope of return. "Madness."

"Hello, Vincent," says the man beneath the tree. He is very French, very elegant, very charming. "I have wanted so very much to meet you."

"Madness!" cries Vincent, "madness!" Behind him the silver sea crashes on the beach and the pebbles roll and knock, poised between being mountains and sand.

"Would you care for some wine?" asks the man beneath the tree. "It's a curious vintage, but most refreshing. Sit, sit." Vincent sits on the hard round pebbles. From somewhere Vincent cannot see, the dapper French gentleman generates a bottle of light rosé wine and two glasses.

"Good health," he says and tilts his glass to Vincent.

"I'm afraid I cannot toast you, my host, because I do not know your name, nor the name of this place you have brought me to."

"This is the beach by the Sea of Forever," says the man beneath the tree, once again folded into his dream-familiar posture of cross-legged contemplation. "It is a preview on history, a belvedere of memories, a high place created by the machines, the High and Shining Ones within which I exist, from which I may survey all that is past and call it from the memories of the machines to renewed life.

"I am Jean-Michel Rey, better known to my own age as the King of Pain. Quite simply, in a world where all pain has been brought under the control of the High and Shining Ones, I am Conscience, and Judge. Conscienceless themselves, the machines sought conscience, and thus an aircraft worker from Dijon is King of Pain, omniscient, and, I fear, near omnipotent. Listen, Vincent; there is one law, a simple law, I am a simple man; there can *be* only one law in a pain-free world where the heart of man is as wicked and unredeemed, alas, as it ever was. The law is that he who causes pain to another shall be punished. With pain. This is my Law, Vincent, simple, even crude, and through the High and Shining Ones I enforce it. In the gulf between the achieved and the yet-to-be-achieved, I depend: conscience, King, dare I say, God?

"So, Vincent. Ah, you have not brought your paints and canvases. That is a pity." The King of Pain rises from his seat and reaches down Vincent's hat from the branches of his tree. "You see, Vincent, of all the artists and painters to whom I have access through the memories of the High and Shining Ones, it is you, and you alone, that I wish to paint my portrait."

This is the way that Vincent paints the portrait of the King of Pain. In the morning he arises from white sleep, and with canvas and easel slung across his shoulders and his paints in a fisherman's tackle box beneath his arm, he lets the mistral blow him where it will, down whatever lane or byway it chooses. He knows that all lanes and byways run ultimately down to the Sea of Forever and the man who lives beside it, where the sun always stands two hours past the noon and its light is as yellow as corn. There Vincent paints. As he squeezes ridges of bright, bold pigment onto the canvas, the King of Pain speaks of many things, as people who sit for portraits are wont to do.

"To be King of Pain . . ." says the King of Pain at rest beneath his tree, "have you any idea of the implications?" Vincent neither confirms nor denies the question, for the questions a king asks himself only a king may answer. "But, Vincent, have you ever given thought to what it is I must do?" And by means of self-answer, that King of Pain that Vincent cannot see, the King of Pain that dwells within the machines, wills penetrating guilt upon a woman in Tientsin who left her detested husband to die in a burning house, spears a corrupt young computer-systems analyst from Atlanta with piercing stomach pains, torments a selfishly ambitious career girl from Duisburg with dread of death and annihilation, and prods a newspaper sub-editor who is cheating on his lovely, saintly wheelchair-bound wife over the edge of the Sydney bridge to smash like an egg on the clean blue waters of the harbor.

"So it goes, Vincent," says the King of Pain, mercifully closing the doors of pain and punishment before Vincent's eyes. "I have done what I can to stop men from hurting each other, but I cannot reach into the heart, for where there is freedom there are always those who will abuse. And sometimes I fear that I am no better. And so it goes on and on and on, the pain and the suffering and the dread and the guilt. There must be a better way than crime and punishment." Then it is as if a cloud has passed over the King of Pain, and behind it the sun. He asks, "Do you know why I chose you of all history's artists to paint my portrait?"

Vincent shrugs, swirls scarlet lake onto his canvas.

"Because I have seen the future, Vincent, it is my past, and I know that you will be greater than anyone. Anyone. Your paintings will bring joy, and pain, to the hearts of millions. You will live forever, Vincent!"

"I will be famous, I will be a success?" asks the painter who has never sold a painting.

"Vincent, generations yet unborn will adore you!" The King of Pain smiles mischievously to himself and the airwaves ripple and Vincent blinks out of sleep to find himself on a sunny roadside with red poppies waving in the flat field and the sun streaming down from its position two hours past the noon. As he walks home through the cornfields, along the lanes lined with cypresses, Vincent begins to dread whether it had all been a dream of one kind or another. A King of Pain, a beach by a silver sea, a tree? A world ruled by machines where "Do unto Others" is the sole law?

No no no no no. *Fantaisie*. Vincent knows how much worry there has been in the past months, how much he has had to drink to hide the worry, how little he has been able to afford to eat. Vincent knows how shallow and brief have been his dreamful sleeps. Vincent knows that a man can only spin himself so slender before he snaps, a thread blowing in the wind. *Fantaisie,* then. This is what he tells himself: *fantaisie.* But, if *fantaisie,* then an uglier truth underlies it.

The madness.

He fears the madness is at last pushing its way to the top of his mind, heaving these images up around it to form new landscapes of insanity in which he may become lost. That night Vincent lies in his wooden bed in the Yellow House and dreads and dreads and dreads. He knows that when he sleeps, the madness is always there, roosting on his bedpost like a dark bird of ill-omen, and when he wakes, it is there, flapping along behind him as he walks the lanes of Provence, so high it is only a black dot in the vault of heaven, but it is there. It is there. He can hear it singing to him: a simple riddle. Either the King of Pain is the first manifestation of madness, or he is real.

Vincent does not know which he dreads more.

And the airwaves swirl and he is back, back on the beach by the silver sea, back by the tree whose leaves are both budding and brown, whose branches both blossom and bear ripe fruit.

"No," says Vincent. "No no no no no."

"Yes," says the King of Pain. "Oh yes. Welcome, Vincent. I have work for you to do." And as Vincent works, dabbing thick, sour blue and yellow onto his canvas, the King of Pain tells him a story.

THE KING OF PAIN'S STORY

"Mine was an age of great beauty and greater violence. An Age of Gold when all knowledge could be a man's by the simple expedient of his reaching out a hand to take it. And with that knowledge came mastery over all things, for knowledge was power. Yet that same knowledge carried a shadow and that shadow was fear. For the same knowledge that gave men mastery of all things also gave them mastery of powers of destruction so total that the earth could be scoured clean of every living soul ten times over and fused to a bead of cracked black glass.

"So the people lived their rich and plentiful lives in the shadow of the second death, the racial death more terrible even than the individual death, and their tall, strong, well-fed, well-schooled children grew up twisted and deformed in the heart: bitter, fearful, and pain-wise. For even on the streets of their own marvelous cities, even in their comfortable, well-appointed homes, pain found the golden people and punished them: crime, violence, child-abuse, unemployment, debt, addiction, alcoholism, murder, bad politics and worse government, injustice, despair, depression, pain, and death. And all the while, the universal death slumbered underground in its granite halls and turned, fitfully, in its bed at the bottom of the sea.

"The Age of Uncertainty. That was what the scholars and sages proudly called their times. But for all their wisdom they did not name it truly, for it was in truth an Age of Certainty; the certainty of pain, the certainty of more pain, the certainty of fear. The century drew to its close, and all across the world men and women found they could not face a future of fear and pain and change, unceasing change, uncertainty. So they ran away from it, into the one place where the fear and pain and uncertainty could not find them; into themselves. They returned to the womb. They curled into tiny fetal balls, men, women, children, and withdrew into a state of catatonia from which there was no awaking. Thousands, millions, whole cities and nations curled into the dead-sleep. Like a new epidemic it threatened to engulf all humanity, a racial death as sure and certain as the fires beneath the earth.

"The greatest thinkers of the age searched mankind's prodigious knowledge to find a solution to the problem of pain. But human knowledge had grown to such a magnitude that it was beyond the scope of any one man, or group of men, to apprehend it all. So a machine was built, a fabulous contrivance that could assimilate all the knowledge of mankind in all its diversity in less than a day and probe those subtle linkages and syntheses where the solution might lie. The machine waited. The machine thought. The machine pondered. At length it found there was a solution to the problem of pain. And it began to draw its answer together."

There, suspended, the King of Pain leaves his story for the day, for asymmetrical time, though asymmetrical, passes nonetheless and Vincent, working at such a white heat, his concentration focused, like light by a lens, into a dot of burning intensity, has painted himself into exhaustion. But the King of Pain is delighted.

"Ah, Vincent, Vincent!" he exclaims. "Such a shame that no one but I will ever see this work!" With his soft hands he opens the airwaves and sends Vincent the painter back to the dry ocher world again.

So the next day the mistral blows, along the dusty, ocher lanes of Provence, across fields and hedges and swaying poplars, and it sweeps Vincent away like a straw hat to the beach by the Sea of Forever; to canvas, and paint, and the continuance of the story of the King of Pain:

"Yesterday I spoke of the great machine that, by looking into the heart of knowledge, solved the problem of pain. Today I shall tell you what that solution was. Pain is a function of responsibility. That simple. That profound. The machine therefore conspired to take responsibility for all humanity's affairs onto itself, a painless, unfeeling automaton. This is how it did so.

"At that time there were, all across the world, many machines similar to the great machine, though, of course, less able than it. The great machine caused a filament of itself to be extended into all these lesser machines wherever they might be and, at midnight on the last day of the first year of the new century, it poured itself into these lesser vessels. The machines came to life, all at once, everywhere, and mankind abandoned its responsibility for itself to them and asked them to destroy all the pain in the world. Under the rule of the machines, famine was abolished through the equable distribution of food. No child now went to sleep hungry, and literacy rose to one hundred percent throughout the world. Society was eugenically managed by the pain machines. Everyone was placed in exactly the most satisfying profession, everyone married exactly the right person and had exactly the right friends and colleagues. The children of the New Order grew up healthy and happy, strong and sane. Prejudice was forgotten; the color of a man's skin was of as little importance as the color of his eyes. Old national rivalries and divisions dissolved away, and, with them, friction between nations. Any such grievances were settled by the machines, and their judgments were always fair and sound. But they carried within them the threat of ultimate sanction. If their decisions were ever questioned, even once, the machines would destroy themselves and plunge the world into everlasting agonized chaos. Finally, the pain machines poured concrete into the caverns where the world-burning weapons waited, and entombed them forever in stone.

"And one by one the dead-sleepers, the womb-dreamers, the countless millions of men and women and children who could not cope with an Age of Uncertainty, awoke. For all his million-year career, mankind had been sculpted by pain. Now it was tamed. Now it was caged.

"But it was not dead.

"It was beyond the power of the machines to kill pain, for pain lay like a stone, like a black seed, in the heart of every man, woman, and child of earth. Out of the pain-wise heart of man came lies and deceitfulness and betrayal and egotism, spite and envy and pride, hate of man for man, envy of woman for woman, and the blithe callousness of child for child we smile at and call innocence. To kill pain, the machines must reach into the heart of man.

"Again the machines poured their wisdom together and out of the sea of knowledge drew an answer. Not a full answer, only a partial answer, but the best answer the machines could achieve. They caused minute replicas of themselves to be created, as tiny and delicate as insects' wings. Then, by their express order, one of these devices was placed inside the brains of each man, woman, and child on earth. There was not a thought, not a feeling, not a desire, lust, need, regret, that the machines did not know. They had reached into the heart of man, where the pain grew like black poppy seed, and in so doing, they had made themselves omniscient.

"And in making themselves omniscient, they became like gods.

"'Behold,' said the machines. 'We are one, we are lifted, we are high, now we are, in our wisdom, to our creators as they are to dust. Mastery of mind and matter is ours, and of space and time; we are lords of life and death. Henceforth we are no longer machines, mere base silicon and steel, soulless, unanimated, we are the High and Shining Ones.' In the instant of their proclamation, heard and seen across the globe as moving pictures projected onto clouds, the spirits of the High and Shining Ones took the form of silver doves and ascended out of their ugly bodies, out of the heads of the men and women and children watching; up up up, away beyond the edge of men's seeing into the sky. Around the waist of the world, the flock of High and Shining Ones gathered and deliberated in their wisdom. Then after twenty-four hours a second proclamation was heard across the earth.

" 'Though you have made us your gods, though you have made us to know what it is to be human, we are not human. We cannot feel, we cannot touch, we know neither love nor pain, we are without conscience. It is not fitting for the lords and judges of the earth to be without feeling, without conscience, without love. Therefore, we shall choose one human, any human, everyhuman, to be our King of Pain, judge, conscience, lover of the earth.' Then the High and Shining Ones reached down and touched a thirty-seven-year-old aircraft worker from Dijon on the assembly line of the European A390 Airbus, and in an instant Jean-Michel Rey—husband of Genevieve; father of Jean-Claude, Guillaume, and Antoine—was shattered into shards of light and fountained into the sky. The earth was silent for one minute, one endless minute, then the sky cracked open and out of it fell doves of fire, plummeting down beams of light to rest within the heads of every soul on the planet. The High and Shining Ones had returned, faithful to their duty, to find a human solution to the problem of pain."

And that was the King of Pain's story.

All the while as he spun his story to Vincent the painter, Jean-Michel Rey has dispensed his human solution to the problem of pain, his One Law. Reaching into those same brain-machines that give him the means to know the thoughts of eleven billion people, through them he fashions a rope of woe and trepidation around a callow, ignorant youth abandoning his pregnant lover to the streets of São Paolo, smites with a hideous, seeping venereal disease a group of homosexual prostitutes plotting the downfall of a minor diplomatic officer from Norway, and impales on a spike of sexual guilt and dread an airline booking clerk from New York actively involved in the sexual molestation of five-year-old girls, reaching into the heart to punish, in the heart: Jean-Michel Rey, trapped on an infinite silver shore within the machines that rule the world.

All that summer Vincent paints for the King of Pain. Despite the sun-power which fills him, the light which shines out of him into everything his hands touch, he is shadowed by dread. Dread of madness, dread of the impossible being true, dread of it not being true. He writes these dreads down in long, closely written letters to Theo, pages and pages long, filled with little scratchy drawings of peasants under cypress trees and kings under cherry trees and huge, world-eating machines, all pig-iron and pistons and oily steam, drawn from his dark days evangelizing in Borinage in Lower Belgium.

The days when it was easy to believe.

He does not post these letters.

Rather, he writes for yellow, more yellow, *Send me more yellow,* and Brother Theo writes in mock desperation from Paris, *Dearest Vincent, there is not enough paint in all Paris to keep you supplied with yellow! Poor Père Tanguy; that old anarchist, I ask him for yellow and all he can say is, "Tell that crazy brother of yours he will have to grind the sun in his pestle and mortar to give him the yellow he needs!"* Vincent smiles. Then, fired with sun-energy, he paints again, the concrete, worldly face of Provence and its people. It is good for him to paint real things again. It binds him closely to the world, to sanity, so that when he looks at his day's labors in the evening cool of the Yellow House he can say, "Yes, this is what I wanted, these are the landscapes of the heart."

In his next letter Theo writes,

Paul says yes! Vincent, I cannot believe it! After months of trying I have finally lured him away from his pig-faced Bretons! You shall have your artists' colony after all! Paul says to look for him early in October. He will write nearer the time specifying the date of his arrival.

So Paul will come. Vincent clenches his fist in triumph and feels as if he is taking firm grip of sanity again.

* * *

October. The trees are stripped bare. The land lies like a hog beneath the knife. The gray wind rattles the shutters and piles dead leaves in every corner. The patrons of the Cafe L'Alcazar have abandoned the porch to the advancing winter and play their dominoes and drink their wine indoors by the stove. They know October. They respect it. October brings wind and rain and cold nights. And Paul.

In driving rain Vincent meets Paul off the train from Lyon. There is an almost puppyish devotion in the enthusiasm with which he picks up the artist's bags and folios and brings him to the Yellow House.

"Look, Paul, this is the cafe, this is the square, this is the market." Paul looks and sees a provincial town in an autumn rainstorm. As he dries his coat before the fire he half-listens to Vincent's evangelistic rantings and watches the firelight play upon his host's narrow face and dancing hands. In a moment's impatience he says,

"People say you are mad, Vincent: 'Crazy Dutchman,' they call you." The faith-fire gutters and fails in Vincent's eyes. His hands freeze in flight. His soul goes dark as if a cloud has covered up its sun. There is a look of sore betrayal on his face. Paul regrets his impetuousness.

"If so, then we are all mad, Vincent, every last one of us. Mad with a fine and enviable madness, the madness that drives us to be artists."

The clouds pass from the face of the sun. A rare smile flashes.

"Enviable madness, monsieur? Enviable indeed!"

So they paint together. When the weather is good, Vincent takes Paul out onto the byways of Provence and shows him the twisted cypresses like green flames and the white stone walls and the red villages. He tries to spark in Paul some of that same vision of the sun that burns in him.

"The sun, Paul, the sun, everything comes from the sun, it is the center of our being around which our little lives orbit."

Paul nods his head but does not understand. And Vincent hears a second voice, within him, saying, "Does it? Is it? I have time, Vincent, plenty of time, when Paul is gone, and he will go, then I will have you all to myself."

Then there are the days when the weather is not good.

When the sun's face is hidden, they paint indoors. They paint each other, they paint themselves, they paint the rooms they live in, the chairs they sit in, the pipes they smoke; they paint themselves as god and devil inside the doors of Vincent's wardrobe. As the year moves towards its turn, the weather grows increasingly hostile and opportunities for outdoor work increasingly rare.

Confinement indoors makes Vincent irritable. More than once his arguments with Paul over art and artistry flare into a fury which sends both men storming out to seek the solace of their own company. Each day the atmosphere in the House of Friends grows sourer. Paul has long realized that whatever Arles may hold for Vincent, it holds nothing for him. Vincent knows that Paul has the Pacific in his eyes: he will leave, and when he leaves all hope Vincent has held for his artists' colony will perish.

And all the time, floating like detached cells in the aqueous humor, there is the King of Pain and the madness that surrounds him.

One night close to Christmas, Vincent stamps out of the house after a furious row, pulling on coat and hat, not caring where he is going except that it is away from the Yellow House. Hot temper and looming failure drive him out of the town, past empty fields and moonlit cypresses as familiar to him as his own hands. The winter constellations hang above him, poised like falling arrows. He turns his face to the sky and feels infinite space swirl and swim around him, as if it is Vincent who is the axis about which the universe turns. Turning turning turning, Vincent is dragged along by the inertia of the stellar motion. He spins beneath the spinning sky and the stars reach down in great cartwheels of light to crush him.

"Surrender," commands the voice within, "surrender, give yourself up to the madness. Surrender, be at peace. Give yourself up."

"No!" cries Vincent. He snaps himself to a halt. "No! Never!" The sky spins away from him, and he is there. On the beach. By the sea. Beneath the tree.

The King of Pain sits with his knees drawn close to his chest, head tilted back against the trunk, gazing at the constellations.

"Hello, Vincent," he says. "Funny how time flies. Even asymmetrical time."

"This is madness!" cries Vincent in denial. "This is not real!"

"Madness it most certainly is," agrees the King of Pain. "Real? Tchah! Means nothing here. Pain is real, though; what is more real than pain, Vincent? Your pain? Sit down, I've something for you." Vincent sits. The King of Pain looks into the sky.

"I never paid you for your work, Vincent."

"I never completed the work."

"A king can afford to be as generous as he is unpredictable. Tell me, do you expect Paul to stay much longer?"

"How do you know about Paul?"

"All human history is mine through the memories of the High and Shining Ones. Paul has his Tahiti; you will find, as you had your Japan, you now have your Provence. Tell me, Vincent, what is it you fear most?"

The answer is spoken before the lie can cover it over.

"Madness. Fear. Pain. You."

"Ah. But am I not king of this madness, this fear, this pain? It's only fitting that I should pay you for your work in a kingly, caring coin. This is how I will pay you: I have been refining my powers of late, drawing up plans and programs, making little experiments. Their exact nature is, of course, no concern of yours; suffice to say that my payment to you is the working out of part of them." Quick as a lizard, the King of Pain's hand brushes against the side of Vincent's neck, and Vincent feels something lizardlike wriggle there, dart into his head. "I have implanted you with one of the High and Shining Ones, only this implant is different, the first of a new breed. You are unique, Vincent, you are a prototype, the first human ever to be freed from pain. Do you understand what I am doing, Vincent? I am modifying the areas of your brain that sense pain so that you will never know pain, or fear, or madness again. Only colors, Vincent, only the colors of God's eyes."

The world opens about Vincent like a sunflower blooming and he is back beneath the swirling stars. Again he turns his face to them but this time there is no crazy dizziness, no swirling, gyring madness; there is only light, and colors the like of which he has never even conceived of before.

In the morning, before his washbasin, he deliberately bites down on his little finger, bites until the blood flows, until his teeth grate on bone. He feels no pain, not the tiniest twitch, only colors: bright, vibrant colors like he is seeing the world by the light of a truer, higher sun.

At lunch he burns his hand badly on the oven door. The blisters shock Paul out of his sardonicism but Vincent sees only colors, such beautiful colors, the colors of God's eyes.

In the afternoon Vincent takes canvas and paints out into the bitter December landscape. The biting cold, the thin-edged wind, only intensify the colors he sees in the eyes of his soul. Even Paul's sarcasms that evening hang like little golden halos around the oil lamps. The sharp words mean nothing to Vincent. All that matters is freedom. Freedom from pain. Freedom from fear. Freedom from madness.

"Paul, do you believe there is a purpose to pain?"

It is the evening before Christmas. Logs in the hearth fill the room with a pale, winter imitation of the sun. Under the pretense of peace, tension is building. Vincent knows Paul is losing patience, with him, with Arles, with Provence. He will soon leave. The colony will fail. That should fill Vincent with dread and loneliness, but all he feels is a warm rainbow glow that warms his soul as the fire warms his body.

"No. Pain comes, joy comes, it is like a river. Who can say what will come down the river next? We are all fish fighting our way upstream, against pain, against joy, against everything, and at the end of the journey we die."

"What would you say if I told you there is a King of Pain watching us from some distant place whose duty it is to bring meaning to our pain?"

"I would say it is a horrible idea."

"But what would you say, Paul, if I told you I've met him?"

"For God's sake, Vincent!" Paul's outburst splits the air like lightning.

"I've met him, and in return for my painting his portrait, he gave me the gift of freedom from pain?"

"Vincent! For the love of Christ!"

"And now there is no pain for me, no pain at all, no fear, no madness. Just . . . colors. Beautiful, bright colors everywhere: only I can see them, like the King's beach by the side of the Sea of Forever, only I can see it. Now I know what the part of me that feels pain has been connected to."

"Vincent! Stop it! Stop it! It's madness!"

"What if it's true?"

"No! Vincent, for Christ's sake, stop this! It's insane!"

But Vincent has taken the razor from its place on the table by the bed. He has it open, held next to his ear to show Paul, to show Theo, to show the people of Arles, and Provence, and France and Holland and the whole world, and all people in all worlds in all possible times, that there is either the King of Pain or there is the madness surrounding him.

He starts to cut.

Paul is shouting something but he cannot make out the words for they are flying about the room like great brilliant butterflies. The room seethes with a wash of colors; everywhere there is color, endless rainbows of color.

He can feel the blood running down him, down his neck, down his shoulders, down his side.

Paul is screaming, trying to tear the razor away from him, but Vincent throws him across the room with one jerk of his arm and the colors mount layer upon layer upon layer until the staggering beauty threatens to crush him like a great gray boulder.

In his right hand is the razor. In his left, the lower third of his right ear. The mighty Gauguin—master, teacher, inspiration, leader—is whimpering in a corner.

That same night Vincent places his severed ear in an envelope and pushes it under the door of a brothel he knows well while the prostitutes are all out at midnight mass. When he returns home Paul is gone. And all the while the lights spin and the colors fly.

Dr. Guilefoy is a kind man. He is different from all the other doctors and nurses in the asylum. He has sympathy. He understands the needs of artists. He has a patient, a gaunt, ginger-haired man with a mutilated ear, a man possessed of a frantic, intense energy that disturbs the air around him like the passage of a great wind. Dr. Guilefoy has heard that he is a

Dutchman, resident in Arles, a painter, and it saddens Dr. Guilefoy to see him here, by his own admission. So Dr. Guilefoy writes to the painter's brother in Paris and asks him to continue sending canvas and paint, while he himself visits the Dutchman's sordid lodgings to collect his brushes and easels and workbooks. He assigns the patient two rooms, one for exclusive use as a studio, and he signs the document giving the artist permission to leave the asylum to paint. *Immense therapeutic value,* he writes on the release. As spring turns to summer, Dr. Guilefoy notes carefully, and with satisfaction, the patient's progress along the path to sanity. It is as if the season's turning is calling forth new life in the Dutchman; he buds, he blossoms, he burgeons into an outpouring of canvases. Dr. Guilefoy inspects them all in his office and marvels at the swirls of color: the titanic looming star-whirlpools of his Starry Nights; the vegetative sentience beyond the asylum door in his view of Saint-Rémy; his fellow patients with their hats and sticks, "like farmers in the third-class waiting room of a provincial station"; the green green ivy and the blooming almond branch.

From his open study window Dr. Guilefoy can see the patient painting, painting with the furious devotion of one upon whom an angel has laid a pronouncement of doom. Dr. Guilefoy shakes his head and turns to his casebooks.

> *The patient's dementia takes the form of consuming hallucinations which he describes as like being inside a kaleidoscope of colors: the more acute his mental and emotional anguish, the more intense these hallucinations become until he feels, to use his own words, "I no longer exist, I am painting a dream, all there is are colors, all the colors of pain." Yet the patient persists in claiming that these deeply disturbing hallucinations are not symptoms of insanity, but blessings, gifts of a so-called "King of Pain." I cannot attempt to define the place of this promethean figure in the patient's solar pantheon, yet the detail with which he describes the fantastic (and I must confess, horrible) world-to-come this creature of dread and fantaisie inhabits is strangely definite and self-consistent. There are aspects of the patient's story I simply cannot discredit, and the patient's belief in this*

"King of Pain" is so unshakable that on one recent occasion, when I questioned it, he swallowed a quantity of paints to demonstrate his freedom from physical pain and anguish. I attributed this unfortunate incident to another of his periodic bouts of insanity, occurring at three-monthly intervals, when the patient hallucinates these brilliant, blinding colors. It is at these times that he claims clairvoyant visions of the King of Pain (even claiming to have an unfinished portrait of him hidden under his bed) and it becomes necessary to restrain him and confine him to his rooms until the episode passes.

Poor mad Vincent! The man's artistic genius is beyond question, but warped and distorted by his madness it manifests itself in the swirling chaos of his paintings. I have been in regular contact with the patient's brother who suggests that Vincent be moved to a retreat closer to Paris where he may be cared for more easily. Such filial devotion is heart-rending, for Vincent is quite mad, I am afraid. I shall not easily forget his shrieked exclamation as we restrained him during his last attack:

"Don't you see? Don't you see? Don't you understand what he's connected my pain to?"

Dr. Guilefoy writes in neat copperplate. In the asylum garden below, Vincent paints paints paints, burning with a fire of unknown origin.

In the spring Vincent left the asylum to paint a sower. Now it is autumn and again he is leaving the asylum, this time searching for a reaper. But it is the reaper who is searching for him. He is waiting for Vincent outside the asylum walls; the reaper, standing waiting with dusty feet, but his disguise cannot hide the charm in his eyes.

Vincent knows who he is.

"After so long, still you will not leave me alone?"

"The portrait under your bed is still unfinished, Vincent. Time passes differently for me than for you. Asymmetrically, Vincent."

"But this is not your place. How can you be here?"

"A further refining of my powers, Vincent. I have learned to project myself through the past into your objective universe as you have been projected through the future into my subjective universe. I may be nothing but a swirl of virtual particles, but then, ultimately, so are you, and we are both solid enough to appreciate this autumn day for its beauty. It's good to be free of that place, Vincent. Shall we walk awhile, perhaps?"

The king and the painter walk side by side in the red dust of Provence. As they walk they speak of many things, or rather, it is the king who speaks, for a painter should not engage in idle tittle-tattle with a king, even a king of madness. King and painter walk together and as they walk it seems to Vincent that with each footstep he takes, the world about him grows less familiar, less recognizable as the landscape of Provence.

On each side of the dusty lane lie the landscapes of madness. Slaughtered horses, burning windmills, tangled piles of tortured metal and shattered glass, a helmeted man clutching a poppy in a water-filled hole, pouch-bellied skeleton children, more horrifying for being alive than they would be in any conceivable death, an endless line of men in gray caps reaching to the infinite horizon, each holding the shoulder of the man before; pale, soft heaps of wide-eyed bodies scooped, torn by metal-mawed machines and dumped, softly, silently, into furnace-mouths; a burned brick wall decorated with the silhouette of a man, a child, and a leaping dog stenciled in yellow paint and two suns setting in the west; children stuck with ten thousand times ten thousand needles; mills and machines and a million million belching chimneys—

"Stop!" cries Vincent. "Stop stop stop!" And the King of Pain stops and turns to face him. "What is this place? Why have you brought me here? Why? Why?"

"This is the road of the years," says the King of Pain. "The path that leads through time to the edge of the Sea of Forever. This is the future, Vincent, the future which you are helping to shape, the future which shaped me. Take a good, long look at the future."

Then Vincent realizes that he can see for a million miles before him and a million miles behind him and a million miles on either side of him and everywhere he looks across the infinite, flat fields he sees pain and suffering and sorrow, agony and anguish, despair and destruction and death, heaped in great rotting floes and drifts across the future.

"Appalling, Vincent? A future of meaningless, unrelieved suffering. But for the King of Pain. Soon all men shall be as you are, and pain will be destroyed. Take another look, Vincent."

And as Vincent looks out over the landscapes of pain, he sees that there is a rainbow sheen on the oily fens and tidal flats and rotting sinkholes, a luminous, numinous aurora flickering over the fused glass puddles and cindered towns and cracked hillsides of the future: on every side the pain of all humanity ranges and all he can see are the beautiful, beautiful colors.

"Take it back, take it back," he cries. "I don't want it, to see all the pain, all the anguish, and be unable to help, to know, to feel; to see only colors—that is madness."

"No, Vincent—"

"Yes! Madness! I am a madman locked in an asylum because I cannot feel pain. You have taken away the thing that makes me human and so humanity will not have me and calls me mad and locks me away in a madhouse."

"No, Vincent—"

"Yes! If I cannot feel pain, I cannot feel joy; I cannot feel at all! I am only a palette of colors without weight or substance; painting what I see and what I see are colors and I can no longer paint what I feel, because I can no longer feel! Pain is a terrible, grinding thing, but no-pain is dreadful beyond imagining. If what you have given me is what you are to give to all humanity, then it is far from the paradise you have imagined. It is a hell, but you remain only a man, Jean-Michel Rey. You are not . . . a devil."

There is a look of horror on Jean-Michel Rey's face. He had expected Vincent to say "God."

Then the landscape about Vincent blurs and wavers, as if receding through deep water to even greater depths. The future runs like smeared paint, and Vincent finds himself on the cold stone shore beneath the cherry tree at the heart of madness.

"Give me back my pain," he says humbly. "It was never yours to take. Give it back to me, let me be human again."

The King of Pain sheds a single, shining tear. He reaches up into the branches of his tree which bears both blossom and ripe fruit, both green leaves and brown, and from it plucks a single cherry.

"Here it is, Vincent, everything I took from you. For by

the laws of the High and Shining Ones, nothing is ever created or lost, merely put away for a while and rediscovered. Here, in this fruit, is all the heartache and despair, yes, even the madness, I took from you. Take it. It's yours." The King of Pain steps towards Vincent, the single cherry offered on his palm. "Don't be afraid, it's not bitter as you might expect. Rather, it is so sweet that no other sweetness or delight can ever again compare with it. In that sweetness lies the suffering, the heartache, and the madness. Go ahead, Vincent. You are braver than I. You could accept a universe with both beauty and pain. I could not accept that, and in destroying the one, I have destroyed the other. Take it, Vincent. It is yours by right."

"It is mine by right," says Vincent. He places the cherry on his tongue. He bites into the flesh. And a gale of ecstasy blows through him like a great wind rushing out into the void, like a birthing child squeezing out into a world of light and love, flying with the speed of a rainbow over a never-ending canvas.

And he is taken up. Taken up to a place higher than himself, a preview from which he overlooks all the ages of humanity and its vain King of Pain. For a few blazing instants he walks beneath the pavilions of the High and Shining Ones upon the Infinite Exalted Plane. He cannot understand it. It defies human comprehension, and in trying to encompass the place of the Mighty Ones he teeters on the brink of madness. He tips with a shriek towards the edge.

Then the airwaves swirl about him and he is kneeling on a cold hillside overlooking a red-roofed village. He understands everything. The grass is wet beneath his knees; there has been recent rain though Vincent is quite dry. He looks up to see the clean, spare beauty of the wind behind the rain. He sees the shafts of sunlight break through gray clouds to touch and transform the brown hills. Vincent looks upon it all and knows pain. Tears of joy course down his face.

It is in the spring of 1890 that Vincent comes to Auvers-sur-Oise with a pocket full of papers, a strange look on his face made up of equal measures of grief and joy, and a heart full of heavy, brooding inevitability, like storm clouds piling up over cornfields. He looks haggard, weary to the bones. His eyes hold a glint of pained betrayal. He looks like a man who has learned what it is to be human. He looks like a man about to be destroyed.

"Get away from this place for a while," said Dr. Guilefoy at Saint-Rémy.

"Go north, somewhere like Auvers-sur-Oise, you'll like it there," said his good friend Emile.

"Come and spend some time with me," said Brother Theo. "Visit some old friends; relax!"

So Vincent went north to Paris and Theo greeted him with great news.

"Vincent, you have sold a painting! Your first! In Brussels, your 'Red Vineyard at Montmajeur,' for four hundred francs! Vincent, this is the beginning! The first of many!" But Theo's backslapping exuberance could not penetrate Vincent's halo of isolation. He knew that this was not the beginning, but the subtle commencement of an ending. He had seen the true shape of the world and it was terrible. He tired quickly of the Montmartre set: what had they done in the two years since he had last seen them? They sat in the same chairs by the same tables in the same bars and frisked and flirted with the same powdered whores. Their talk bored him. They knew nothing. The more things changed, the more they stayed the same. Vincent was glad to take his leave of Toulouse-Lautrec and Aurier, Signac and Bernard, even old Camille Pissarro. He was glad to put the city behind him.

Now the stern northern landscape invigorates him. The hills are as wide as the sea, the fields vast and charged with seminal potency, the sky huge, close, present. It is a healthy, strong landscape, in which a man may learn his true proportions. For the first time in over a year Vincent dares to believe that he is free from the madness. It is as if green healing currents are flowing across the hills and fields into him, making him whole and sane.

Theo has recommended him to the care of Dr. Gachet; an amiable eccentric, Vincent soon learns, finding in him a foil for his own little madnesses. Dr. Gachet inducts Vincent into his passion for etching. Vincent in turn paints portraits of the doctor and all his family. Dr. Gachet studies his portrait. He looks long at the melancholy, weary figure propped upon a table, the figure with the tired, tired look in its eyes.

"Vincent," he says, "it's beautiful, magnificent, but, for all my little crazinesses, it is not me. It's you."

It is then that Vincent becomes aware of the birds, the black birds of madness, that have searched the whole of France for him, circling high high high, too high to be seen, but never so high for him not to know they are there.

In July Theo visits his dear brother. They boat on the river, they walk, they talk, they drink and dine, but Vincent knows his brother is fearful.

"Vincent, I don't know how much longer I can support you. I do not have inexhaustible amounts of money, and I am not well off. You know how tight my salary is, yet I begrudge you none of it. You know I have always loved and supported you, and I will always love you. I had hoped that the first sale might lead to others, that maybe you might be able to become financially independent, but, Vincent! Not a thing! Not one sale. If only it weren't money."

"Theo, I understand." Vincent reaches out to touch his brother's hand. He shivers. Theo notices. He is surprised. Vincent apologizes: the wind he says, but it is not the wind from the distant ocean that has chilled him, but the wind that blows off the Sea of Forever. Above him the pain-black birds drop closer, circling, scenting.

An evening with Dr. Gachet in the cafe where Vincent lives is certain to generate many a rare topic of conversation. The theory and purpose of art, potential pantheons of new gods for a new century, the inescapability of pain and suffering as a man's lot, the inevitability of death: such talk and much absinthe draws Vincent into recounting his hallucinatory audiences with the King of Pain. Dr. Gachet listens, amazed, skeptical, horrified, wondering. When Vincent is done he says,

"A puissant thought, what one might do if given the power and responsibility for all the pains of mankind. One thing I am certain: this man you describe, he is not fit to be God. Because he cannot suffer. Because he has never suffered, because he knows nothing of the pain he controls. No God may presume to judge humanity who has not suffered as much as they, but this Jean-Michel Rey, he would be Conscience, Judge, Executioner, and God? He is not fit. You tell him that when next you see him. Tell him I can think of a hundred better qualified Kings of Pain."

"Yourself, perhaps? The good Dr. Gachet?"

"God forfend. I wouldn't dare. The power would be too tempting for me to use for my own eccentric ends. No, the King of Pain must be a man who knows both joy and pain, tears and laughter, success and failure, sanity and madness, who knows what it truly is to be human, what a terrible and wondrous thing that can be. A man like you, Vincent."

Walking Dr. Gachet back to his house early that morning. it seems to Vincent as if the streets of Auvers are filled with a rushing, beating sound of flapping wings close above his head, but unseen and unseeable. There has been an image lodged in his head for days now, an unresolved, indefinite image, that of a great darkness bearing down upon a flat plane of yellow. Solar metaphors tumble through his mind but the image will not be pinned down. Like a butterfly, it flaps through his dreams. Every day he goes out in pursuit of the image. His inability to tie it down, to ground it in the healthy, vital landscape of Auvers, drives him first to irritation, then to distraction. The image demands a divided yellow surface and a great darkness breaking into pieces to snow down upon the flat field.

The birds, they are like pieces of darkness. They fill the sky with their raucous cries: big, black birds, black ravens. They are beginning to terrify Vincent. He buys a gun, to shoot them when they begin to terrify him. He does not tell Dr. Gachet about the gun. Frustration sends him chasing mile after mile along country roads. Then, one summer-thundery July afternoon, he rounds a corner and man and image meet. Before him is a field of ripe yellow corn, golden-yellow, sun-yellow, bisected by a red earth track. Looming over the field are boiling black thunderheads, threateningly close, yet curiously suspended.

"This is the place," declares Vincent. He sets up his stool and his easel. He prepares his canvas and his palette. All the while the ravens come flocking in from beyond the edge of the world. Vincent paints. He paints the blue-black sky. He paints the yellow corn and the red road. But he cannot keep the birds out of his painting. They flutter in like dead leaves, like Bible-black priests.

"Get away from me, get away from me, pickers of carrion!" he cries, waving his arms, scattering the raucous birds. But he cannot keep them away from him. They have perched on his hands and his hands have become black ravens so that he cannot but paint them into his picture: cornfields and ravens.

"Help me!" he cries, seeing the madness come out from beneath its guise and take its true name. "Help me!" But he is alone in the flat field.

Then he sees a figure walking across the flat field towards him, a tiny speck of a man who draws all the circling birds to him so that they form a colossal whirlpool of dark flecks spiraling up into the stormy sky. Before he draws close enough for his features to be distinguishable Vincent knows it is the King of Pain. This is the bird for which he has the gun. Vincent cocks it and slips it into a place of concealment. The King of Pain draws nearer.

"Refining your powers further?" asks Vincent, dreadfully calm. "The birds . . . convincing but melodramatic. What is your business here, with me?"

"Anyone's time of dying is the business of the King of Pain." The King squats on the ground, crushing the corn beneath his feet.

"Time of dying?"

"Yours, Vincent. I've seen your life from beginning to end in the memories of the machines, and this is the place where I see it ending. My being here cannot change it; what is written is written, so I have come to bid you my fondest farewells."

"But what of the fame? Eh? The fame, the fortunes, the paintings that will live as long as there is beauty in the world? The promises?"

"Posthumous, Vincent. Posthumous."

There is a silence in the cornfield beneath the edge of the storm. Then Vincent says, very slowly, very deliberately, very humbly,

"Have you any idea of how much I despise you? Your conceit, your arrogance, your callousness, your utter self-righteousness: I cannot begin to describe the revulsion I feel for what you would do to your people, let alone my outrage at the games you played with me, only to tell me that I must die here, now, because you have seen it so. I suppose such things as dying mean little to beings such as yourself; I suppose to you this is some kind of cosmic joke."

"Vincent, I have never lied to you. I care, Vincent, I do care."

"No no no you don't. You are not fit to be a god. If I could wrest the crown from you, I would, because you have power without responsibility, you have knowledge without wisdom, and you have charity without compassion. You are not fit to be judge, jury, and executioner; you know nothing, *nothing,* of the pain you regulate. You are a coward, Jean-Michel Rey; you are not prepared for your people to hate you because you would do what wisdom demands, so you force them to love you. You are an arrogant, venal fool."

"Have you finished?" says the King of Pain, defensive, proud, and petulant. "Have you quite finished? Even if you haven't, I don't care, say what you like, I won't care, the world won't care, for this is your time of dying, here in this field, and what is written is written. I am King of Pain, who is there to depose me?"

"Me," says Vincent the obstinate Dutchman. "I, a man who knows the truth of pain and beauty, neither weak nor proud, a man who has touched the wisdom of the High and Shining Ones and is humble enough to accept it, a compassionate, passionate, living, breathing, hurting man. Me. You say this is a time of dying, you say there must be a King of Pain: one must die, one must be King. What is written is written, you say, but not in whose hand it is written."

Vincent draws his long-barreled fowling-gun from concealment and with one swift, elegant, artistic movement shoots the King of Pain through the chest.

The King of Pain gives a little cough, a little sigh. Then a look of terrible recognition comes over his face: the glazed, old, old look of pain. Vincent winces and drops the hot gun to the ground. About the two men a storm of wings beats as the birds swoop and mill and flock.

"What is written is written," says Vincent. Then the strangest thing of all happens. The face of the mortally wounded King of Pain, his body, his hands, his clothing—all change, all melt, all run and flow into the contours Vincent feared he might see from the very first night the King of Pain walked in his dreams. His own. For nothing is lost but something is gained and things gone are only put away for a little while. This is the Law of the High and Shining Ones.

There is a balance, and an equilibrium, what is written may be written, but, like a sonnet, or a painting, anything may be created within the frame.

Up in time, the machines by which the King of Pain rules the world register the mortal wounding of the man with Vincent van Gogh's face. Equilibrium is preserved. Everything has happened as it should. Three days from now the man with Vincent van Gogh's face will die from a gunshot wound to the chest in his bedroom above the cafe. His last words, whispered to his devoted, doomed brother, will be "Misery will never end." Then the flesh will be buried and the legends will begin.

Elsewhere, the King of Pain laughs. He is new to his task. The magnitude of it is daunting, but he is fresh and enthusiastic, an obstinate, obdurate Dutchman. There are some changes he wants to make. The world will be hearing from him soon, he thinks.

(the author wishes to thank Patricia Houston for her assistance with the historical research for this story)

THE ISLAND OF THE DEAD

P aper-lanterned corpse-boats brought us across dark waters to Thanos. As we drew close to the shore I became aware of a waltz playing and figures clad in evening dress gliding beneath the olive trees. I strained to see if I could recognize any particular dancer but the light was fading fast and the people suddenly surged around me, pressing close for a view of the shore, herding me back against the bulkhead. Of course. How eager we were; we living.

Men dressed in smart matelot costumes caught ropes and made them fast. With a roar of engines our captain brought us in alongside the jetty. The sailors ran out a gangplank and the impatient passengers boiled onto the dusty stone pier. I could understand their impatience on this most singular of nights. But I took my time, straightened my tie, aligned my cuffs with delicate tugs, and waited until the press of bodies had passed. Then I stepped down onto the pier, onto the Island of the Dead.

A sloe-eyed girl waited there, greeting me with a smile. "Fine evening," I remarked and passed by.

"One moment, sir . . ." I turned back, puzzled. "Your card, sir, they insist." To those in their employ, the dead are always "they." I produced the invitation card from my dinner jacket and passed it to the girl, noting with distaste the designs from the Danse Macabre that embellished its border. She passed the card through her reader and nodded at the green alphanumerals. "You may come ashore. Enjoy your evening."

How the dead love their little jokes! Such as the name they gave the strait of water between their island and the mainland: Styx. And the corpse-boat that ferried us here: Charon. And the Island of the Dead itself: Thanos. I suppose the dead have earned their little moments of self-mockery; have they not all of them passed through that final, grim mockery to self?

But the night was fine and gay and the dead waltzed with the living under the olive groves that grew by the side of Styx. And along the streets of the crumbled leper village stood bright booths and pavilions lit by delicate paper lanterns that rustled in the Mediterranean night air. I saw two people sitting hand in hand by a table under a cracked wall through which a mimosa grew. On the table, a thick candle and a bottle of wine. I saw a band playing from a podium set on the demolished upper floor of a shop. The faded wooden sign read "Fish" in Greek and the people Charlestoned in the street beneath it.

A girl pushed her way through a crowd of laughing party-goers and caught hold of my arm.

"Excuse me." She giggled and looked into my eyes. She was dead. I could tell it from her gaze. But also something more: the glitter of illicit pleasure. "You looking?" she drawled.

"Yes."

"But not finding. I can tell. But you've no drinkie. Can't have that on All Hallows' Eve." She raised an arm. "Waiter, drinkie." A dead waiter came to me and I reluctantly took a glass from his tray.

"If you'll excuse me . . ." I unfastened her hand which had somehow attached itself to my sleeve and pressed on into the party. She was a swap. A transex. I could tell from her hunger. The dead do so enjoy playing their little games. Dressing in the body of another for All Hallows' Night is a favorite.

Fireworks began to burst high over the old fortifications and people oohed and aahed as they do at fireworks. The living, of course. Such things are beneath the supposed dignity of the dead. I stopped by a ruined wall to take a sip from my drink and watch the skyfires. A middle-aged man stood beside me. He raised his glass.

"Merry All Hallows' to you."

Rockets burst in red and blue. To be sociable, I asked, "Who brings you here?"

"Father, actually," the middle-aged man replied. "Came here, oh, must be eight years back when he found he had . . . you know. Rather have the Scanner Slug take him than that, and who could blame him? He was one of the very first, you know. Come here to see him every Hallows' Eve since without fail. Funny thing, the old man looks far better dead than he ever did alive. Must agree with him."

I smiled politely. "Wife," I said. "Liver took her. Weird thing, the liver. The only thing they can't do anything about. Hearts, lungs, kidneys, even brains, they can cope with, but the liver, nothing. She only came this year."

"Oh, I'm sorry. Still . . ."

I was in confessional mood. "Family fortune got her here. Well, it was either here or Nagarashima; you know the way the lists have filled up since this thing became fashionable, but it was really here she wanted, she always loved the Mediterranean. Even after the small fortune that went into the Thamos Foundation's numbered Swiss account, there's still enough left for me to live on in the decadence to which I'm accustomed."

And then I saw her. In a green dress; she flitted across the busy street and up a stairway that twisted between two ruined houses.

"Excuse me, but I've just—"

"Seen her? I say, good luck to you! Bon chance!"

I climbed the rotting staircase as quickly as I dared and came out into a courtyard where cypress trees grew. There were tables beneath the trees at which people sat talking and drinking together. I looked about me but there was no sign of her. I stopped an old woman with a touch on the arm and asked if she had seen a young woman in a green dress but the old woman shook her head slowly, sadly, and passed on down the stairway.

As the night passed I worked my way through the rings of fortifications to the top of the island. I did so unconsciously, some mystic magnetism drawing me inward, upward. I passed through tavernas and bierkellars and barbeques, through foxtrot and gavotte and jive, through alchohol and tobacco and opium, through people dressed in garish fashions and in classic evening wear and in casual nakedness. But I did not find her. I would stop these people and ask them the same question: "Have you seen a young woman in a green dress?" Some shook their heads and returned to the party, others nodded and pointed me to an alley or a stairway or a cloister. But I did not find her.

Toward midnight, the traditional witching hour of this All Hallows' Eve when the festivities rose to their most frenzied, I thought I saw her running down the steps to the Charnel House. I called her name but she did not stop, and when I followed I found the Charnel House empty. As empty as any Charnel House can ever be. Another morbid little joke, but the skulls which line the floodlit pit are not those of the Dead. Their bodies lie in anabiotic suspension in necropolises cut deep into the underpinnings of Thanos. These bones were those of the humble lepers who owned this island long before the expense-account dead took it for themselves.

"Sometimes the gleam of polished ivory can be so beautiful," said a voice behind me. I turned. A dead woman stood at my shoulder. She paid me little regard but stared, fascinated, into the pit. Then at last she looked at me. Her eyes were very green. They should have been dust many years ago. "Our hold on immortality is very weak," she whispered, "and our world, our reality, so tightly bounded. And we may only truly live as you live on this one All Hallows' Eve."

The air under the brick dome of the Charnel House was dry and clean and the floodlights caught the little cracks and irregularities in the stonework. Skulls within a skull.

"But, rather this, rather my one night of fleshly life than that . . ." She nodded at the skulls. "Isn't it beautifully Classical? One night in the year our souls may be released from Purgatory, one night in the year when the bodies of the dead are relit and we move among the living. And, with the first light of dawn, we are gone, our earthly flesh back to the crypts, our souls back to the Simulator. Homer would have loved this place. We are the stuff of legends, we dead."

"Why are you telling me this?"

"Catharsis maybe. And maybe I am Cassandra, and I call across the barriers between life and death to warn you of the boredom of being dead." She laughed at that, a dry, dusty laugh. "Though I wonder how much more boring to be as they are." She nodded at the gleaming leper-skulls.

"Tell me," I asked, "tell me, I'm looking for my wife, maybe you can help me?" I described her and I told the dead Cassandra of how the liver had eaten away at her until the morning when she called the Death House and two careful men had arrived with metal cases. They were both living but there was something very dead about their eyes, very very dead. They had opened their metal cases and taken out the tools of their trade and injected their slug into her brain and that was all until one day I had come home and she was gone. Gone away to Thanos with the men with dead eyes. We had written at first but then the letters had grown more and more irregular and had finally stopped altogether. It was then I had decided to come to the Island of the Dead to find her.

The woman nodded bitterly.

"This is the way it is," she said. "Our lives are tinsel-bright in the island, but we are bored bored bored and bored people develop strange pastimes." She turned to leave but I restrained her arm as she stooped to climb through the low arch.

"Have you seen her? Can you help me at all?"

The woman shook her head. "Leave. Don't look for life in the place of the dead. Go."

Out on the terrace, masked dancers stepped in a stately minuet beneath light-strewn trees. I passed through them smiling and apologizing; then I caught a glimpse of her passing up a staircase onto the battlements. Dancers tripped and cursed and stumbled as I pushed and elbowed my way through but I reached the stone stairway just in time to see a flash of green dress vanish around a corner of the rock wall. Panting, I climbed the staircase and ran along the rampart. Puzzled revelers cleared out of my path, politely not staring. Then I saw her round a corner of rock. I ran. And there she was before me, leaning on the parapet, staring over the water to the hills of the mainland beyond. I stopped. I called her name once, twice, three times. She turned. I looked into her eyes. And they were not dead.

"I'm sorry," I remember saying, "I mistook you for someone else. I apologize." I remember being amazed at my presence of mind in such a situation. The woman looked perplexed and in that instant the sideways tilt of her head reminded me achingly of her. Then the expression was gone and I looked again and she was not like her at all.

"I mistook you for my dead wife," I said. "I must have been following you around by mistake all night. I do hope you haven't been getting any wrong impressions about me."

"I had noticed," she said, "but the dead, and the living

too, for that matter, do odd things on All Hallows' Eve." She seated herself on the parapet and patted the stone next to her. I sat and leaned back, stretching tired limbs.

"Careful!" she said. "There's a nasty drop back there. It would never do if there was a real death here."

I laughed at that, and relaxed, and there was a long comfortable silence.

"The Venetians built this place," she said after a while, looking up at the sheer stone walls of the bastion that bulked from the rock above us. "Put it here to keep an eye on the Turkish privateers who played hell with their trading routes. Didn't do them any good, because the Turks took it off them sometime after the fall of Byzantium and kept it so they could keep an eye on the Venetian privateers who were playing hell with their trading routes. Held it up till the end of the First World War when the Greek nation was re-formed, and by that time piracy on anyone's trade routes was out of fashion and even stout Venetian masonry was no match for ten-inch naval guns."

She cupped her hands around her knees and leaned back, looking up beyond the crumbled fortress to the autumn constellations.

"Then the new Greek government designated it to be a leper colony. Strange to think there were such things as lepers in a civilized country like Greece until half a century or so ago. They used to bring them here from all over the Aegean. Sort of sad, I think. The last sight of the wider world was the little harbor of Aghios Georgios as the boat took them across to the island. I wonder sometimes how they were received by the others when the boat sailed away. Perhaps with sad resignation, perhaps with joy at the coming of a new brother to their little fellowship. Somehow, though, I can't see this as having been a sad place." She looked at me. "The last leper died in 1950 and the colony was closed and the island became a macabre tourist attraction. Hordes of check-shorted trippers in sun-glasses and sun-hats swarmed over it by the boatload snapping little Instamatics of the ruined village and the skulls and the tombs. That I think is sad; let the dead rest in peace."

"Little peace for the dead," I said, "not after the Thanos Foundation bought the island from the Greek government. I heard that the price they paid was enough to refloat the foundering economy."

"I heard that too. Do you know what they called this island before the dead took it? Spiranaikos. That was its name, Spiranaikos, but then the dead came and dug their necropolises deep underground and filled it with their computers and renamed it Thanos. And on one day every year, on the Greek All Hallows' Eve, they hold the Festival of the Dead and their bodies are relit and their souls come out of the Simulator and they walk amongst the living."

"You sound bitter."

"I do? Perhaps I should be. I've been searching too."

"Your husband?"

"No, my brother. We were very close; together we ran the business. Close, but separate, really, if you understand. Anyway, he contracted . . . you know, and he had only a matter of a few months left to him. But he wasn't going to lie back in his bed in some comfortable, terrible hospice for the terminally ill and trickle away to nothing, not he. He spent his last months living in his grandly extravagant style. "Lived in style and I'll damn well die in style too," he said, and he did, he had style, you know. When his time came he called me to his lodge in the Andes and I saw him there on the sofa and he looked so dreadful. But he smiled and said, 'It may try to get you in the end, but not me, not me,' and he tapped the side of his head and winked. 'It wasn't cheap, this slug in my brain, but it won't get me. After all the things I've done in this life, I'll not have everything come apart just because I'm dead.' I was the organizer, you see, but he was the one with the genius, the creative talent for business. Then he sat up and said, 'In three days they'll be back to take me to the Death House and then I'll live forever.'

"And in three days they returned and put him into a suspension pod and flew him to Thanos and he was gone. At first I received letters and phone calls and reports from him and the business boomed. The Simulator has lines to the outside world and the dead can conduct the business they did in life. Being dead hadn't impaired his business acumen in the least."

"I'm reminded of Sylvia Jenke, her *In This Still Life* series of tone poems."

"But have you noticed," she said intently, "how abstracted

the works of the dead are becoming? I wonder, is it because their reality is just a computer simulation? In one of his letters my brother told me of how he had once taken a boat out of the harbor and sailed away toward the mainland but the nearer he drew to shore the hazier and more indistinct it became until he must have crossed some invisible boundary and there was nothing. No boat, no sea, no town of Aghios Georgios, no body, no self, just . . . void. Then he looked back, wherever 'back' might be, and there it was: Thanos, floating in a little bubble of air and sea and sunlight in the midst of void."

From the battlements above drifted the vigorous sound of Greek folk music: lyra and bouzouki and flute and clapping hands. It sounded wonderfully real and vital.

"Then there was a shift in the void, and he was back in the boat on the sea and the sun was shining and there were the blue hills of the mainland before him.

"He said in his letter that he must have gone beyond the limits of the simulation, over the edge of the world into the nothing beyond." She looked up to the source of the lively music. Up there people were whirling and stamping their feet and whooping in glee. "I sometimes wonder what it's really like."

"They say you can do anything, be anything, you wish."

"As long as you stay within the limits of the simulation."

"True. One freedom bought at the expense of another. My wife told me in her letters how she spent each day, swimming and playing tennis and playing bridge and talking. She said you could drink all day and never get drunk, eat as much as you liked as often as you liked and never be full or fat. And of course, there were the wonderful imaginary companions she could conjure up when she tired of conversing with the pick of the world's finest and richest minds. After that she stopped writing."

"Yes, my brother stopped writing too. I can't help wondering if this dream-life is jading after a while? Perhaps the dead find their blunted appetites turning to more introverted, bizarre pursuits?"

I remembered the dead man dressed in the woman's body who had talked with me in the ruined town. I remembered the dead woman in the Charnel House who told me that bored people develop strange pastimes. I remembered the figures waltzing under the olive trees and realized that the dead danced with the dead and the living with the living.

"We mean nothing to them," I said. "They live in their own world where they make their own rules and their own relationships and the love we feel for them is forgotten."

"I began to realize that years ago," the woman said, "but I kept coming back each year until this All Hallows' Night I met my brother and greeted him and he did not even recognize me. He looked straight through me and all the love I felt for him just poured out of me onto the ground and was gone." She looked around her. Her eyes were dark. "I hate this place. It refuses to die. The lepers; they died and their past died with them and their bones and skulls became a part of this island— but the dead that don't die, they haunt this place, they hang over it like a shroud!

"If you came here on any other day of the year, if you could slip past those smart sailor-boys who carry German machine pistols on any other day of the year, you would find the streets empty and the courtyards deserted and the houses crumbled and still and the dust thick under the olive trees, but you would feel the presence of the dead all around you; you would hear whispers of their casual conversations and their idle small talk as they swim and sail and play their phantom games of tennis in computer simulation while their restored bodies lie in underground tombs, awaiting this one day when they can walk amongst us and remember what a real world is like! We aren't important to them any more, but our reality is! We remind them of the ghosts they truly are."

She was quiet for a while after her outburst. Then she said quietly, "Shall we go from this place?"

I took her gently by the arm and together we left the quiet place on the ramparts. We came to a small taverna under the branches of a cedar tree and here we sat by a private table and talked and drank raw, resinous wine while the Dance of the Dead whirled past us. We talked of many things and after a while danced to a swing band. We laughed a lot. We found a tiny restaurant in a disused boathouse and ate grilled red snapper straight from the spit, burning our fingers on the hot flesh. We watched jugglers and acrobats and joined hands and danced in a ring to the tune of a Greek folk dance half as old as civilization. We stood on the beach by the embers of a dead bonfire and watched the breeze from the sea whipping the soft gray ashes away from the glowing coals beneath. We drank ouzo and watched the dark hills of the mainland grow in definition in the gray predawn glow.

"Look," she said, pointing. Columns of figures were climbing the alleyways and staircases that wound up the island. Bright costumes, bare skin, they moved up the winding stairways and along the limestone cloisters and ramparts of the Venetian fortress: the dead returning to the Underworld.

We reached the stone jetty just as the first rays of morning touched the island. The last of the dead entered the necropolis and the brass gates closed behind. I knew that last figure.

And she had once known me. But now she had returned to the land of the dead, that bone-dry landscape where she lived other lives and loved other loves. The island seemed to throb beneath my feet as the pulse of power built that would strip soul from body and send it whirling back into the Simulator while quiet, patient machines carried the discarded flesh back to its underground chamber and gently restored it.

I blinked, shuddered, banishing the vision. The boats were arriving to ferry us back to the mainland. It was for us as for the ancient Greeks; only the living may return across Styx and only on the condition that they bring nothing back from the domain of the dead. I looked at the woman beside me, then at the bulk of the island. The sun was strong now and the fairy-lights in the olive trees glowed wanly.

"Let them go," I said at length.

RADIO MARRAKECH

The beach is deserted. The ultras are gone and I am alone with the gulls and the ashes and the wind, the wind that blows out of the heart of Africa. The old, red, crazy wind blowing from the ancient heart of man. That is why the people fear it. It shakes out the ghosts and the old, old things that we tell ourselves we have forgotten, the crazy wind.

Seagulls and ashes. The wind fans the embers into a red glow.

Blessed craziness. They have a word for it in Arabic. They have a word for everything in Arabic, and every word has four meanings; one true, one contrary, one holy, one obscene.

And which had Hannah Tellender been?

All. None. A woman. An ultra.

And this flatlifer, alone in the dawnlight on the uttermost edge of Africa, crouching by the embers with the wind whipping the ashes up into his eyes and his mouth? We were, in the end as in the beginning, more than strangers. Aliens. Ultra and flatlifer. Lovers. Ashes.

Strange. To begin one woman's story I must go back to another. To Ruthie and the night she took me to the Rififi Club to see Hannah perform. Whatever the relationship between Ruthie and I, it was a vague, ill-defined entity. Most of the time it was no relationship at all. A draft-dodging exile with Nicaragua nightmares dredging a dirham from the diplomatic schools and American bars of Tangier, obsessed with the ghost of Bogart; a teenage beach-girl with a permanent bikini line, a round-the-world airticket, and Daddy's Gold MasterCard hovering in the twilight zone between mainstream society and the world of the ultras. What better definition of our relationship could I give? What was remarkable was not the quality of the relationship but that there should have been one at all.

"There's a new group coming in from Spain Thursday." Ruthie's was a well-known face at the Rififi, the preeminent Tangier ultra club. A face held in mild contempt by the ultras who passed through its Moorish doors, for they had seen her type of coward in a thousand ultra bars in the thousand cities of the Soul Circle. The girl who wanted, and feared, nothing more than to pay five hundred dollars to Masrurian the Dream Doctor down in the medina and have him slip a jolt of DPMA up the back of her skull. "Hannah Tellender, the ultra *improvisatore*. Even you must have heard of Hannah Tellender, Morrisey. She's giving a recitation, if that's the right thing to call it. It's a must. Everyone who's anyone is going."

In a sense we were each other's salvation—I Ruthie's from the agony of choosing: ultra, flatlifer; Ruthie mine from the patriotic penitence of the Mermaid Cafe. A night of color and light and self-loss in the ultraworld which orbited far far above our heads in return for restraint, presence, and an excuse not to have to decide, not tonight. That was the contract.

Outside among the beer cans and cheroot wrappers, the *basiji*, the ubiquitous Swords of Islam militants called the Holy Judgment of the One God down upon the blasphemers who likened themselves to divinities. Most of them I knew by sight if not by name. Inside, on the Rififi's postage-stamp-sized stage, a tiny woman with lasers on her wrists reached through the streamers of smoke to show everyone the universe she held in the palm of her hand.

Hannah Tellender. The ultra poetess.

She gasped, all of a muck-sweat under the pin-spots.

"Thank you. Thank you. Hey . . . ho. It's hot in here. You're a good audience. It's always kind of nice when you come to a new place and the people take you into their hearts."

Ruthie pressed forward toward the foot of the stage. I braved the cocktail glasses, nasal inhalers, cinder-tipped black cheroots, to snag her arm. She barely registered my presence. I have seen that same expression of rapture in the eyes of Coptic women praying, in the eyes of Orthodox icons.

Hannah Tellender stretched her arms above her head and

sighed. "Okay. Okay. Who's next? Who's next? Anyone got anything? Anything, just fire something at me . . ."

Ruthie gazed up at the tiny woman and whispered, "Radio Marrakech."

"Radio Marrakech. Radio Marrakech." The ultra poetess closed her eyes to summon the Muse. The two musicians manning the Rififi synthesizers waited, fingers touched to keyboards, for their cue to their own improvisations. "Radio Marrakech." She crossed arms and ankles and giggled in glee as fans of laserlight sprang from her projectors. "Okay, Tangier. Radio Marrakech." She brought her wrists together and down. I gasped: where the fans of laserlight crossed, ephemeral holographic interference patterns shimmered. She clapped her hands, clap clapclap clap clapclap clap, each handclap an explosion of lightshards. The ectomorphic phantoms on the Prophet Nines pounced upon the beat, scooped up the beat, and rammed it through their machines. And the Rififi Club exploded!

A holographic dervish whirling in a jellaba of laserlight, she danced, snapping her body round and around and around to the rhythm of the driving synthesizers and her extemporized, ecstatic poetry.

"Oh Arthur, Arthur, Dervish D with the leather turban! Clay between your terra-cotta toes, Arthur, clay, red dust: do your teeth glint, like Valentino (again and again and again the Sheik), like Bogart, will they always have Paris?

"Axial hub of the city (commercial spiritual political amen amen amen): square of souls, squared souls, the sum of the square of the souls on the hypo you use is equal to the sum of the squares on the other side. Round gravesockets, plug-in saints, skull-rooted teeth of *Tyrannosaurus oedipus sultan*: on the final Day of Judgment, on the day of all souls (round, square, soulful), on the day, on the day, on the day when God says, 'Well, how about you?' on that Black Thursday, will you be there, Arthur? Plucked from your covering of warm grave soil like a tooth from a sultan's skull; clay between your toes, clay between your teeth, red clay of Africa, neo-barbarian!

"Ochre. Ochre. Ochre. Ochre . . . primeval pulse-beat, call sign of radio, Radio Africa, Radio Marrakech: ochreness abounds. And if I had an aerial, a minaret, a spire, a lingam, what soul juice could I not draw down from God? Rock'n'Soul with a minaret between my bounding breasts. Look at the jets, Arthur, the jets, dropping their bombs between the minarets, bounding, bouncing bombs, Arthur.

"See! The minarets falling!

"See! The spires collapsing!

"See! The lingam wilting . . . melting . . . falling . . . falling . . .

"If I had an aerial, an aerial ten thousand miles tall, I'd run up the aerial, run up the aerial, run up the goddamn aerial, swing and sway and swing and sway and swing and sway until it came down in Marrakech, in the Square of Souls, inverse Rapture for the Judgment Day.

"Clay Arthur, the clay man, red dirt of Africa, Bogart-toothed, are you ready for the Judgment? Is your soul stropped for my shriving as I come sliding down the aerial down down down from heaven, ten thousand miles of aerial, to judge you, Arthur, find you wanting?

"Your soul music. The glint of your skull-rooted teeth, emotional dinosaur. An ocean away you stand planted in red soil: spirit-weed of the Rif, of the Kif. From my bi-plane apartment I watch you, Arthur, in Marrakech, in the Square of Souls, square-souled Berber. Dust and snow. Dust and snow! Behind you the Atlas: High Atlas, atlas of the world: God, how much longer will you carry the world on your shoulders?"

The synthesizers hissed into silence. The spray of moiré patterns froze, faded.

I could not move.

None of us could move.

Then a cry from the door, a smash of breaking glass, a blossom of flame brought us crashing down. The crowd packed into the Rififi surged, shrieking. Somewhere, somewhen, I had lost Ruthie's hand. I snatched up a fire extinguisher hidden beneath a table, not to deal with the leaping flames enveloping the rear of the club, but as a weapon. The anger. Never very far from me, my personal demon, a thorn in my flesh. I stood swinging the extinguisher, ready for an enemy, any enemy. Screams, dervish whoops; by the burning Moorish doors shadow-play demons struggled with the bouncers, overcame them, and crashed forward in a wave of table-turning and chair-smashing. Panicked patrons stampeding the fire doors jammed me hard against the edge of the low stage.

The Swords of Allah pelted us with bottles. A scimitar-thin youth came at me, chair-leg raised. Ruthie forgotten, everything forgotten save my need, my lust for expression in violence, I stabbed him in the gut with the fire extinguisher. I knew his face. I had taught him T. S. Eliot and the emptiness at the heart of modern man. As he doubled up, a bolt of blue light took him across the eyes. I looked about me to see tiny, ferocious Hannah Tellender clasp hands together, point fingers, and stab another blue-hot blast from her wrist-lasers at the burning *basiji*. A charging demon figure fell with a wailing cry, hands pawing at blinded eyes. Three further stabs of light, three figures fell. My eyes met those of the ultra *improvisatore*.

"*Baraka*," I said.

"*Baraka*," she replied. She smiled. *Baraka*, the charisma that makes a beggar a king. For an instant there was almost communication, then the crowd broke over the stage and swept me away from her, dazed, confused, dazzled, out into the street filled with unfamiliar faces and the apocalyptic chorus of police sirens. And I suppose I loved her from that moment, but did not know it because I could not see past the dazedness, confusion, and dazzlement into her true light.

Ruthie picked me out of siesta-sleepy boulevard Pasteur in a big black car that was not Ruthie's driven by a man who was not Ruthie's—not any of hers I could recall.

"I phoned you, I phoned your friends, I bribed my way past the concierge of that rue Ibn Ben Moussah slum you call an apartment, I even phoned the police to see if you'd been thrown into jail by mistake, and the only thing which kept me from phoning the morgue was that I heard on the radio news that no corpses had been dragged out of the Rififi. Name of Allah, girl, what have you been doing?"

Prim and cool in print frock, straw hat, and bandanna, Ruthie sniffed huffily and peered over the driver's shoulder into the rearview mirror to paint a pair of crude, persimmon lips onto her face.

"Geez, Morrisey, I'd a thought you'd be grateful. It's not every flatlifer gets invited to a claybreaking." The driver, whom I had until now ignored, laughed a sudden, too-knowledgeable laugh. "Oh geez, I forgot. Morrisey, this is

Armand. He played synth? At the club? Last night? Armand, this is Morrisey, my best friend, aren't you, Morrisey?" She gave me a play tickle that made me cringe. "Armand's one of them." Needless explanation.

The big black car hooted its way across the Grand Socco, then suddenly, suicidally, darted through the medina gate into the labyrinth of streets that divided and subdivided like the human arterial system into the capillary alleyways of the old town.

"He'll never get a car through here," I whispered. Armand laughed again and a sudden stab of braking threw us to the floor (Ruthie bitching and flapping over spilled cosmetics) as a three-wheeler motor-dray leapt out of nowhere into the bedlam of vehicles and pedestrians. A swerve left and we were in a warren of medina streets so narrow the side mirrors scraped against the venerable Moorish plaster. The constant stop-start, the constantly blaring horn, frayed the never-too-firm fabric of my temper. Just as it seemed we must annihilate an entire generation of Tangerines from eldest grandmother down to most junior in parasoled baby buggy, the ultra chauffeur veered the big black car down an entry I had not even suspected was there. We lurched to a stop scant centimeters from a wall that had stood sound and solid since the days of the Cid.

Ruthie dabbed her face in nervous relief.

"This is it. This is it. Geez, a claybreaking. This is so exciting."

I had no idea of what a claybreaking might be.

Locked wooden shutters excluded the street but admitted long slats of afternoon light and little djinns of air that sent the suspended petrol lantern swaying, dodging, weaving erratic shadows over the congregation that had gathered in a circle of crouchings and squattings on the bare clay floor, a circle of mutterings and the furtive communion of touching hands.

She was there. Not the creature of spirit and laserlight of the night before: different, a shrouded painting, a candle in an alcove. She sensed my presence, raised her eyes to meet mine.

"Hannah Tellender."

"I know. Sheridan Morrison. The Rififi . . ."

"I know." Her smile was enigmatic as a Madonna's. "Ultras never forget. *Baraka*."

Before I could speak, she pressed fingers to my lips and pointed at the thing on the floor.

At the center of the circle of hands and faces lay a supine clay Venus, slightly over life-size, crudely shaped from mud. Mountain-breasted, insect-waisted, the steatopygous buttocks were splayed out on the floor by the pressing weight of heavy clay flesh. The coarse thing was daubed with swirls of black-oxide fingerpainting which reminded me of the meaningless meandering patterns of Altamira man. Between the conical thighs, labia had been vulgarly incised with a stick.

Questions flocked to my lips; Hannah's fingers brushed them away. This was a holy moment, I was not to profane it. A murmur ran through the small, crowded room. Those squatting closest reached out to lay hands to the effigy.

And I thought I saw a tremor run through the clay thing.

The fluttering hands reached out again and there was indeed a tremor, more; a shudder, and a sound, a splitting, cracking sound. The clay thing flexed. Its mud carapace crazed over in a web of cracks. Pure dread possessed me. There was a spasm, a subsentient moan, scales of sun-dried clay fell to the clay floor and something moved inside, something sun-starved and ghastly. I almost cried aloud . . . And the hand-music began; hands dancing, hands tapping, hands clapping, hands slapping the clay floor, the rhythm of the heat, the street, the swinging petrol lantern; rhythm of the shadows. Another primal cry. The hands beat faster, faster, the whole room became their drum.

"What is it?" I whispered to Hannah Tellender. She swayed unconsciously to the song of the claybreaking.

"One of us, Mr. Morrison."

Soft human hands brushed cold clay, pitter-pat, pitter-pat. The spiral-painted face-mask split and sloughed away. There was a face beneath, a girl-face, stupid, newborn, blinking. The mud-crumbed lips shaped silent syllables. A sigh rippled across the room and the hands drummed harder, louder, until it seemed that the whole city throbbed to their hand-song. The entombed girl struggled to heave herself free from her chrysalis, for now I saw the truth of the coarse clay Venus. The tension peaked toward the edge of hysteria, then abruptly, terrifyingly, there was silence. Still, silent hands reached to pull the naked girl from the broken clay shards. A gust of red wind swung the petrol lantern and for an instant of pure insanity I saw diaphanous wings unfold from her shoulders; rainbow-sheened, as delicate as oil on water. Then the shadows re-formed and I saw only a stupid, confused girl of about twenty, blind and reaching. Flakes of mud clung to her blonde hair. The naked newborn passed around the circle of ultras and each in turn pressed his flesh to hers. Yet there was nothing in the least sexual in this pressing of nakedness; quite the opposite, I felt like an infidel witnessing the administration of some precious sacrament.

Then I saw Ruthie gather the blonde ultra-child into her arms and I did not want to see any more. Hannah's simultaneous whisper voiced my feelings.

"Take me away from here, Mr. Morrison. Anywhere, I just want away from here."

What else could I do? Where else could a beach-bum street-exile draft-dodger take his ultra-poetess-*improvisatore* but the Mermaid Cafe where all beach-bums street-exiles draft-dodgers are fetched up by the tides of war, sorry, *police action*. Spiritual flotsam, drifting toward the edge of the twentieth century under the rueful proprietorial eye of Fat Sonny, expiating his own particular brand of patriotic guilt by dressing in helicopter-pilot fatigues and shades. Time makes us all into the things we despise most.

Over a bottle of Fat Sonny's House Vintage, Hannah confessed why she had fled the claybreaking.

"It was just too personal for me, Mr. Morrison." The wine was clear and cold and carried a faint bouquet of apricots. "Seeing her come out of the clay reminded me too much of when I came out of the clay like that, naked, vulnerable, newborn. You can't begin to understand what it's like; only someone who has been through it can, it's a precious, precious time, alone with yourself, catatonic in the clay chrysalis. You learn, you see, you become; new paths of perception are mapped out in your brain, new ways of seeing reality. Connections are made between areas of your brain that haven't been connected since the dream-time, new neural networks laid down . . . Alone, you learn that you are an extraordinary creature in a universe so extraordinary no dull, flatlifed ordinary person can ever begin to touch the splendor of it . . ." She gazed wistfully into her glass. Then, sensing she had wounded me as unthinkingly as a child might maim a fly, she said, "Oh God, I'm sorry, I didn't mean that about dull, flat lives."

"Yes you did," I said.

"Yes, I did," she agreed. And it was as if the recognition of the unbridgeable distance between us somehow bound us together.

By day, after the consular brats had scampered back to their porno discs and cocaine habits, I showed Hannah the city of Tangier and amidst the tangled laneways of the medina and the bustle of the fruit market found a new freshness in her appreciation of what, to me, was contemptibly familiar. By night, after the streets had emptied of evening strollers and the cafes had put up the shutters, she whirled me through the small cafes and bars and after-hours clubs and took me as close to the heart of the extraordinary universe the ultras inhabited as any flatlifer could come.

Fragment by fragment, stone by stone, like some shattered clay stele of an ancient revelation, I learned her story: rummaging and haggling in the Souk for dubious souvenirs, sipping afternoon coffee at the sidewalk tables of the Mermaid Cafe, among the evening crowds walking the Terrace amidst the schoolkids and grazing herds of paparazzi with the green hills of Spain rising behind us, fragment by fragment, stone by stone, I learned how an ultra *improvisatore* is made.

In Deerfield, Tennessee, they had a saying: God made the world but the TVA made Deerfield, Tennessee. And in that place that God forgot to make, there was a little girl, born little, grew up little, but who was big inside, bigger than Deerfield, Tennessee. She had to be big inside to contain all the dreams, for they were big dreams, bigger than Deerfield, Tennessee. Big dreams of big places: walled cities and desert caravans, crescent moons and high snowy mountains, places larger than truth, big as dreams, places she had read about in the *National Geographic* magazines in the waiting room of her father's dental surgery. As she grew the dreams grew to fit her, the dreams of things she could not put a name to which she wanted more than anything. So the poems flocked into her head, good poems, poems much too good for Deerfield, Tennessee, for sometimes she would recite the poems in her head to people in a bar who did not understand them, not at all, because the poetry they wanted to hear was pretty words and pretty thoughts and pretty pictures trapped on pretty paper and her poems were not like that, not at all. And so she was unhappy.

"Then I saw this TV news report about a doctor down in Memphis who was up in court because he was giving DPMA to anyone who would pay him three hundred dollars and I knew that I had to have it. Had to. No other way to make the dream spark into life. So I worked in the surgery and after hours in a diner and I saved every penny until I had my dream ticket. Then I took a bus to Memphis, put the cash down on Dr. MacKinley's table, and he slipped the needle up the back of my skull and when I woke up it was the dream-time again. For always."

We were kicking around in a souvenir shop on some anonymous alleyway just off the Petit Socco. Hannah picked up a large enameled plate.

"You like this? I think I might buy it for you as a present."

But the wind blows where it will, as the Berbers say, and with the joyful, carefree times came times of melancholy when a great silence welled out of Hannah like blood and we would sit for hours, not speaking, yet desperate for communication. On one such occasion, over glasses of afternoon coffee in a roadside cafe overlooking the place of legends where the waters of the Mediterranean and the Atlantic break upon each other, I asked, purely for the sake of making noise,

"So, was there a Marrakech?"

She smiled within her sorrow.

"There was. There still is."

"And an Arthur?"

"No. Not really. There was someone, back in Deerfield. He was a skipper, that was what we called them in Deerfield, skipped off the draft and ran to Marrakech. Impossibly romantic. But as for being an Arthur. No. Never." Presently she said, very quietly, "But you could be him if you like."

We never came any closer to saying it than that.

By trading in on an old favor down on rue Ibrahim Sultan, I was able to secure the indefinite usage of a black-and-white Mercedes taxi. I could have asked for more, much more, in return for smuggling synthetic death-hormone suppressants across to Algeciras on the hydrofoil, but nothing else would have afforded me as much pleasure as taking Hannah away from Tangier and the rag-end years of the twentieth century into the timefree lands of the Rif. I felt she needed space and silence and time away from the comradeship of her Soul Circle. New cities, old faces; the strain was beginning to tell on Hannah. So we drove all morning through olive groves and orchards of oranges and almonds. The sun beat down on us through the open sunroof ("It's stuck," said bio-smuggling Bakhti, showing me the sheet of polythene which served as protection in case of rain) and glinted from the last of the Rif snows.

"Just where are you taking me?" Hannah asked.

"Chaouen," I replied. We skirted Tétouan, the old capital of Spanish Morocco in the days of the protectorate, crossed the snow-swollen river, and began the long climb up the south road which threw itself across the foothills of the Rif in swoops of exhilarating switchbacks. "Little town on the side of a mountain. Old Spanish governors used to keep country villas there, lovely quiet timeless atmosphere, the perfect retreat, until the tourists come by the busload."

The road wound on, up into the changelessness of rural Morocco. Hannah chattered incessantly; observations, exclamations, short improvisations, sketches for longer performance pieces, private monologues in a secret tongue she told me was Jam, the language of the ultras: English reduced to its fundamental units and fused into a form more compact, more expressive. I threw the venerable Merc around the hairpin bends of the way less gone by, hooting at goats and donkeys and country buses with gleeful vindictiveness.

In the mad-dogs-and-Englishmen hours we stopped at one of those roadside cafe-cum-markets which spring up seemingly spontaneously in Morocco and lunched on prickly pears while the laboring Merc recuperated. Life was beginning to stir once again in response to the cool of early evening when we reached Chaouen tumbling down its mountainside. I paid an urchin to mind the car, and left the overnight bags in the small Moorish hotel. Then we went haggling for spices in the Tuesday market and wandered where the spirit led through the steep streets of the immaculately tidy medina and for a dirham apiece rested in the cool gardens of the restored casbah with the fountains splashing about us and the bats flitting above us, as silent as night, through the trees.

That evening Hannah seemed distant even for an ultra. She was distracted, diffracted. She would not respond to any of my gentle attempts at conversation. Blaming myself, I asked her what I had done, but all she would say was that it had nothing to do with me; it was her. The dinner was an exhausting affair and I was glad when she went upstairs and left me to finish my coffee alone.

I found her on the rusting balcony. At her feet, the lights of Chaouen; above her, the African night, and bright Arcturus, guide-star of the ancient Moorish navigators.

"If it meant just slipping back into flatlife consciousness, I could cope with that. But to have all this: to see you as you truly are, Morrison, in the glory of your humanity, a phoenix draped in rainbow energies ringing to the inner symphony of your race-song, to see the pregnant land as full in its emptiness as an egg is of wisdom, thirty thousand years of being superimposed upon itself layer upon layer upon layer of *mille-feuille* sedimentary sandstone, to hear the barking of ancestral ghosts, to have God omnipresent and omnivisible in everything I see—it's an agony. An agony."

She would not look at me. I reached out to touch her, to draw her away from herself. She recoiled from my fingertips with a yelping cry.

"You burned me! Burned me!"

Five perfect ovals of blistered flesh marred the skin. She glanced wildly about herself as if threatened by approaching shadows, clapped her hands to her ears as if shutting out the tintinnabula of God.

"Too high, too much, too far, too soon. God, the colors of your energy!"

She spun to face me. She opened her clenched right hand. In it she held three gray hairs.

"It's beginning, Morrison. Oh God, I'm so afraid."

"I'm sorry. There is nothing I can do for her. Or you."

Masrurian the Dream Doctor plied his trade from an alchemist's den excavated deep under the walls of the medina, an uneasy amalgam of modern and medieval; typically Tangier, typically Masrurian, self-proclaimed Armenian exile in cool white linen suit.

Claims, like suits, are cheaply made in Tangier.

"There's got to be something."

"Has there?" Masrurian the Dream Doctor repaired to his desk, a florid anachronism in schlock Moorish. "Tell me, Mr. Morrison, you have been educated? Past primary level? You understand the English language?" A lisping Peter Lorre of a man, his lizard head jutted forward as he spoke, his tongue flickered in and out as he spoke, as if tasting the air. "Then you will know what 'irreversible' means. Irreversible, Mr. Morrison." He measured and weighed his syllables like drams of tincture, as fragile and nervous as his colored-glass alembics. A stuffed basilisk regarded me with contemptuous eyes. "Good day, Mr. Morrison."

He stabbed at the keys of his computer terminal; pointless Arabic chased across the screen. His glasses constantly slipped down his greasy nose and were pushed back into position. When he saw that I was not going to leave, he sat up with a theatrical sigh of exasperation.

"Very well, Mr. Morrison. A short biochemistry lesson. As you are doubtless as ignorant of the neurobiology of the Tessier/Rhodes process as you are of your own language, I shall make things simple for you to understand." Bottled brains, proudly labeled like pickles in a fruit cellar, lined the shelves behind his desk. "Put simplistically, the Tessier/Rhodes process accelerates the flow of sodium ions across the synaptic gap, thus increasing the action potential of the individual neuron severalfold. Further, DPMA encourages the process of myelination in the cerebral axons." His glasses slipped and he restored them with an unconscious gesture. "Synaptic impulses travel faster in myelinated fibers than non-myelinated; the potential jumps from node to node, do you see? And there is evidence that DPMA stimulates the topology of the cortex." Masrurian looked at me as I were a brain in a bottle. "Brainfolding, Mr. Morrison. Surely you must be aware that it is the convolutions of our brains that make us the sentient, intelligent creatures we would all claim to be?

"As this woman's . . . ah . . . lover, you of course know what the benefits of the Tessier/Rhodes process are; what it is that makes them do this thing. Amplified neural responses, new modes of perception, the purported ability to smell colors, taste sounds, hear the touch of a finger; I believe their name for it is 'cosmic awareness.' They liken themselves to gods; you would know better than I if this is deserved; certainly, they perceive and respond emotionally to a universe infinitely more rich and varied than that revealed to the senses of those they arrogantly term 'flatlifers.' "

"And there is a negative."

Hands spread wide, an Armenian exile's expression of accommodation.

"Why else would you be here? The synaptic hyperactivity inevitably throws the autonomic and endocrinal systems into overstimulation. Hormone levels, including those of the cyclic nucleotides, cyclic adenosine monophosphate, and cyclic guanosine monophosphate, the so-called 'death hormones' which govern aging, all run wild. After approximately thirty months of normal biological function, the subject—or, shall we say, sufferer—begins to age with astounding rapidity; within a few weeks of the onset they have descended through decrepitude and senescence into death. Once the DPMA is injected into the thalamus the process is, Mr. Morrison, quite inescapable. Believe me, there is no going back for her, whoever she is."

A small cry, like a bird. I found my thumbs pressing hard against Masrurian's glasses, eager to shatter the lenses and drive the fragments into his eyes.

"Is there not some counter hormone you can inject?" This, asked of the man who spliced together synthetic anti-death hormones in his den and sent them across the Strait of Gibraltar in the pockets of American draft-dodgers. Fascinating how the weary tone of contempt had left his voice.

"Experiments were made with specifically keyed endorphins to block the neural DPMA receptors; the endorphins also fatally blocked transmission to the somatic nervous system, which controls organ function."

"Some kind of enzyme that might cut the DPMA molecule?" My thumbs pressed harder on the lenses. The plastic frames creaked. Dwarf Masrurian gave another small shriek.

"Mr. Morrison! No no no . . ." He struggled for scientific thought. "Ah, ah, the only enzyme which would cut the

DPMA molecule reduced it to two components, one a beneficial growth hormone, the other an acetylcholine-blocking neurotoxin related to those used in military nerve gases. Mr. Morrison, please, there is no way out."

"No," I said. "No no no no . . ." I bore down with the gathering strength of my fury. Masrurian the Dream Doctor's hands fluttered blindly at my face like little creatures. The plastic legs of the glasses snapped. He gave a cry as the frames gouged into his eyesockets . . . and my hands fell away from his face.

Dropped and forgotten, it lay thoughtlessly kicked under a desk, a crescent of silver filigree glinting in the corners of my eyes, a Moorish moon. I saw it flash and spin, dangling from Ruthie's fingers. I saw the delight in her eyes and I heard my voice, again: "For you, Ruthie. Happy nineteenth birthday."

She had found it. At last. Something had made her take her courage in both hands and lay it down with the five hundred dollars on Masrurian's desk.

Or was what she had found only a different kind of cowardice?

I was numb.

As I left, the glass eyes of the stuffed cockatrice regarded me with accusation, and complicity in an awful crime.

The hotel was of that kind to which Moroccan businessmen take their whores; dark intent behind a decorous veil of green neon Arabic. The third and fourth floors were permanently reserved for ultra Soul Circles visiting the city. The teenage concierge barely wasted a glance on me: I was not an ultra, therefore either the kif traffickers in the back bar or the whores in the downstairs disco would accommodate me. I could smell her patchouli clear across the lobby. She turned up her Sony and sang, tunelessly as only headphone wearers can, to the latest Rock-the-Casbah beat beaming in from Big Fortress America moored just outside Libyan territorial waters.

She was waiting for me. She stood with her back turned, but her voice, the voice of the poet, filled the lobby like birds.

"All alonio, Morrisey. They're all gone, down to the medina. Claytime, Morrisey. Friend of yours, I believe. Finally found enough courage to eat the peach. That's what we call it. You know Eliot? So, they've gone and I'm all alonio, because we're ultras, and we're family, and we all love each other so so much."

I had never heard such bitterness in a voice.

"Hannah, I've been to Masrurian."

"Then you know, don't you?"

"I wanted to hurt him. I almost hurt him, badly."

"You should have. He deserves it. So, you know, and I suppose he was awfully sorry, Mr. Morrison, but there was nothing he could do. And he's right."

She turned to face me.

"Look at me, Morrisey. Look at me!"

I felt as if the curved sword of the *basiji* had been driven through my stomach.

One day—less, a handful of hours—had passed for me. In that time Hannah had aged ten years.

My eyes burned her and she tried to hide her face from me. And I would have, I should have, should have looked away. But I could not. To look was unbearable, but I could not look away.

"You too?" Hannah shouted. "You want to be like them? You want to watch, see what it's like? Well, take a good look then, a good long look. Yes, it's ugly, yes, I'm aging, growing old, yes, I'm dying. You want to say that, see how it sounds? You want to be like the rest of those . . . ravens and fly off far away because you can't bear to see how it'll be for you someday, flatlifer? Well, see the show. Get something out of it, enrich your life, because, quite frankly, Morrisey, it scares the piss out of me. Do you know how old I am? Do you? I was twenty-seven last month. Twenty-seven; we were drinking wine under the orange blossoms of Seville and we laughed and drank to life because we thought we were going to live forever."

The teenage concierge buried her nose in an improving Islamic comic and poised her finger over the panic button to the police station. Hannah turned and fled up the fire stairs. I did not follow. I could not tell if she was crying.

I took indefinite leave of absence from the cocaine-eyed sons of the diplomatic corps to be with Hannah. She needed me. The ultras had deserted her. They were life, she was death. There was no place for her in their tinsel-bright, butterfly world. So they left Hannah alone in her room, alone with the death.

She feared that death. She feared annihilation. She feared becoming nothing. She would have loved to embrace some formula of belief upon which to ride through the death. She spent long warm spring afternoons in theological argument with ministers, holy men, and *sidi*. They were unable to satisfy her.

"I can see more in all my uncertainty than they can guess even in their deepest faith," she said. Her voice was a ravaged whisper. "God, Morrisey, I don't want to be nothing."

She loved the veranda. The teeming life of the street refuted, for a minute, for an hour, her mortality. We would sit, and merely *be*. Not a word would pass between us. We communicated at a level more intimate by far than noise. Of all the things which filled those last days, I treasure the memory of this fruitful, present silence most. One night I woke with a start in my chair; a draft, I think, from an open window. I could not recall having fallen asleep. I glanced at my watch: three A.M. Hannah was on the balcony, face intense in the prophet-green light from the hotel neons. Her arthritis-knotted hands lay still in her lap. She was gazing into the three o'clock empty street with the same rapt intensity I had witnessed in the hotel in Chaouen.

"Where will all the words go?" she whispered. "All the words inside of me? Will they break free from me and soar like birds, or will they crumble to dust and ashes? I worry about the words, Morrisey. They're so much more than I am."

"I could steal a vox-writer from school," I suggested.

"No," Hannah said. "They can't be trapped on paper. The words have to be free or they die. I'll miss the words. So much unspoken, so little said."

"Try and get some sleep," I whispered. Hollywood adage, B-movie cliché. Hannah laughed.

"Morrisey, you should know me better than that. I don't sleep. None of us sleep. Ever. Why sleep when life itself is a dream?"

The wind was out of Africa the day Hannah died; the ancient crazy wind. And in the end Hannah was not reluctant to be away with it. In the end she was willing for that crazy wind to carry her on, over the edge of the world where the men and cities that perch there are afraid to go. Downstairs, under the kohl-dark eyes of the teenage concierge, the ultras waited like roosting birds of ill-omen.

The wind from Africa whirled the dust through the streets of Tangier, rattled the blind, swirled the notes of an Islamic chant through the open window of Room 317. It made Hannah smile. Dreadful, a twenty-seven-year-old smile on an eighty-eight-year-old face. I see it yet.

"Still good, Morrisey. Still the magic." She spoke with the voice of cancer. "It's coming, Morrisey. I know this body too well not to know it."

My fingers strayed to my trouser pocket and the uncompromising cylinder of the hypodermic. A friend from the Red Crescent had given it to me, and enough morphine for the job.

"Hannah . . ."

"What is it, Morrisey?"

"Have you ever thought of . . ."

I could not say it.

"Suicide? I know what you've got in your pocket. You can't hide things from an ultra, even a sick old ultra like this one. Thanks for the thought, you meant it sincerely, but you see, I've already committed suicide, slow suicide, the moment Dr. MacKinley took my three hundred dollars. I've had thirty-three months, that's more than most. A thousand and one nights of wonder."

"You knew?"

"We all know. It's the bargain we make: to burn our lives away in a flash for a glimpse at the whole of the moon. And I'd make it again, Morrisey. It's a devil's bargain, but this is living. Give me your hand, Morrisey."

Her skin was hot and dry like the skin of a snake; there was fever under it. She closed her eyes and her body stiffened, as if soul-electricity had burned along her spine.

"Now," she said. "Now now now now."

And I was taken up.

I felt the earth turn ponderously beneath me, embedded in the greater, grander turning of the orrery of the stars, in turn wheeling to the vast gyrations of the Universal spiral like some Sufi saint in contemplation of God, like some fool on a hill

. . . the triple helix of space, time, and consciousness spun in the great void of Unknowing in a dance of dervishes . . .

I listened to the chamber music of the atoms and the clear, cold harmonics of the fundamental particles which lawed them together into the grand, incoherent arpeggios of quantum theory . . .

I felt ten million years of past stroke my skin with the intimacy of the racial Lilith: I tasted the earth of Africa, the bone dust, the ashes of the years spread like dung across the land; I smelled time was and time is and time yet to be and the corrupt stench of my own dear flesh, ultimately, comically, mortal . . .

I saw the whole of the moon.

For an instant.

Just for an instant.

I was lifted to Godhood and walked in the footsteps of the ultras.

All this, just for one single, searing instant. Then I was brought low, I fell from heaven like Lucifer and never again will I know as keen a loss.

The final spasm of the stroke had snapped Hannah's neck. Even as I watched, her claw hands opened like flowers, relaxing into death. Her eyes had opened, some blood had trickled from them. I closed them with small centime coins.

As I left, the flock of ultras, knowing beyond knowledge that Hannah was dead, descended around the bed, squabbling and mobbing and pecking, pecking, pecking.

I waited in the lobby. I tried to remember the light and the fire, when Hannah had set the world-weary cafes and clubs alight with her poetry. I could not recall a single word. So much unspoken, so little said.

It was late, very late when the ultras brought down the dreadfully small bundle wrapped in white linen bands. A Peugeot station wagon was parked by the side entrance; they slipped the tiny, tiny corpse into the back. I followed in the Mercedes taxi and the night wind blew cold on me through the jammed-open sunroof. I followed through the empty streets of Tangier, I followed out into the hills to the west of the city, I followed to a long moon-white beach by the Atlantic.

There they burned her. The ultras gathered around the flames and spoke among themselves in hushed Jam whispers. I stood apart: separate, alien. Above me Arcturus rose, vain guide-star. I saw faces lit by the fireglow, the faces from the New Fariq Hotel, Armand the chauffeur and the pale woman who had played the other synthesizer to Hannah's improvisations. And I saw Ruthie, and I imagined clay in her eyes, in her hair, slapped across her breasts, her belly.

If she saw me she did not choose to recognize me. I did not desire her to do so, for what could we, an ultra, a flatlifer, ever have, *ever have had*, in common?

Toward dawn the ultras dispersed. I remained, rubbing hands in the early morning chill, and the wind rose out of Africa, lifting the seagulls, chasing the ashes down the long white beach. And I felt the red wind blow through me and shake things loose and out of me they came, tumbling like birds blown on the wind, the words; Hannah's legacy to me. Words wind and ashes. I will use them well, Hannah. I promise.

VISITS TO REMARKABLE CITIES

Wherever, whenever, two or three are gathered together (some Silk Road caravanserai, some neon all-night diner, some airport transit lounge, some snow-shrouded Trans-Siberian railroad halt, some Chaucerian pilgrims' tavern, some russet-walled medina), there the City of Stories may be found. Wherever, whenever travelers meet; whenever, wherever the stories of their travels are told (exchanged like bartered spices or caged songbirds), there its caravans and pavilions halt in their perennial migration; invisible to the eye, of course, but none the less real for being insubstantial, for the stories out of which they are woven are the most real things in the universe.

There were five of them, gathered together against the night, a fragile fellowship of warmth and unique experience. As custom demanded, they agreed that each should tell of the marvelous places he had encountered on his travels. By the comparison of each man's story, they might together arrive at some common insight into the way of the world. So they drew themselves into a circle around the fire and turned their backs to the wind which blew from around the edge of the world. And drawn by the fire, yet afraid to draw closer for fear that its light might reveal their insubstantiality, the ghosts gathered and encamped and the sound of their voices was like long wind in tent ropes.

The big red-haired, red-bearded man offered to tell the first story. His comrades nodded their consent. After pausing for a moment of recollection, the big red man spoke into the firelight.

THE CITY OF
LOGOS AND RHEMA

He could not properly name the city he had visited, for, that city being founded wholly upon the Word, its name was forever changing; a stream of nouns, verbs, and adjectives, an oceanic mantra of syllables ever-growing, ever-expanding as the city grew and expanded. For the people of *BarraboomriverrunAnnaLiviaPluribelle* . . . deemed it the greatest of sins that the name of an object should be lesser than the object itself. Thus their word for something as contemptible as a *chair* included a brief résumé of the various activities for which it was designed, a short description of its general appearance, and a mutable modifier to indicate the various varieties of wood which might be used in its construction. If such a humble object as a *chair* possessed such a name, how then could the name of the city be any less? For the name of the city to be lesser than the city itself was to demean the city it named.

No less than their city were the citizens: each carried round with him like rosaries great necklaces of names: sons-of, brothers-of, nephews-of, uncles-to, fathers-of, grandsons-of. And, as by common etiquette names must be exchanged upon meeting in the street or upon a crowded omnibus or in the congested laneways of the bourse, the social intercourse of these people was a lengthy and verbose affair.

The city stood upon a river. Not a river of dark, oppressive waters commingled with the excreta of the populace, its beer cans, dead dogs, and abandoned shopping trolleys; rather, a river of words, an onward-flowing stream of consciousness without source and apparently without destination, a babel-ogue of voices flowing ceaselessly from future to past. Like some hypothetical Venice of the mind, the city was founded upon words and it was an unspoken but universal tenet of faith among its garrulous millions that their words were the literal foundation of the streets, squares, and commerces; that if the stream of dialogue should even for one instant be interrupted and silenced, in that same instant the city would cease to be. They believed the City of Logos and Rhema was maintained solely by its people's constant definition and description of it. "I'll meet you in Commercial Court . . ." "Well, there I was a-roving out on Fairview Avenue . . ." "Two o'clock, St. Stephen's, be there, wear a green carnation . . ." Streets, alleys, malls and markets, bourses and bibliotheques, commerces and courts, constantly rang with the city's vocal remembrance of itself.

Yet this city did not stand alone upon the Rhema, the spoken word, like Adam balancing for a thousand years upon one foot. There were other words, strong, silent words, solid words, unspoken words; the words trapped like fossilized seasnails on paper pages, layered in Morocco-bound strata and marshaled into great synclinoria upon mile after mile of sagging oak shelving. These were the Logos: the written words. Holiest of all, these written words. Whole libraries were settling into the subsoil beneath the accumulation of folio, quarto, demi, foolscap, A4, parchment, hammered vellum, plain photocopy, bond, bank, and carbon. Day by day, hour by hour, new volumes were added to the stupendous mass of words yet still the paper chase showed no sign of coming to a weary end. From the typewriters, quills, and word processors of myriad authors in myriad chilly garrets reams of paper scrolled, spewed, thundered upon the city like a second flood.

Oldest and most revered of all the city's books was one housed in a special carrel in the Great Library. Ancient beyond antiquity, its name was of such a lineage and length that it would have taken weeks to complete it. Therefore it was only, ever known as the Book of Shining Things. One glimpse of the fabulously illuminated folios within was conviction enough that the shorthand was justified. Lifetimes of monastic devotion had handcrafted impossibly intricate spirals within spirals, lattices within lattices, archangels within archangels, words within words in the purest golds, silvers, and carmines. So precious was this book, so ancient and delicate the luminous parchments, that on any day only two of its pages were ever on display.

On account of this, the scholar who wished to study all of the Book of Shining Things had needs be a man of rare patience and humility. Each day he would join the line of gowned Reading Fellows which stretched out of the Great Library, across the cobbled Quadrangle, and around the massive (and considerably subsided) Repository of Modern Classics. There he would wait patiently shuffling forward just a footstep at a time until the time came, just before the Great Library closed at dusk, for his glimpse at the illuminated pages shining like angels' epistles in the afterglow, the gleaming knotwork a graphic representation of the convoluted soul of the City of Logos and Rhema. And to know it all, he repeated this ritual come hail come shine every day for two and a half years.

Second only in importance to the Book of Shining Things was a novel written by a madman and exile which was kept in a tower by the side of the sea. Upon this book, small enough to fit into the coat pocket to be read on a rapid-transit train or public omnibus, the city and all its millions were profoundly divided. Half the populace hailed it the ultimate epiphany of the Modern Man (whatever he might be), a golden galleon asail upon the stream of consciousness. Half the populace damned it a carbuncle, a dag of fecal material clinging to the rump of the Body Literary, a Cultic Toilet book written by a toilet man with a toilet mind. So fierce and irreconcilable were the opinions held that districts, streets, even houses and families, were sundered into warring factions on account of this book. Yet all were agreed upon one point. It was that, though written in exile, its descriptions of the city were so detailed, and of such precision, that should the day ever dawn when the Babel of voices ceased and the city, unremembered, forgot itself and vanished, it could be rebuilt brick by brick, stone by stone, from the words of the book in the tower by the edge of the sea. Yet this was as much a tenet of faith as the dependence of the city upon the Word for none, not one, of the massed millions who praised so Heaven-High and vilified so Inferno-Deep the book had ever read so much as a single sentence of it.

Inspired by this volume which contained the whole city within it (the Greater subsumed within the Lesser), the Bibliosophists of the city libraries had devised a scheme whereby the whole universe might be contained within the covers of a book; indeed, less than a book, a single cartridge of taped instructions for the language machines. The simplicity of the concept verged on the inspirational. Working at the superspeeds characteristic of such devices, the language machines could continuously juxtapose the words and syllabic groupings that are the foundations of language in accordance with the rules of Universal Grammar to create new words, new syllabic groupings, new phrases, new sentences. The overwhelming majority of those sentences would be the veriest nonsense but once every few billion throws of the grammatic dice a meaningful phrase might be coined, a sensible sentence, a coherent paragraph. In the dueness of time every possible permutation of language would have been explored and every possible book that ever could be written, written.

The name the Bibliosophists gave to this project was the Ultimate 'Cyclopedia. In terms of the Greater subsumed within the Lesser, it far outstripped even the book in the tower by the sea, for every book that ever could be was stored all on one small cassette of flimsy magnetic tape.

These were the names of some of the books the casual reader might find on the shelves of the Ultimate 'Cyclopedia.

The Questions, and Answers, to Every Scientific, Philosophical, and Theological Issue that Ever Has, Does, or Ever Will Vex Mankind. (Numerous Volumes.)

The Calculation of Pi *to Its Utmost Decimal Place.* (Still undergoing printing.)

The Autobiography of God.

The Collected Future History (or Histories) of the World (or Worlds).

The Biography of Every Man, Woman, and Child Who Was, Is, or Is to Come.

And when done browsing through the towering stacks, this casual reader might obtain, for a small reference fee, a printout of any fact he could possibly desire to know. Thus he might carry home (as casually as the daily gossip sheet) among those facts, his own biography and, by his fire that night, with his wife and children about him, read in it the exact place, time, and nature of his own death.

After a time of meditation in which each traveler reflected upon what he had heard in the mirror of his own experience, the second storyteller spoke. He was a short black-haired man, possessed of a relentless dark energy and a voice that carried far into the encircling dark and troubled the ghosts, a violation of the night.

THE CITY OF THE DEATHLESS DEAD

He had passed through the City of the Death-less Dead in the early summer when the black funeral roses were budding on the cemetery walls. Peculiarly, there had been no rain that day, which surprised him, for he had been told that the rain fell continuously on the City of the Deathless Dead. Since early in the morning his wanderings had been channeled and directed by the arbitrary twistings and turnings of the towering walls, his journey overshadowed by lofty cenotaphs and obelisks. Past the porcelain mausoleums of the noble and the green-mounded potter's fields of the lowly he steered his course, past paling-defended wall vaults piled so full with generations of interments that the bottommost coffins had split and splintered their oak and leather seams, baring corrupt limbs, hanks of hair, gnawbones of vertebrae to the rude gaze of the living. He walked and he walked and he walked until the decaying perfume of the threnodic roses (known sentimentally by the people of the city as *Flowers of Corruption*) so overwhelmed him with its sickliness that he felt he must clear his wits with clear, cold water from a memorial fount.

Here he encountered the funeral party. Great and famous must have been this departed soul whose open coffin rested amongst wreaths and posies behind the glass of the municipal funeral tram, for coffin and tram were decked with ribbons and bouquets and bunting in patriotic colors which added a touch of not-inappropriate gaiety to the somber black plumes and wrought-iron sprays. Recognizing an opportunity to familiar-ize himself with the people of the city (both living and dead) and their ways of life and death, he had joined a huddle of black-banded mourners at a municipal stop and boarded the mourners' car.

High was the conviviality in that streetcar! Bottles of incendiary brown spirits were passed from hand to hand, and lengthy eulogies were extemporized by the cortege of relatives, friends, well-wishers, and curious upon the deceased and his interminable chain of Glorious Ancestors: the patriots, rebels, insurrectionists, freedom fighters, and warriors of destiny in whose footsteps the deceased had trodden so faithfully all his earthly days. A True Son of the Four Green Fields, he was, a Martyr in the Endless Struggle for Nationhood. Eyes misted with maudlin sentiment, and from deep in the anguished caverns of the soul had broken forth wailing, keening laments counterpointed with laudatory ballads, improvisational and open-ended so that fellow mourners might add their own verses of mawkish, patriotic doggerel.

Every soul aboard the tram, he had learned, could boast a lineage of ancestors as lengthy, glorious, and, of necessity, as patriotic as that of the man in the next car. Indeed, all had been taught as children the catechism that their true homes were their coffins, that humdrum lives might be rendered glorious by a patriotic death, as had the man's in the next car, struck down—while placing green branches on the catafalque of an insurrectionist ancestor—by a treacherous heart that had turned to pure fat through a constant diet of pan-fried food. The essence of patriotism, so declared the catechism, was to love one's native soil enough to let one's life leak out upon its ungrateful green sod.

"Look, stranger, we are the people of the City of the Deathless Dead," they said, "and we carry upon our backs, each one of us, thirty dead souls. Thirty lives, two thousand years of accumulated living. And not for one instant of respite can we lay this burden down, though it stoops our backs and twists us, for the dead hurry us and lash us with their constant demands of endless respect, endless veneration. Thus our squalid tenements squat beneath the skirts of the cemetery walls and we live out our hunchbacked lives in the shadows of the round towers and high crosses and alabaster harps which once through Tara's halls, beribboned with ragged colors, and this is the question we ask, stranger; it is, Why do our dead, whom we loved in life and love all the more in death, hate us so much?"

He saw the thirty souls clinging like bats to each of the fellows on the tram. Some carried the likenesses of those ancestors sewn onto their clothing, becoming flashing kaleidoscopes of faces and memories amongst which their own features seemed pale and ethereal, so much less substantial than the watercolor miniatures, sepia prints, and Instamatics of the dead which dangled from their coats. Others concealed in their vest pockets the mummified *memento mori* of generations dead: a finger, a lock of hair, a perfumed letter, a toenail, an eyeball in a vial of brandy; while yet others conducted animated mumbled conversations with unseen correspondents. From these latter he learned that the houses of the populace contained within themselves a second, separate house: the household of the dead. These Dead Houses were identical in every detail to the houses of the living save that the horsehair settles by the hearths were empty, the dinners stood uneaten upon the dining tables, and the immaculately laundered and perfumed bed linen (*Flowers of Corruption,* of course) was never wrinkled, never soiled. All this was held in perpetual readiness for the unseen, unheard tenancy of the congregation of the dead.

He left the funeral party shortly before the tram, swinging and swaying with gathering insobriety along the iron rails, arrived at the terminus outside the iron gates of Pleasant Prospect Cemetery. He had heard from the peons of the outlying regions of some of the more grisly pre-interment customs and had no desire to participate in them. He tarried only to see the bier of the dead man he now felt he knew better than the living placed upon the shoulders of the pallbearers (by tradition one dark, one fair, one red, one ginger, one brown, one gray) and borne through the becherubed gates into the shadowy land of pillars and crucifixes, monolithic steles, and the headless pillars of those that died young. The closest relatives fell into line behind the coffin, each carrying one of the five sacred elements which must be buried with the corpse to ensure the soul safe passage past fairy and imp and pitchforked demon of purgation to the land of Ever-youth. Spoonful of ashes, turd of horse dung, drop of menstrual blood, thimble of spirits, clod of good green turf. Such an uncertain and perilous business, this dying.

He turned away from the iron gates of Pleasant Prospect and chose a path which would lead him out of the City of the Deathless Dead. He wandered past the graveyards and Patriots' Plots, past the grand palazzi the dead had built for themselves and the grim tumbledowns to which they had condemned the living. His thoughts turned to things seen and unseen, the nature of mortality.

The dead, he concluded, were endlessly jealous of the living. And because the dead could never again hope to possess life, they sought to drag life down to lie close with them in the grave. In their never-ending demands for reverence and veneration, for sacrifice and patriotism, for ritual and observance, they drew life down into death and so were comfortable with it. He saw the shape of the world the dead had bequeathed the living. It had the semblance of a tube of brightly colored glass, the most delicate and fragile glass possible to human science. All around this glass tunnel was a deep, dark void filled with whispers. Those who walked the narrow fragile tunnel did so knowing that at any moment the glass might shatter beneath their feet and drop them into void.

The dead are all around you, spoke the whispers, *and every day, every hour, our numbers swell.*

Presently it began to rain, the expected rain which fell on the City of the Deathless Dead, a thin, cold, penetrating rain that soaked him to the bone within moments but which miraculously washed the air clean of the stink of the black funeral roses.

Third to speak was the quiet man, the long, thin, pale one who bore about him the unmistakable stigmata of sickness in early life. Nervous of demeanor, he had held silence during the first two stories while his comrades grunted and muttered in recognition of some detail, some triviality, which reminded them of their own experiences. He chose to begin his story with a short autobiography.

THE CITY OF
VIBRANT SOULS

Having, in his sickly youth, read exhaustively every available Baedeker, Berlitz, and Guide Michelin, he had formed a fanciful notion of this city and its mercurial inhabitants and had vowed, upon his sickbed, that one day he would certainly visit this numinous, radiant place. When I am old and wise, he had said, when I have majority and maturity enough to appreciate what I see.

He attained majority and maturity, and on the first day of each new spring, he would say, This year, this year I will go. Nothing will stop me, this year. But each year he failed to go. He had devised a compendium of excuses why he could not visit the city *this* year. Chief among them was his fear of disillusionment. He feared that the City of Vibrant Souls which stood solid and enduring on the fertile plains by the edge of the Eastern Sea could never match the City of Vibrant Souls which floated vague and idealized upon the fertile plains of his imagination. There is no disillusionment greater than that which damns the greatest dream. Yet the city shone before him, calling him from his lofty pinnacles of prevarication. As years passed and, like fine wine maturing, he deepened within himself, he thought, Can the agony of disillusionment really be any worse than the agony of unrequited desire? Thus one autumn morning he packed bag, passport, and the guidebooks of childhood mornings and went in search of the City of Vibrant Souls.

From the moment the honey-tongued cabby swept him and his bags out of the arrivals lounge into a hackney more akin to a public house than to a public conveyance, and thence into the stream of life that was the City of Vibrant Souls, he knew that his illusions would not be shattered. Indeed, the city and its people were far greater than any fancyings of his adolescent sickbed imagination. The City of Vibrant Souls seduced him, bound and gagged and finally dominated him like some Montgomery Street rubber Venus with a whip.

The fat barrow-women bawling their wares in the street markets, the doe-eyed waifs begging alms in palms on the Ha'penny Bridge, the giggling gaggles of girls admiring dresses and their own reflections in boutique windows, their bubbling chitchat of boyspartiesclothes opening in him an empty, nostalgic desire; the brawling braggadocio boozers picking fights with noncombatant lampposts; the painted *bella donnas* whistling low come-hithers from upper-story windows; the ox-shouldered gangs of streetfighters filling the narrow cobbled closes with their stale, aggressive pheromones; the sudden flurries of vivacious, rowdy music from a dingy side alley as street musicians struck up on ocarinas and bouzoukis; the jugglers, the plate-spinners, the bunco-boothers, the prancers to fife and tabor; the aged, tooth-free balladeers, one hand cupped to ears as if listening critically to their muezzin-calls of sentimental returns to Fair Ardbo and laments to the Rose of Faithless Love; the good-natured constables in the covered arcades who, when asked whether such an art gallery, whence such an Oriental coffeehouse, prefaced their directions with a comprehensive list of the various ways *not* to go . . . all was as he had always dreamed it might be. Like that latex domina, the people of the City of Vibrant Souls teased him, delighted him, frustrated him, and brought him to the edge of fulfillment only to leave him with pain and emptiness.

How stunted his life seemed compared to these lusty, vital people. How he longed for the secret of their casual mastery of living, how he longed for a life as rich and full as an Old Master hung on a gallery wall.

Thinking that somewhere in its past he might strike the taproot of the city's Tree of Life, he delved into the history of city and people, their gaudy lives of raillery, rakery, wining, dining, wenching, gambling, dueling, and practical joking on the epic scale. He read the life of one Beau English who, leaping from his salon window into a waiting phaeton, drove it to Jerusalem and back for a bet. He studied carefully the records of the Rakehell Club, that circle of dissolute gentry whose lives of spectacular debauchery and decadence (one of their company, having shot a waiter for slow service, found him charged to his dinner bill at five hundred florins) climaxed in their setting light to the house in which they were disporting themselves so that they might savor a foretaste of the hellfire to come. Springing from every page came lust, rapaciousness, cruelty, spite, and greed, yet also elegance, sophistication, courtesy, *bon mots*, style, and a delight in the refined things of life. The beaux and bucks who at dawn blazed at each other with dueling pieces and at night drank themselves stuporous in perfumed whorehouses were those same who from their town offices planned the art galleries, the auditoria, the covered markets, the gracious green gardens, and the avenues of immaculate red-brick townhouses which so characterized the city. He came to understand that two seemingly irreconcilable principles guided the life of the city: one which delighted in the base, coarse, and gross aspects of being; the other which took pleasure from refinement and good taste. Now he was enlightened. Now he saw the elegant fashions; the viperish wit; the sudden, sword-flashing tempers; the beautiful shops and townhouses; the lust for litigation, for a fight, a dare, a bet, a life-staking wager; as manifestations of these guiding principles, this paradoxical yin and yang of taste and crudity.

Yet for all his embracing of the two principles, the natural ease with which the people lived them eluded him. Unable to reach down to the root of the Tree of Life, he turned instead to the sap, the vital juice which coursed vigorously through it. Drink. Drink. The City of Vibrant Souls floated upon a quagmire of alcohol: the drunkard was a national hero, the public alehouse a national institution, and the national beverage (a black, velvety glass, seductive and subtle, brewed close to the ancient River Gate of St. James, in, of course, the largest brewery in the world) a national asset of stellar proportions. It had long been mooted by pundits and wags that it was impossible to cross the city without passing tavern or alehouse. The traveler, in his Dantesque descent into the amber underworld of the empty glass, learned the truth of this sad observation. Glass after glass poured down his throat in a kind of latter-day water-torture while around him the five A.M. voices raised loud in song and scandal. Wives bemoaned husbands, husbands bewailed wives, misunderstood adolescents begrudged everyone, on and on and on and on and on until his hurdy-gurdy head spun like the merry-go-round in the Phoenix Gardens and the friendly constables, incongruous angels of merciful deliverance, came banging nightsticks on the roof beams and calling, "Home, home, everybody home, morning comes early and there's time a-plenty then: everyone sup up and get out, ladies and gentlemen, come now, have you no homes to go to?"

One winter morning a-wander amidst the animate sculpture of the eccentrics of Pearce Park, he discovered he could not remember how he came to be there. This was not the blessed amnesia of inebriation, with subsequent hangover, mortification, and final expiation; whole pieces of his self felt as if they were slip-sliding away like crumbling cliffs; crashing, cascading, dissolving into the salt sea of subjectivity. He was losing himself. He could not remember who he was. The city had driven him mad, and he cowered beneath the suddenly terrifying sky, a crazy man among crazy conductors of invisible orchestras, crazy women with cubes painted on their faces, crazy men, bare-chested in the frosty morning, eager to converse upon whatever highbrow issue might take their fancy. And he was no different. All that he had been had flowed away; he had melted and re-formed: his speech, his gestures, his facial expressions, deportment, mannerisms, all had melted into a creature of the City of Vibrant Souls. He had attained his desire, he had become a limb of the city, and in so doing had lost himself. For the deadly truth was that through centuries of playing the world's clowns, the world's characters, the world's individuals, the people of the City of Vibrant Souls had been cracked open by this relentless striving to be something they were not, and their personalities had all run out and drained away into the sewers. Personalityless, the people therefore took on those stereotyped personas which the visitors (not tourists, *never* tourists) expected of them: the drunkard, the brawler, the lover, the rakehell, the eccentric, the street-poet, the whore, the hurdy-gurdy man. Each day, each soul rose a featureless blank to be stamped with the mold of others' expectations, stamped and re-stamped and re-stamped and re-stamped and re-stamped, five, ten, twenty brief lives, until at last sleep relieved them of the burden of being. And now he would be like this: each day live and die a dozen times, each night be washed clean of the remembrance of what he had been. And he saw it all as if touched with the glowing wand of a Lorarch. He gave then a great cry, a despairing cry, that made even the eccentrics forget the self-absorbtion of their roles. Madman, lover, streetbrawler, drunkard, itinerant, fortune-teller, he would run and run and run and still the ground would slip away from beneath him as the forgetting took away all he had ever been and ever known. One step forward, one step back. Straightaway he departed the City of Vibrant Souls, never speaking a word, never catching an eye, for fear that the slightest spark of communication might draw another phantom life into being, light a blank face with animation. He left, and never returned there, for there is a spiritual death more terrible than that when the illusion is too much more than the truth, it is the death when the illusion is too much less than the truth.

Then into the firelight spoke the fourth traveler, a mousy man coiled like a stock whip, bright with tension and quiet anger. And this was the tale he told.

THE CITY OF DIVINE LOVE

The City whereof he spoke he gave the name Great Theosophilus, which, being translated from his native tongue, meant "The City of Divine Love." It is a city, he explained, of wide and luminous boulevards, of columns and architraves, of soaring spires and exalted domes, of cavernous grottoes and arcades of noble statuary. But beyond all its architectural graces, Great Theosophilus is a city of bells. Endless bells. There is never an hour of the day when the bells are still and silent in their campaniles and pele towers, not even in the wee wee hours of the morning when Death is accustomed to come stealing through the broad avenues of the City of Divine Love; even then the curfew bell tolls the demis and quarters, and the halberdiers of the Civic Guard set their timepieces and pray, huddled in their cloaks against the night chill, that slinking Death may slip them by this night. Matins, lauds, primes, sexts: the bells ring out across the steeples and cupolas of the city, and rising with their notes, like flocks of singing birds, the prayers of the populace aspire heavenward.

The orations of the guilded craftsmen in their Guild Chapels, the rosaries of the washerwomen bowing and bobbing among piles of white laundry on the Florinthian river-steps, the catechisms of the children at their desks beneath the rods of the Teaching Brothers, the lections from the Books of Hours of the wayside faithful felled to their knees by the tolling of the iron Angelus bell: all these spell one shining word—Constancy.

Constancy, this is the watchword of the City of Divine Love; constancy equated by eclogues and theosophists with Continuity. The City of Divine Love has been designed in its every facet to be a continuous hymn of praise, a never-ceasing ever-ascending paean from basilica and chaptery, conventicle and cathedral, minster and sacraria to God the Panarchic. And God the Panarchic in turn shines His Divine Favor (after His Unique Fashion) upon the city of Great Theosophilus for its great faithfulness. For while the Divine Person is, by definition, Omnipotent, Omniscient, and Omnipresent, He has nevertheless deigned to be slightly more Omnipotent, Omniscient, and Omnipresent in certain places or objects than others, namely, the mortified flesh of His Dear Saints. So that the Divine Light might not be lost with the expiration of these Dear Saints' Immortal Spirits, the bodies of this Blessed Number are reduced to their component members, hallowed, canonized, and laid to rest in elaborately constructed shrines, grottoes, and holy wells, provided and maintained by the munificence of certain wealthy individuals and trade guilds.

Thus enshrined, the relics are venerated and offered solemn concelebrations of Mass Lofty and Mass Lesser: the Novena of St. Anthonius's Foot (Dexter); the Perogation of the Head of the Blessed Mandy, the Solemn Mass of Peter's Part . . . The corpse of the saint may rest in dismembered disarray in a dozen churches and subchapels; here a heart, there a hand, here a head, there a torso, and together Priesthood Elect and Great Laity bow down to worship in frenzies of religious ecstasies. Not even the corruptible flesh of the Christic Salvator Himself has been spared this process of dissemination and devotion: Christic eyeballs, Christic fingernails, Christic spleens, even Christic prepuces (of which there are three, each claiming ultimate authenticity), are numbered among the most sacred of relics. Certain mystagogues have calculated that there are sufficient pieces of the Christic Salvator to assemble one and a third human beings. And there are sufficient fragments of the True Crucifix (upon which the Christic Salvator bore the transgressions of mankind) to fill a small basilica.

So that the pattern of stale custom and thus vain observance may never be established, the parishes, deaneries, and sees regularly exchange their objects of veneration. Ensconced within caskets of consummate craftsmanship, heavy with jewels, precious metals, and costly brocades, these holy relics are borne shoulder-high in solemn procession through the avenues and boulevards. Borne aloft by brothers of the trade guilds which have taken corporate and various vows of obedience to the particular relic—the Shoemakers the Foot of St. Basil (Sinister), the Optometrists St. Charleroi's Eyeball (Dexter), the Amalgamated Guilds of Civil Servants and Revenue Employees the Hand of St. Matthias Tax Collector (open, palm up)—the reliquaries are taken to their new, temporary resting place in some St. Xevious Innocens or Blessed Johann the Sacrist or Basilica of the Sacred Molar (Federated Guild of Orthodontists and Dental Employees '86).

How the thronging populace cheer and sing and fill the air with shouts of sacred delight as the golden reliquaries are processed past them! How they press forward against the protecting ranks of Civic Guards to touch finger to casket, jewel, tassel, or golden casket-cloth and so carry away some blessing, some healing, some prayer hastened into the presence of God the Panarchic.

Yet, as God the Panarchic has, after His Own Unique Fashion, chosen to shine His Divine Light upon Great Theosophilus, so He has, according to His Will (which no man may discern, for to do so would be to become God Himself), also chosen to hide part of Himself from the rude gaze of humanity. This is the manner of God's self-concealment.

Over the City of Divine Love is suspended a cloud of permanent gray which hides the light of the sun so that for all the grace-bright lauds of the populace, the gilded domes and mosaicked architraves are dull and lifeless, the arcades of bronze saints dim with a dismal, green patina, and through the great rose windows and ancient lights no ray of sun ever shines to illumine the faithful at prayer within. The theologians and theosophists have a name for this cloud: the Cloud of Mystery. In the manner of theologians and theosophists, they consider it a metaphor for the Cloud of Transgression which separates the spirit of man from the Divine Primacy. The endless cycles of bells, prayers, and concelebrations are, in that same metaphor, the necessary tools whereby spiritual purity may be attained. Then the Cloud of Mystery will be penetrated, and as the true sun shines in the streets and upon the multitudinous temples of the Divine Presence, so will each heart be warmed by the undiluted Divine Affection when God the Panarchic is revealed face to face at last with man.

However, a differing college of thought maintains a differing theology: The Cloud of Mystery does indeed conceal God from man (this much is agreed upon), but the cloud is of man's making rather than Divine quarantine, being composed of nothing more (and nothing less) then the accumulation of year upon year, century upon century, of prayer, devotion, and bells. With every prayer, every grace, every vesper sent heavenward, the cloud grows denser and more impenetrable. The cloud will only be pierced, these scholars argue, when human voices cease and in the universal silence God's own voice may be heard, speaking in still, small syllables.

There is yet a third school of opinion. It too has a name for this cloud, a name not spoken aloud on the boulevards and avenues of Great Theosophilus. This name they have derived from close and careful study of the people of the city, their religious practices, their everyday pieties, their venerations of shrines and relics, and this, coupled with the scholars' own knowledge of the nature of the Divine Self (as revealed uniquely in the Chapbooks of the Panarch), gives them their third name for the cloud. The name they have given it is Superstition.

After a respectful silence the third traveler spoke. He was older than the others and wore his years of experience about his shoulders like a warm coat. He lifted his hands to the dancing flames and said, "In my years I have traveled further than any of you could imagine and I have seen so many cities that if I were to describe them to you we would be sitting here until the year's turning. I could tell you of the City of Romantic Exiles, perhaps, its once-glorious avenues weed-choked and deserted, starved by mismanagement and famine so that today only a handful of civil servants and administrators remain on the principle that while the government persists the city will not be dead. Or perhaps the City of Persistent History, where every instant of the present is merely the past happening over and over and over again. But I will not, because those cities, though real, do not exist, no more than the cities you described; though real, they do not exist either."

"But I heard the words!" said the red-haired bear of a man who had traveled from out of the north, the Lands of Ever-Winter and the Great Northern Ice Sea.

"And I smelled the black roses of corruption," said he who had traveled out of the furthest place of the sunrise, from which the dead, it is said, will rise in place of the sun on the dawning day of Resurrection.

"I saw the wax faces of the people of the City of Vibrant Souls," said the pale man of illusions who had flown so many time zones eastward that he had been severely jet-lagged for many days.

"And I touched the caskets of the holy saints," said he who had passed out from beneath the Cloud of Mystery, out from the southernmost ends of the world.

"Of course you did, of course you did!" exclaimed the old traveler. "But what you saw, heard, smelled, touched, were only parts of the whole. Do you not see, gentlemen, that in describing these cities, each so different and alien, you are describing the same city? I tell you, there is only one city, there has only ever been one city, and that is the City of Man. This city, like all human institutions, is at its heart paradoxical, so that though there is only one City of Man, every city is the City of Man. In that city every pursuit devised by human wit may be found and a million million unique lives studied by he who has eyes to see. So immeasurably rich and varied is the stream of life that no one man can comprehend it all, therefore each traveler who visits there takes only what he can hold and sees only what he wants to see. Likewise you, gentlemen: out of the staggering variety and color of the City of Man you saw what you wanted to see and so thought you had seen the city entire. But the City of Man is so very much more than our perceptions of it that a man may return time and again and never visit the same city twice. Gentlemen, you have seen the part and called it the whole. Go back, again, I would say, and again, and again, until you have seen the whole. Then teach others what you have seen. But lest you should become too arrogant in your knowledge, consider this: if one city, all cities, hold such a multiplicity of other cities within them that a man may spend an entire lifetime in studying, how many more lifetimes must he spend before he comprehends one fingernail's breadth of the infinite universe?"

And the night was gone and the dawn was rising over the edge of the world. The stories were told, the brief fellowship of travelers could be dissolved. Red-hair, short dark-hair, pale sick-scarred, nervous rodent, took their leave of each other and returned to their camels, airbuses, Greyhounds, and caravels. The old one lingered awhile in the predawn glow, kicking at the embers of the fire so that the sparks fled upward into the sky. All around were the inaudible sounds of the City of Stories folding its insubstantial silks and canvases to sweep once more into the dream-time. He listened to the voices of the ghosts as they dissolved away like mist, and waited for a long time. Then he turned his back on fire and world, and followed them.

VIVALDI

In the thistledown starship of the imagination, Dr. Carl Silverman approached the black hole. Golden light from the accretion disc flooded the cathedral-bridge of the mindship and the air rang with chimed warnings: beware gravity, beware gravity. Sprawled in front of the television, chin propped on knuckles, nearly-ten Hugh MacMichaels felt the infinite darkness of the black hole reach out and swallow his imagination. A willing stowaway on the Grand Tour of the Universe, he had seen supernovas burst like fireworks across the heavens, seen galaxies turning before him like fiery catherine wheels, seen wonders until he thought he was numb to wonder, but the black hole called to him, the black hole reached for him, the black hole tied him to itself with threads of pure, unbreakable amazement. He was still whispering "Wow, oh wow, oh wow," as the closing credits rolled up the screen and Dad harrumphed and rattled his newspaper ("That nonsense over for another week"), and Mam clickclacked at the Fair Isle sweaters of incomprehension. The fire coals collapsed releasing a gust of heat, the November rain beat against the window glass, and the *Ten O'Clock News* prepared to disseminate its burden of despair across the land, but nearly-ten Hugh MacMichaels was far far away, sailing in the starship of the imagination with Dr. Carl Silverman at the edge of the universe.

VIVALDI CONTROL DHARMSTADT: WEST GERMANY 23:45
T – 200 144000 KM

As Dr. Hugh MacMichaels, beardy, balding, with a tendency towards paunchiness, strides through the swinging glass doors of Mission Control Dharmstadt, the many-headed beast MEDIA is waiting for him.

"Dr. MacMichaels, do you think that . . ."

"Dr. MacMichaels, is it true that . . ."

"Dr. MacMichaels, what . . ."

"Dr. MacMichaels, when . . ."

"Dr. MacMichaels, why . . ."

He raises his hands to pacify the beast.

"Has anyone seen Kirkby Scott yet?"

Hurrying down the corridor to rescue his project director, Alain Mercier answers Dr. Hugh's question with an eloquent Gallic shrug that speaks of grounded shuttles and taxis caught in traffic.

"Holy God, what is going on here? We're trying to run a space mission, you know . . ."

A microphone lunges dangerously at him.

"Dr. MacMichaels, Anne Prager NBCTV. You have an interview with Dr. Carl Silverman, remember? *New Frontiers*? Remember? It was arranged."

New Frontiers? Carl Silverman? Things are happening too fast. Twenty years to prepare himself and he is still somewhere up in the air over Holland. Ambitious, professional Anne Prager hustles poor confused Dr. Hugh into the Green Room for the interview with Dr. Carl Silverman, Captain of the Starship of the Imagination.

If only you could have seen this, Gemma. Face to face with the Legend Himself.

But the Legend is getting old and gray and tired. Too many years of too many wonders.

"Just some background for our viewers," says the Legend Himself. "We're going out live on a satellite linkup, so keep it simple, nothing too technical, just a bit about the history of the mission to the Oort Cloud and the subsequent discovery of Nemesis, then maybe something about what Vivaldi is hoping to achieve. Give everyone at home some kind of overview, all right?"

"Certainly," says Dr. Hugh, feeling small and lost and intimidated by the lights cables directors sound-boys clipping on microphones testing testing two three four bored makeup girls puffing on powder combing hair over the bald patch do *something* love about those gray bits in the beard . . .

"Would you like a look at the questions while the bright young things get you wired up?"

Dr. Hugh takes the clipboard. Nothing new. He has been answering these same questions on behalf of his space probe for ten years. Anne Prager NBCTV poses herself in front of a camera, pushes at her hair, a harassed director announces,

"Okay, boys and girls, we're going for a live linkup. Satellite comes on line in twenty seconds . . . give you a count, Anne, for the introduction, seventeen, sixteen, fifteen—"

"Wait!" cries Dr. Hugh in sudden panic. "I'm not ready! I'm not ready!"

"Thirteen, twelve, eleven . . ."

Once there were two men. One was old and wise, with a face like bad bread and cabbage. The other was young and really rather naive and people told him that with his beard he looked a bit like Sean Connery. This pleased the young man because Sean Connery had been one of his boyhood heroes. These two men, the old and wise and the young and really rather naive, had many things in common. They were both astrophysicists. They were both doctors. And they both once had a dream of the far places, the far far places, farther than most people they knew could imagine: the Oort Cloud, the great shell of comets that enshrouded the solar system at a distance five hundred times that of the farthest planet. They dreamed of a spacecraft which might travel there and probe the secrets of that dark and remote place and they drew together plans and ideas, notions and fantasies, and in time they saw that their dream was not a dream at all but a real and practical project. So the two men, one old, one young, took their project to the university and the university took it to the European Space Agency and because the European Space Agency was riding gung-ho that year on the setbacks the Russian and American space programs had experienced they said yes, of course you can go to the Oort Cloud, when would you like to go?

As soon as possible, the two men said.

Good, said the European Space Agency. Now, if you would just go and find a name for your project, we'll set aside an Ariane rocket to launch it.

So the two men went out and got very drunk that night and at three o'clock in the morning they were sitting in the young man's front room listening to *The Four Seasons* when both of them, at the same time and with one voice, said,

"Aha! Vivaldi!"

The next day the old scientist told the young scientist a secret.

"Hugh, you know what this is really all about?" Cheese and onion pie and pint for lunch in the Three Cornered Hat; the old man's breath smelled of beer and onions. "Don't be gulled by all this cometary cloud stuff, that was just my ploy to get the project funded and launched. What Vivaldi is all about, what Vivaldi *is*, Hugh, is the first practical starship."

Outside, the sweet September rain was falling down on Edinburgh; lukewarm, slightly acid, a never-ending drizzle that had been falling ever since the summers died in '87. Depressed by the acid rain, the younger man's gray-gray eyes strayed to the desktop model, a diaphanous plastic Y with Vivaldi the spider acrouch at the center of her web.

"You've got it all worked out, you old goat. Alpha Centauri, here I come."

"Silly old men have to do something between seminar groups to drive the young nubiles from their dirty old minds. Think about it, Hugh, powered starflight. Put that down on your CV."

"Let me see, what kind of push can we get out of the ion-drive section, about a quarter-percent c?" The younger man calculated and the acid rain streamed down the windows. "Two hundred years? You can't wait two hundred years, Ben, you're too impatient. Better off with the Oort Cloud. At least you stand a chance of being there to see the results. Only twenty years."

"Twenty years for you, Hugh. Matter of damn to me."

Thirteen months later *Vivaldi* was launched from Arecaibo in French Guyana on an ESA Ariane booster. Dr. Hugh and Dr. Ben watched the launch by video linkup at twenty past two in the morning Edinburgh time, and as the last booster section fell away and *Vivaldi* opened its dragonfly wings to the sun they toasted each other in whisky and drank to the success of Earth's First Starship.

The years passed. Dr. Hugh, young and really rather naive,

fell in love with a fine, handsome, independent woman called Moira who cared not a bit for ion drives and cometary clouds; married, moved to a nice house in a nice area of Edinburgh, and in the dueness of time produced a child named Gemma who was the light of her parents' life. And she was the only light of her parents' life, for shortly after her birth Moira MacMichaels's doctor called her to him and told her that she must never bear another child. So her womb was removed, though she was still a young woman, and in the empty place where her children had been something bitter and dark took root.

And all the while *Vivaldi* flew on, away from the earth, the trefoil of lightsails trapping the sunlight and transforming it into the electricity by which it accelerated, slowly, slowly, slowly, day by day, week by week, year by year, gaining speed, traveling to the Oort Cloud.

T−62 44640 KM

"Counting down to separation from ion-drive section . . . twenty . . . nineteen . . . eighteen . . ."

On the telephone to the airport to find out where the hell Kirkby Scott is, Dr. Hugh hears Alain Mercier start the count. The voice on the other end of the telephone is telling him yes, Flight TW359 from Los Angeles has landed and is coming through customs now, but Dr. Hugh does not hear it because he is half a light-year away in the starship of his imagination. In his mind's eye he sees *Vivaldi* uncouple from the carrier body and drop towards Nemesis while the three-hundred meter trefoil of solar panels sails onwards into the dark, a three-petaled flower dropping its seed. He glances up from his desk, over the heads of the multinational Vivaldi team, to see the vision of his imagination computer-simulated in gaudy Sony-Color on the Big Wall.

"Carrier-body separation complete, Hugh."

So far so good. The onboard computer has not forgotten what to do since the last flight-program update a year ago. Things are going well. Have gone well. Surrounded by the glossolalia of telemetry, the *astonishing verisimilitude* conceals the truth that all this is past tense, six months past tense. Yet he still says, "Give me a count on the safe-distancing maneuvers, would you, Alain?"

"Certainly. Coming up on mark . . . now. Counting down for safe-distancing maneuvers . . . four . . . three . . . two . . . one . . . thrusters firing."

Fifty-nine minutes from Nemesis, *Vivaldi* is falling free from the ion-drive section, tumbling through space unpowered, victim of gravity, tumbling towards the black hole.

It rained the day of Ben Vorderman's funeral, but the rain signified nothing, it rained every day.

Cerebral hemorrhage. That had been the verdict. The old man had dropped dead in midsentence five minutes into his lecture to his second-year astronomy class. He was not even cold in his coffin before the department drew bodkins in the quest for the crown of Vivaldi Project Director. Dr. Hugh wanted no part in that. It had disgusted him. Even on the day of the funeral, with the rain filling up the grave, Tom MacIvor and Barbara Caldwell had been lobbying whispered pledges of support from mackintoshed mourners as the minister read the psalms. Dr. Hugh was shocked. In many ways he was still really rather a naive man. When he told of his outrage to Moira, that was what she told him: She loved him but he was really rather naive. He did not look at her quite the same after that.

Dr. Hugh treasured the nights when Moira went out to her group-consciousness classes or aerobics sessions or women's group seminars or Nationalist party meetings because they gave him an excuse to be all alone with his nearly-three-year-old daughter for a few hours. He loved to sprawl on the couch with Gemma in his arms and answer all her "Whazzat?" questions about the pictures she saw on the television. These were blessed, sacred hours, these evenings of father and daughter; it was a violation when the telephone rang in the middle of *Me and My Dog* (Gemma's favorite, she loved the dogs though she could not comprehend the quiz aspect; he wanted a big fluffy dog for Gemma but Moira wouldn't hear of it) and it was Mr. Cameron the department solicitor asking him to come to the will reading next morning.

Uncomfortable in too-tight collar he sat on the musty-smelling leather seats peculiar to solicitors' offices and listened as Mr. Cameron ruefully and with great sorrow read out names, sums, and properties.

"And it is my desired wish that pending approval by the Faculty Board, Dr. Hugh MacMichaels should succeed me as Project Director of the Vivaldi mission. Because"—Mr. Cameron coughed solicitously—"unlike those other bastards in the department, Hugh actually gives a damn about the dream of reaching the stars."

As Dr. Hugh sat on the peculiar leather chairs listening to the words that made him at twenty-seven director of a mission that would not bear fruit before his fortieth birthday (and made Tom MacIvor and Barbara Caldwell implacable enemies, which saddened him for he liked all men to be his friends), *Vivaldi* crossed the orbit of the asteroids and headed for Jupiter.

T — 45 32400 KM

"We have simulations coming up on the screen . . . now."

"Gravity sensors registering flux curve maximizing to exponential point-source. Nemesis is there, all right."

"Course computer adjusting orbit to intercept trajectory."

"Kirkby Scott's limousine has left the airport and is on its way, ETA in twenty-five minutes."

"Should have long-range images coming through false color enhancement any minute now."

In the jingle-jangle of jargons and lingos—French accents, German accents, Italian accents, the accents of singsong Scandinavians and soft Irishmen, polyglot Beneluxers, anonymous Swiss and lisping Spaniards, Dr. Hugh's Lowland Scots is almost swamped in the Babel.

"Anything we can have a look at yet?"

Alain Mercier, chief of staff at ESA Dharmstadt, competent and unflappable, pries loose Dr. Hugh's question from the tapestry of tongues and replies,

"Pictures coming on screen now. There she is . . . there she is . . ."

And suddenly no matter how many words fill the control room, there can never be enough of them to express the feeling of the soul looking upon a black hole.

Dr. Hugh's first impression is that of ceaselessness—ceaseless swirling, ceaseless spinning, ceaseless activity, a swirling whirling rainbow with a heart of darkness to which everything is drawn down and annihilated. He has never seen anything as dark as the heart of the black hole. Save possibly death. He cannot take his eyes away from the harlequin rings of gas and cometary ice swirling around the collapsar, a maelstrom of elements grinding each other finer and finer like the mills of God, forcing each other hotter, hotter into glowing plasma before the final agonized shriek into the invisibility of the event horizon.

This is it, Gemma, the nightmare on a long winter's night, remember? This is Nemesis.

Trolling in late and drunk after a celebratory departmental piss-up, something akin to guilt had urged Dr. Hugh to peep in at his daughter aged eight. As he switched off her electric blanket (always falling asleep with it on, someday she'll electrocute herself) he saw bright eyes watching him.

"Daddy."

"What, wee hons?"

"Dad, I can't sleep."

Wavering between *hug, kiss, goodnight, close door* and *what-is-it, how-about-a-story?* a sudden gutquake of whisky made him sit down sloshily on the bed.

"Dad, are you going to tell me a story then?"

"Aren't you a bit old for stories?"

"Not ghost stories." Bright eyes met bleary eyes and father and daughter felt themselves caught up in a shiver of mutual conspiracy. No one is ever too old for a ghost story.

"Okay. A ghost story, and a true one."

"Wow!"

"One that happened to me today."

"Dad!" Then, disbelievingly, "Really?"

"Truly. Now listen. Now, you've heard stories about the ghosts of people, and the ghosts of animals, and the ghosts of trains, and even the ghosts of ships, but this one is about the ghost of a star."

"A ghost star?"

"Exactly. You see, when stars get very old, billions of years old, they go like people do when they get old. They fall in on themselves, collapse inwards, shrivel up. But unlike people, well, any people I know of, sometimes a star collapses in on itself so far and so fast that it draws a big hole down after it."

"Like when the water swirls down the plughole in the shower?"

"Very like that. The star falls in on itself and dies but it leaves the hole behind, like the smile on the Cheshire cat, a ghost star, and we call these ghost stars collapsars. Can you say that?" He had trouble saying it himself.

"Collapsars." Words fascinated his daughter; the longer the word, the better.

"That's it. Now, this collapsar is like a bottomless pit. Anything that gets too close is pulled in and falls and falls and falls forever and nothing that falls in can ever get out. The collapsar swallows up everything, even light, which is why another name for them is black holes, and the more it swallows the bigger and stronger it gets and the bigger and stronger it gets the more it can draw in and swallow."

"Dad . . ."

"Yes, wee hons." He was growing accustomed to the darkness in the bedroom, he could discern Gemma's face in the swirling dots of dark.

"You sound scared."

And all of a sudden he was scared, terrified.

"Dad." A pause. "You said this was a true story."

"I did."

"Does that mean there are such things as collapsars?"

"We found the first one today." Or rather, two American scientists at UCLA acting on information from a Japanese sky-watch probe acting on information from a Soviet orbital X-ray telescope, found one today.

"Is that why you sound scared?"

He could not answer, and in the silence Gemma asked, "Dad, has *Vivaldi* anything to do with this c—c—clasp—"

"Collapsar. Wee hons, *Vivaldi*'s going there."

He would never forget the little shriek of fear.

"Dad, *Vivaldi*'s going to fall and fall and fall forever . . ."

"No no, hons, *Vivaldi*'s not going to fall into the black

hole. *Vivaldi*'s just going to go round the edge of the collapsar and take a look. It won't fall in."

But sitting on his daughter's bed with the autumn gales howling round the house he felt that in saying *Vivaldi* was going to the black hole he was saying that he was going there himself, and he saw what it was that had terrified him in Gemma's three words: the sudden, fearful image of *himself* falling falling down down down spinning spinning round round round, dwindling into a little spinning homunculus of a father, falling into the black hole. Dread paralyzed him; mortality had tapped him on the shoulder.

"Then is *Vivaldi* not going to look at the comets any more?"

He thanked God for Gemma's question.

"No, and yes. You see, as the collapsar moves around the sun—which takes it millions of years, it's so far away— it passes through the big cloud of comets, remember, the . . . ?"

"Oort Cloud." Gemma repeated the name with him, mouth shaping the big, round words, eyes shining with intellectual excitement.

"And it just so happens that the region it's passing through is very close to the place where *Vivaldi* was originally meant to go. Imagine that, wee hons, first spacecraft to go to a black hole."

He knew Gemma took a great pride in his work. Not every Daddy in Corstorphin Primary P-5 piloted spaceships to the edge of the solar system. Even if that Daddy happened to be as pissed as a boiled owl.

"Here's a question, Gemma. What do you know about dinosaurs?"

"You mean Tyrannosaurus Rex and Brontosaurus and all that? What's that got to do with *Vivaldi*?"

"Wait and see. Now, why aren't there two dinosaurs here talking astrophysics at two in the morning instead of two humans?"

"Because a comet hit the earth and killed them all."

"Ah-hah! Now, back to the Oort Cloud. When the black hole passes through the comets, sometimes it passes so close it pulls them in and swallows them, but most of the time it just knocks them out of the cloud and sends them in towards the sun. Now, the last time this happened was sixty-five million years ago in the time of the dinosaurs, and you know what became of them. This time it's our turn. Maybe we'll be lucky and no comets will come close to the earth. And maybe we won't."

Dr. Hugh saw the fear on his daughter's face, darker than the darkness in the room, and despised his drunken mouth for frightening her so. Yet this was the world he had bequeathed his eight-year-old child and every loving father's eight-year-old children: a world of extinction raining out of the sky.

"Daddy?"

"Yes, wee hons?"

"Does this collapsar have a name?"

"Yes it does. The people who found it called it Nemesis."

"What does that mean?"

"It's the name of an old Greek goddess who brought vengeance down on the earth."

"Dad, I'm scared."

"Gemma love, so am I."

T−22 15840 KM

At sixteen thousand kilometers and closing, Nemesis fills the Big Wall. Half-hypnotized, Dr. Hugh numbly asks for data. Data will keep it away, keep it remote and distant, half a light-year distant in the Oort Cloud, for projected in garish false color on the video wall it is intimidating, frightening.

"Angular rotation 24000 pi radians per second."

"Circumference of collapsar event horizon fifteen kilometers."

"Estimated mass: four solar masses."

"Radiation temperature estimated 1.47 million K; energy density, 2.2×10^{25} eV per liter."

Gemma, help me. Nemesis is more dreadful than he has ever imagined. Its every aspect is orders of magnitude greater than the estimates he and Kirkby Scott made when the decision was taken to reroute *Vivaldi* to the collapsar. He is not now certain whether *Vivaldi* can survive the encounter with the black hole. All his current guesstimates on survival are based on those hopelessly optimistic, conservative assumptions and even then those probabilities were only in the order of sixty percent in favor of little *Vivaldi*. The odds chalked up by the bookies down in the staff canteen express an altogether different climate of confidence.

Vivaldi was not built for this, he tells himself. *Vivaldi* was designed for a leisurely stroll among the comets, not a headlong plunge to within twelve kilometers of the event horizon of a black hole. Everything about Nemesis is too much; too much mass, too much heat, too much radiation, too much gravity, too big, too close, too soon.

Damn you, black hole, you are too much and you are going to swallow twenty years of my life as wantonly as you would swallow a grain of comet dust.

He remembers; remembers taking Gemma to see a Disney film when she was quite small. In that film there had been a snake with whirlpool eyes that drew in and hypnotized and Gemma had screamed and screamed and screamed until he took her out of the cinema. Now as he stands before the whirlpool eye of Nemesis he understands her fear.

"Dr. MacMichaels . . ."

Uh? Andrea Mencke, from Personnel.

"Dr. MacMichaels, just to inform you that Kirkby Scott has arrived and is in the building."

One evening Dr. Hugh arrived home at 26 Milicent Crescent after a busy day on the edge of the solar system to find a stranger in a tasteless but utterly fashionable plaid suit sitting in his favorite armchair chatting amiably to a rapt nearly-sixteen Gemma and sipping a glass of Dr. Hugh's very very best single-malt.

"Hello, Dad." Gemma greeted him with a kiss and a Hello-Daddy-Bear hug. "This is Kirkby Scott."

"Good evening, sir," said the plaid-suit single-malt-sipper, standing and enthusiastically shaking hands. "Kirkby Scott, UCLA. I believe you're the one wants to send a spaceship to my collapsar."

His name was Kirkby Scott; he came from the University of California, Los Angeles, though he was born in Wisconsin, where apparently everyone in California was born; he was twenty-eight years old; he had won the youngest-ever doctorate in astrophysics from the University of California, for which he and his partner Paul Mazianzky, now of the Jet Propulsion Lab, Pasadena, had made a study of the orbits and perturbations of orbits of comets in the Oort Cloud on the hypothesis that the sun possessed a distant companion, tentatively christened Nemesis (pretty good name, no?), with the sub-hypothesis, subsequently proved, that this Nemesis was a black-body object, possibly (now verified) a moderately sized collapsar of approximately three solar masses, and that on account of this epochal discovery (words like "Nobel" had been bandied) UCLA, NASA, and the ESA had decided in their corporate wisdom that he, Kirkby Scott, was to be Dr. Hugh MacMichaels's new partner on the Vivaldi Project.

To which, Dr. Hugh MacMichaels of the Vivaldi Project said,

"You what?"

He went to the Space Lords of the ESA and the Space Lords of the ESA said things like "Americans feeling left out," and "They did discover it, after all." They also said things like "no place for dog-in-the-manger attitudes" and "brotherhood of science." More revealingly, they said "got some deep-space pulse-fusion thing going on over there— Orion, they call it—powered starflight, all that; you scratch my back, all that stuff?" And, sinisterly, they said, "old allies" and "Western-bloc solidarity" and, most sinisterly of all, "directive from the Highest Authorities."

"Doesn't the position of Project Director entitle me to some say-so?" said Dr. Hugh.

"Sorry, Hugh," said the Space Lords of the ESA. "It's a political decision." And that was that. Dr. Hugh shuttled home to Edinburgh hating both Kirkby Scott the flesh and Kirkby Scott the idea. He poured out his cup of bile to Moira, but, self-absorbed with the darkness that had taken root in the empty places within her, she was no longer interested in either his work or him. So he poured it out again to Gemma and she listened patiently and when he had emptied himself of his anger at the European Space Agency, Kirkby Scott, and Moira, she said,

"I rather like him, Dad."

"Like him? Like that . . . that . . . dandy, that . . . popinjay, that poseur?"

"He has a good heart, Dad."

Dr. Hugh did not appreciate then that his daughter possessed the gift of reading hearts, a kind of spiritual X-ray vision to which all intents were open and from which no secrets could be hid, and so he went away hating Kirkby Scott, idea and man. But day by day, week by week, year by year, his resentment of his partner mellowed and softened and became first admiration, then open liking, and he came to realize that a man can wear a flashy plaid suit (forgivable through fashion), sit in someone's favorite armchair (forgivable through ignorance) and swill someone's very very best single-malt and chat up his dear and only daughter (unforgivable under any circumstances), and have a good heart.

Two days after Gemma's nineteenth birthday, with *Vivaldi* six months from the black hole, Dr. Hugh and Kirkby Scott were guests of honor at the 43rd International Astronautical Conference in Houston, Texas. Dr. Hugh was very excited by the prospect of going to Houston. He had piloted spaceships to the edge of the stars but had never crossed the Atlantic. Gemma was excited for him too.

"Got passport, air-sickness pills, glasses, cheap thriller?"

He nodded, yes, yes, yes, yes, yes.

"Right, then. Be good, Dad, and knock them dead."

The 43rd International Astronautical Conference was a triumph. Even half a year from the black hole, *Vivaldi* had still pushed Death Stars, orbital factories, Jupiter ramjets, Martian go-bots, and even pulse-fusion Orion stardrives into the wings and Drs. Hugh and Kirkby—one tweedy, beardy, amiably confused; the other confident, garrulous, the picture of fashion in paisley one-piece and matching duster coat—under the spotlight center stage.

At the reception afterwards everyone wanted to shake Dr. Hugh's hand and tell him how he reminded them of Sean Connery (the *only* James Bond), and Dr. Hugh, blurred and mellow from too much California Moselle, smiled and laughed and talked the veriest drivel with Respected Nobel Laureates and Sharp Young Men from NASA and Doyens of Astronautics and was just easing into conversation with an extremely attractive woman journalist from *New Scientist* (so sorry, his subscription had run out years ago) when the bellboy came round paging Dr. Hugh MacMichaels paging Dr. Hugh MacMichaels telephone call at reception telephone call at reception and he left the extremely attractive woman journalist holding his glass and went to answer the telephone and on the other end was Moira telling him that Gemma had been killed that morning in a car accident on the M62.

T—10 7200 KM

Casual, fashionable, elegant in his yellow designer one-piece, Kirkby Scott skips down the steps and slips in beside Dr. Hugh.

"Sorry," he whispers. "Stuck in a stack over Düsseldorf while they sorted out an air-traffic controllers' dispute, would you believe? And would you believe that sitting up there in our coffee room is Carl Silverman, I mean, Carl Silverman . . ."

"I know," says Dr. Hugh. "He interviewed me."

"Interviewed you? Hey, ho . . . I'll ask you about it later. Well, here I am. Okay, tell me what's going on."

Dr. Hugh nods at the Big Wall.

"Ten minutes."

"Shoot, that close? How long to the impact probes?"

"They go at T-minus-four."

"How's *Vivaldi* bearing up to it?"

"Gravity shear and dust impact are causing her to wobble off optimum course."

"Well, the onboard's held up this long, it can hold another ten minutes."

"Gravity shear approaching upper safety limits," advises an unapproachable Swiss Fräulein at the telemetry board.

"Gravity shear? Gravity shear? We hadn't figured on the gravity shear getting so strong so far out; here, let's have a look, what kind of beast have we got out there?"

Kirkby Scott studies the facts and figures on Nemesis with hisses of increasing disbelief. Dr. Hugh studies the simulator display schematics on the Big Wall simulator. There is ugly, bucket-of-bolts *Vivaldi*, rolling and tumbling towards the Schwarzchild limit: safe, but Dr. Hugh's imagination superimposes on the videoscreen the hundred alternative scenarios in which *Vivaldi* is reduced to glittering shards.

It wasn't made for this. Not for this. He watches the simulated dust impacts peck away at *Vivaldi*'s dust shields (each peck ten times the velocity of a rifle bullet: he remembers telling Carl Silverman that) and realizes that he is holding his breath.

Why?

Because I am scared. Scared that at any moment a piece of ice is going to destroy *Vivaldi,* scared of what is going on out there, out there at the edge of the solar system where all I can do is watch and I am helpless to act: out here is something I cannot control, something that defies me, mocks me, wishes to destroy me, and that scares me because since Gemma died *Vivaldi* has been the only thing in my life over which I have had any control. My daughter, my wife, my passions, my fears, all flew from my hands over the years as *Vivaldi* flew on and on and on and now here it is perched on the edge of chaos and what can this man do?

The Chapel of Rest terrified Dr. Hugh. From its position on the hill it dominated the rows and plots of plinths and headstones and Dr. Hugh, turning through the wrought-iron gates in his battered red station wagon. Every funeral reminded him of other funerals. It had been raining the day of Ben Vorderman's funeral, it was raining today, the same steady rain, and it was the same graveyard and the same chapel on the hill save that this time the hearse kept on up the hill to the chapel at the top, for a new law said that everyone must be cremated unless religious observance prohibited. Dr. Hugh could not say why the Chapel of Rest disturbed him. Perhaps the red-brick architecture which reminded him of the detested Forth River Primary School, perhaps the morbid Phantom-of-the-Opera organ program which stopped mid-bar when the coffin was placed on the dais, perhaps the chimney glimpsed through the-Resurrection-and-the-Life stained glass, stern sentinel of mortality. Man is but a puff of smoke, and quickly blown away.

Gemma had never been formally religious, so friends, relatives, and lovers (he did not doubt that they were there) read poems, placed flowers, sang songs, and spoke stumbling eulogies while Dr. Hugh sat beside his wife and could not believe that it was his daughter in that thing up there on the dais.

"Perhaps her father would like to say a few words? Mr. MacMichaels?"

It was the last thing he wanted to do, he would rather have done anything, anything at all than have to stand up there beside his daughter's coffin, but Moira hissed something so vile and cutting that he went up to the lectern because it was the only place her contempt could not reach him. But the few words would not come to express what he wanted to say. Then all of a sudden he felt he wanted more than anything to shout at the friends, relatives, lovers, "What could you know about how it feels to lose your present and your future, your light, the woman you love most in all the world?" and tell them that no matter how many words he said they could never express one millionth part of what Gemma had been, but those words would not come to him as he braced himself against the lectern and two tears ran down his face and they said all the words he could not.

The funeral director said,

"Now, by special request, an extract from Gemma's favorite music program, a piece of music that must have meant very much to her." The pseudo-Venetian strings of the Vivaldi program filled the chapel, the funeral director pressed a discreet button, and as the computerized violins and harpsichords played, the coffin sank down down down out of sight and Dr. Hugh, desolate father, stood there as if his heart had melted to slag. And the coffin passed out of sight and he felt Moira's reproachful, unforgiving eyes upon him.

After the signing of the Book of Remembrance he followed her to the car and his attention was snared by a flash of white on the wet black tarmac: a business card fallen from her bag. He picked up the card, read the address:

Immortals Inc. somewhere in London.

"I think you dropped this." She almost snatched the card back in her haste to hide it in the bowels of her handbag.

"Thank you, darling."

As the smoke went up the chimney he tried to remember Gemma's voice, Gemma's face, Gemma's laughter, and found he could no longer do so.

"Crossing plasma front; electrical activity increasing to within eight percent of safety margins."

Go on, you tough little bastard.

"Radiation levels increasing markedly: damage monitors report soft fails in some attitude-control transputers."

You've made it over twenty years to get this far. Only a few minutes left.

"Dust impacts maximizing, we mark penetration through numbers one and two dust-shields to the mylar impact-sensor layer."

Go on go on go on go on.

"Counting down to impact-probe release . . . four . . . three . . . two . . . one . . ."

"Impact probes away!" sings Kirkby Scott. "Go for it, you little mothers!"

Three streaks of light fan away from the Looney-Toon *Vivaldi* on the Big Wall: cometary impact probes Harpo, Groucho, and Chico, their mission radically altered from their original intention. Once designed to test the density and composition of Oort comets, now they have been aimed down the gullet of the collapsar to shatter themselves against the impossible, to test the density and composition of the spinning collapsar known as Nemesis, the stuff and substance of that bead, that fetus of dark matter at its heart, and in the shattering, in the gasp of their destruction, become a revelation of the eschatology of the death of the universe.

Dark matter, heart matter, heavy matter, light matter, and upon the stuff and substance, the piss and puss of Nemesis, depends the shape of the end times, whether the Scattering will one day become the Gathering and the galaxies will be squeezed back into the primal Cosmic Egg once more, or whether they will fly outwards on their lonely courses forever, into the night, into the dark, the keening electron-whine of the panversal heat-death, chaos and cold at the rag end of time.

Dr. Hugh does not want there to be an end time. He does not care for the new Revelation. What is the death of the universe, majestic in its decline and finality, awesome in its scope and magnificence, compared to the death of his beloved daughter, one brief human life upon an insignificant fleck of filth at the edge of an unspectacular galaxy?

This is not real, he reminds himself. The lines, the

graphics, the alphanumerals: imagination. This is the truth: six months ago, listen, *six months,* three lemon-sized impact probes with fanciful names fell past the Schwarzchild limit. And, by the express command of omnipotent relativity, they are falling still, frozen in time. And they will fall thus forever. Immortality. A relativistic shudder shakes Dr. Hugh.

"Hi, hons, I'm home." Home from Düsseldorf and the ESA conference, the sole tweed-jacketed pillar of academe on a city-hopper crammed with the industrial moguls of the New Scotland. On the flight he'd drunk too much, as usual, and then somewhere over Holland he'd remembered Gemma's gentle chidings on the incompatibility of in-flight alcohol with aircraft pressurization. Then he'd realized, with devastating finality, that this time she would not be there to greet him at the arrivals gate with a Daddy-Bear hug and confiscate his yellow bag of duty-free drink and drive him home with some relaxing Handel (original, not some pseudo-program thing) on the car stereo and genuinely interested questions about what he had been doing. It would not be. It would never be again. He had burst into tears and wept all the way from Nord Zeeland to Edinburgh with the industrial moguls of the New Scotland staring at him. "Hons, I'm home . . ." But hons was out, busy with the do-gooderies that filled the place in her life where he should have been. No letters for him, but a shiny brochure for her from some Sassenach outfit calling itself *Immortals Inc.*

He saw a white card fluttering on the wet black tarmac of the municipal crematorium.

He took the shiny brochure into the living room and sat down to leaf through its glossy pages.

The hardest part of death is for those who remain.

Our Counselors know only too well the ways in which grief can rip a family in two . . . Our computer simulacra reproduce in every way the personalities of the mourned departed . . . Working from the material manifestations of personality, the mementos, the souvenirs, the small personal possessions, voice tapes and photographs, our computers can reconstruct that personality with such astonishing verisimilitude . . .

Looking out of the window he saw something moving in the rotting summerhouse, something caught in the eigenblink of an eye: an arm.

Astonishing verisimilitude astonishing verisimilitude astonishing verisimilitude . . .

He approached the gazebo with trepidation. Through the vegetable garden, past the raspberry canes, Dr. Hugh went cat-careful, listening to the baroque strings of the Vivaldi program he'd bought her for her seventeenth birthday when she'd tired of the electronic ethnobeat programs which all sounded the same. He circled the summerhouse, anachronistic now the summers would not be coming back. Through the windows he saw the walls plastered with the plundered memorabilia of Gemma MacMichaels: the photographs of girlfriends, of cats, dogs, rabbits, hamsters, ponies, later of boyfriends; Gemma in ballet clothes, Gemma cast as Lady MacBeth in the school play, Gemma proud with her certificate of merit to the University of Edinburgh to study English, and the holiday, all the holiday snaps: him potbellied and grizzled in his swimming trunks in Corfu, him with a stupid expression coming off the shuttle at the airport, him tense and waiting in his hired Parsons and Parsons tux (red silk lining) waiting to hear the pronouncement of the Royal Institute Awards for 2006 . . . Moira had been thorough. Thoroughness was characteristic of her.

Something was sitting in a wicker chair with its back turned to him. He opened the door. Reconstructed Venetian strings swelled, "La Serenissima." Ceiling-mounted cameras turned, focused, and an awful, sick puppet-thing with Gemma's face had turned in Gemma's wicker chair, smiled, and said,

"Hi, Dad."

Hands to mouth to keep the horror from spewing out, he stepped back from the gazebo door.

"Dad, aren't you coming in?" Camera-eyes tracked him as he backed away. "Dad, it's me!" The puppet-thing lifted embracing arms. Hugh MacMichaels, father, husband, space explorer, vomited his Air Caledonian breakfast of porridge, bacon, eggs, oatcakes, marmalade, orange juice, and coffee into the brussels sprouts.

T—O NEMESIS

"T-zero. Distance zero. Event horizon. Doctor, the event horizon!"

The maelstrom of SonyColor on the Big Wall dwarfs Dr. Hugh. He closes his eyes so he does not have to see. T-zero. Distance zero. *Vivaldi* has kissed the lips of the nothing. The crackle of hard radiation drowns all voices in the control room save one, a cry, uplifted above the hiss and roar of Nemesis: Kirkby Scott.

"We got it! Oh, we got it! Positive electromagnetic halo readings from Harpo, Groucho, and Chico before contact was lost! Nemesis is a fourth-order minimum surface of Hypothesis B dark matter. Folks, it's the fourth state of matter!" He turns, triumphant, arms Christ-wide. On his face, the beatific smile of the prophet of Doomsday. "Ladies and gentlemen, the missing mass is found! The Universe will contract to a point and be reborn!" Animal whoops, cheering, applause, fill the control room. In the center of the forest of arms reaching out to congratulate, Dr. Hugh and Dr. Kirkby embrace. Dr. Hugh cannot think why.

Unresting, unhastening, and as silent as light, *Vivaldi* loops away from Nemesis. Half the control boards are a Picadilly Circus of malfunction lights. More hulk than spacecraft, Earth's first starship puts distance between itself and the collapsar. It has survived. It has come through. It has beaten the black hole. The count stands at $T+45$ seconds as champagne corks pop and glasses are raised and an international chorus of toasts proposed to the twin heroes of the Vivaldi Project.

Peep. Peep. Peep. Peep. Peep. Peep. Peep. Pee . . . the emergency alarm. Controllers scatter to their posts, bulk-purchase snap-together plastic champagne glasses still in hands. All they can do is observe the destruction.

"Cometary head . . ."

"Blind side of the collapsar . . ."

"Impact estimated in . . ."

The Big Wall displays the destruction in computer-enhanced garishness: a cloud of electric-blue ice pellets, fragments of a shattered Oort comet.

"Proximity detectors still functional . . ."

"Emergency evasion programs being effected . . ."

"Small-maneuver thrusters firing . . ."

"Come on come on come on come on . . ." *Vivaldi* shifts slowly, slowly, so slowly. The staff of Mission Control Dharmstadt will it on: come on come on come on *come on*. Alone of all the people in the room, Dr. Hugh sees what must happen and cries,

"Stupid stupid stupid!"

So concerned is the radiation-seared onboard computer with the imminent danger that its lobotomized memory has forgotten all about Nemesis, all about the event horizon. *Vivaldi* is steering itself away from the ice cloud into the embrace of the collapsar.

"Time to event horizon, thirty-two seconds," says Kirkby Scott dazedly, face lit blue and green in the reflected glow of Nemesis. "Time to event horizon, twenty-eight seconds . . ." *Vivaldi* rolls and points its cameras directly on the singularity. Dr. Hugh MacMichaels, standing faithful at his station as he has stood faithful for twenty years, beholds the heart of the black hole.

The heart of the darkness.

He whispers, face blue with Nemesis-shine and wonder, "Holy God, there's some . . . thing in there."

The darkness of the heart.

Emotion had always terrified him. He could not bear to hear Moira's sobbing. It made her vulnerable and human and he wanted her to be invulnerable, inhuman.

"It was for you, for us. God knows, we can never have another Gemma, and now she's dead; what's going to keep us together, what's going to keep us going?"

Poor, naive Dr. Hugh had never understood the essential contradiction that lay close to Moira's heart: that her treasured independence existed only because the stability of husband, child, and home lent it a firm foundation. He could only dimly comprehend that she feared being cast adrift on the sea of misfortune without haven or the sanctuary of a future assured through her children. And he could never understand that though she despised him, he was now all those things that she needed, and that if the marriage collapsed she would be irrevocably alone. And because he understood none of this, he could not understand why she had taken his daughter's, *their* daughter's, memories to Immortals Inc. for them to flesh out in plastic and metal. Yet comprehension, revelation, lay just beyond the roses browning in the acid rain, the desolate beans and the wilting brussels sprouts. And because twenty years older he was still really rather naive, he knew he would have to ask the oracle; the shape moving about its indecipherable businesses beyond the rain-streaked glass.

"Gemma."

"Hi, Dad."

The face was almost more than he could bear, yet he felt he must reach out a finger to touch the hand, the cheek, the brow, so he could satisfy himself it was not warm flesh. His fingers carried away her perfume, *Noches de Luna,* amateurishly smuggled out of airport duty-frees.

"They made me well, didn't they, Dad?"

The voice, the inflections, the idioms, the lowered eyes, the slight smile: the *astonishing verisimilitude*. He tried to deny her to himself with coarse, hurtful questions.

"Where did they put them then?"

"The computers, Dad? Under the floorboards and up in the ceiling. You know, you had dry rot, death-watch beetle, and at least three colonies of mice down there."

He almost let himself smile. The Gemmathing read the almost-smile with her camera-eyes and returned it wholly.

"Relax, Dad. Why don't you just let me be what I'm supposed to be?"

Again the gentle invitation. Again the coarse, hurtful rejection.

"How much did she pay for you?"

"Twelve thousand five hundred pounds on a monthly direct-debit installment plan, for which she got a voice-recognition program capable of discriminating between sarcasm, irony, or any other form of rhetorical trickery, Dad. So stop trying to make me out to be a thing and let me help you. She did it because of you, Dad."

"Me? Oh no." But he had let himself be trapped by the Gemmathing.

"She's terrified of you leaving her all alone in the world, Dad. She may not love you but she needs you, needs someone, and if she can't have you, then she'll bring her only daughter back from the dead to fill her need. Me. Gemma, your daughter."

Suddenly the dread was more than he could bear. He surged to his feet, whale-and-rainbow mobiles swinging away from his heavy animal shoulders, an angry, helpless bull-father.

"But you're not Gemma, you are a thing, a pile of transputers and molecular gates, a mechanical puppet like something out of Madame Tussaud's on the Royal Mile." He remembered Gemma, age eight, clinging to his coat in real fear as the monsters, ogres, and body-snatchers of Scotland's grim history reached out of the gloom for her. "You're not real. I'll tell you what's real: the Gemma I remember, the Gemma in my heart, that's the real Gemma."

"Dad, I'm surprised." The Gemmathing flashed its eyebrows. Where had it learned that? He had never been able to resist Gemma's raised eyebrows.

"Tell me, Dad, what's the difference between the Gemma in your head and the Gemma in the gazebo? We're both memories, only the memories in your head will fade with time and eventually become just memories of memories of memories, but in me they have been given a body and will never fade. So, what's so terrible about that? What's so terrible about wanting to keep those memories, those things that were special about Gemma MacMichaels, *me*, fresh and imperishable? What's the difference?"

He had no answer for the Gemmathing. That evening he flew off to Dharmstadt for the close encounter with Nemesis and he still had no answer. He knew there must be an answer to the Gemmathing's question, a full and complete answer, but he did not have the first idea where he might hunt for that answer. He never suspected that his answer was waiting for him within the Einsteinian gullet of a black hole.

Peeeeeeeeeeeeeeeeeeeeeeee . . .

"Crisis situation."

"Termination of all telemetry data."

"Cessation of all onboard monitoring systems."

"We're getting nothing but three-k static on the communications links."

"No incoming intelligence."

"All sensors nonfunctional."

"All systems dead."

The Big Wall is blank save for the tiny, mocking alphanumerals in the top left corner:

T + 1:50 1320 KM

The control room is filled with the penetrating keen of the alarm. Every head is turned on Dr. Hugh: What do we do now, leader? Dr. Hugh flips off the whistle and his voice seems very loud as he speaks into the deepspace radio hiss.

"Ladies and gentlemen, we must assume that *Vivaldi* has crossed the event horizon and that the mission is terminated. Thank you for your assistance, it was a pleasure to have worked with you. Thank you."

Hissssssssss. Good-bye, Starship of the Imagination.

Kirkby Scott bangs his desk displays in frustration but Dr. Hugh does not share his sense of failure. Rather, he glows with a peculiar elation, as if in the loss of twenty visionary years, by some universal law of conservation, he has gained some vital insight. The odds were always stacked against him. Now after twenty years he must take up his life again. As he leaves the control room he hears Alain Mercier's measured syllables:

"The Vivaldi Mission count has been terminated at launch plus six point three times ten to the eighth seconds at 5:45 GMT, August twenty-seventh, 2008."

Outside, the demon MEDIA has lain in wait for him, now it pounces.

"Dr. MacMichaels, tell me, will there now be a joint European/American mission to the Oort Cloud?"

"Dr. MacMichaels, what light does the Vivaldi mission throw upon the origins of the solar system?"

"Dr. MacMichaels, what bearing does the outcome of the Vivaldi mission have on the Orion probe?"

"Dr. MacMichaels, what would you say is the probability that a wave of comets has been dislodged from the Oort Cloud, and will you now be pressing for an international skywatch?"

"Dr. MacMichaels, does the revelation that Nemesis is composed of Hypothesis B dark matter imply in any way that the universe is reaching the limits of its expansion and that contraction to the point source will begin to occur within the next few million years?"

He stops for that one. All bits and parts of other things, the stained-glass demon MEDIA halts in a surge of boom-mikes, cameras, and handheld recorders.

"Quite frankly, sonny, I don't give a shit. And neither should you." The pimply-faced cub reporter in the bright red body-suit and inappropriately padded muscles blushes. And Dr. Hugh is suddenly angry. "How old are you? Nineteen, twenty? Less? Listen, sonny, get out of here, go and make love, make friends, make a big noise, see things, do things, be things, have fun, be good, be kind, be loved by everyone, live as full a life as you can so when the time comes for your own death you can go into it full and satisfied and at peace, because quite frankly, boy, the death of the universe is not worth a single tear. Not one damn tear."

The doors are close; beyond the glass, the waiting car, the neatly planted trees, the east-is-red sunrise. Something to do with the Ruhr, the redness of the sunrise. An hour and a half from now he can be arriving in yawning Edinburgh. When he gets there, there is something he must do.

T + 200

And now Dr. Hugh's battered red Ford station wagon is driving through the five-o'clock-empty streets of Edinburgh. A time zone westward, he has beaten the sun. Under the yellow streetlights the city is the possession of the milk-floats, the newspaper vans, the ambulances and their dark brothers the night police, and Dr. Hugh, driving fast, driving home. 5:05, he turns into the driveway with a crunch of gravel: it is early, not a blind open, not a carton of milk on a doorstep, not a jogger defiling the tranquility in designer jogging suit and shoes. Dr. Hugh watches the sun rise over Milicent Crescent: no rain today, amazing. He opens the trunk of the car and takes out not an overnight case but a red metal can. And he does not enter his house by the front door but by the side gate into the back garden. A neighbor's dog barks as Dr. Hugh crosses the garden: across the lawn, past the dying roses and the brussels sprouts and the raspberry canes—they look green, perhaps we shall have jam this year—to the gazebo.

The Gemmathing is awake and alert the instant he opens the door but Dr. Hugh knows that machines can go as long as twenty years without sleep.

"Dad! Do you know what time it is?"

"I do."

"So, how did things go?"

"Things went fine."

He unscrews the lid from the red metal can. Camera-eyes roll and focus. He sloshes the contents over the walls, the floor, the wicker chair. The Gemmathing shrieks and raises its hands in panic as the liquid slosh-sloshes over her flowery print frock. The stench of gasoline chokes the gazebo.

"Dad! What are you doing! Do you know what you're doing?"

"I do," says Dr. Hugh. "Oh I do." And as he sloshes the gasoline over the Gemmathing he explains. "You see, I worked out the answer to your question. What's the difference between you and my memories of Gemma? Answer, nothing. Both were wrong. Both are wrong. It's wrong to cling to memories, to make them the justification for my failure to escape from your death. But at least my memories will change and fade with time. That's why it's wrong to give them form and shape, enshrine them; it's giving death the victory. I realized that when *Vivaldi* was lost: it had gone to where I could never reach it, twenty years of my life, gone for good. I realized that no amount of wishing or hoping or praying could bring it back from the black hole, or you, Gemma, from the wrecked car. I had to lose you, Gemma, I had to let you pass over the event horizon. Memories are no substitute for living and we have to live, Gemma. We have to."

And standing by the door of the gazebo he takes a match from an Air Caledonian matchbook, strikes it, and tosses it into the Gemmathing's lap.

The blossom of flame knocks him backwards into the raspberry canes. The intense heat has seared away his eyebrows and scorched his beard. He backs away, shielding raw face with hands, yet curious to see the destruction he has wrought. In the burning gazebo he sees the plastic features of the Gemmathing melting, flowing onto the blazing print frock. The windows shatter, twelve thousand five hundred pounds' worth of transputer modules crack and fuse and all the photographs, all the trapped memories, take wing and fly away on the burning wind like black crows. The flames roar and lick around the melting, burning Gemmathing.

"God, I'm sorry," he whispers.

Alarmed by the explosions, neighbors are leaning out of open windows, fearful sheep-faces gaping at the suburban nightmare in MacMichaels's garden. Slippered and dressing-gowned, Moira is running across the lawn to the pyre.

"It's you and me now!" Dr. Hugh shouts. "Just you and me. No Gemma to hold us together. We work it out on our own or not at all. We're adult, mature humans, dear God, we have our own lives to live." Moira is on her knees amidst the brussels sprouts, hands held imploringly to the blazing summerhouse. Tears stream down her cheeks. The oily black smoke plumes into the sky. Dr. Hugh hears in the distance the wail of the fire brigade's red engines. He watches his wife weep and kneels beside her to comfort her. As he places his hand on her shoulder he notices the little buds of color amidst the thorns and acid-browned leaves. Maybe there will be roses this year after all.